BREAKING NEWS:
LOCAL HEIRESS DEAD

CHARLOTTE MORGANTI

HALFDAN
PRESS

For every woman with a soft spot for Calamity Jane

Chapter 1

IT TAKES two and a half days to remove a body from a barrel of concrete.

And once the victim is identified, it takes an instant for your life to plummet from a Hallmark movie on downers to an Agatha Christie film scripted by Tarantino.

In hindsight, of course, I should have seen it coming that day at the lake. The signs were all there.

IT WAS SHORTLY after noon on the second Monday in July, and I sat in a borrowed canoe a hundred feet off the south shore of Donner Lake. Not more than four oar-lengths away, a police boat rested at anchor. My estranged husband, Dom Bertucci, was one of the three cops on board. They stared at the silver winch cable drawing an angled line from the boat's stern into the depths of the lake. I cradled my camera in my bandaged hand and calculated the odds of a front-page story. Pretty solid, I figured, since I was the only reporter at the scene, thanks to a tip from Dom.

"Olivia," he'd said on the phone, "some teens diving at Donner Lake think they found a body."

"Think?"

"They're freaked out, not making much sense. Something about pirate treasure and mannequins. We're sending divers down. I thought you'd be interested."

Other cops might not give reporters a heads-up, but they were not Dom, nor were they politicking to be welcomed back to our marital bed. Other women might reject a cheater's offerings, but they were not me, nor were they depending on his morsels as a source of breaking news.

The police and I bobbed in our boats, waiting for divers to connect the winch cable to whatever they'd found eighty or so feet below. Although we were close to shore and everyone wore life jackets, Dom clutched the winch controls with both hands. I knew his palms would be damp and his heart racing. Water deeper than a footbath did that to him.

Sweat trickled down my breastbone, partly from the heat, partly from nerves. Like any reporter, I love a good cops-and-bad-guys tale. But when I'm in a canoe in Donner Lake, I hyperventilate. As spectacular as the lake is, it carries with it an atmosphere of desperation that always reminds me people will do anything to survive. To calm myself, I steadied the camera and snapped a quick succession of pictures—marshmallow clouds that during squalls became dark, menacing fists; protective mountains whose impassable winter drifts sapped the will to live from the unprepared; and the calm water that summer storms whipped into a deadly chop.

I'd just captured a shot of Dom's teenaged witnesses—a bedraggled foursome huddled together on the pier—when a diver popped up and signaled. Dom engaged the winch and the cable slowly retracted, glistening drops of water falling from its length. A rush of bubbles appeared on the lake's surface, and I readied the camera. Several seconds later, two more neoprene-capped police divers appeared. They removed their scuba masks, revealing grim faces.

The harnessed load finally broke the surface with a sighing

whoosh. I snapped pictures rapidly as the winch's burden swayed and spun over the water. The dripping black straps enveloped a concrete-filled green and yellow barrel. I lowered my camera as the rotation of the winch's load slowed and the barrel's open end came more distinctly into focus. Two jean-clad legs protruded from the concrete like pens in a pencil cup.

I focused my camera on the shoes on the body's feet, zeroing in first on the stiletto heels, then on the straps securing the shoes to the feet. I counted six narrow straps across the arch and a seventh around the ankle. Even wet, the shoes' distinctive color stood out like a signature. "Dragon's fire," I said under my breath and my stomach did the little flippy thing it always did when adrenaline hit my system.

I glanced at Dom. His face told me I wasn't the only one who recognized those shoes.

Chapter 2

I BEACHED my canoe and approached the clutch of swimsuit-clad teens, not one of them over fifteen, sitting on the public pier, shivering despite the heat, their eyes glued to the police boat and the load hanging from the winch.

"I heard you discovered the barrel," I said.

A skinny blond boy nodded. "Near the edge of the shelf. We were looking for stuff, y'know? Like we always do. Notes in bottles, fishing rods, cell phones."

"We've been diving here almost every day," the freckled girl next to him said. "There was nothing there yesterday or the day before." She turned toward her friends, her braids swinging with the movement. "Right? We'd have seen it for sure. It appeared overnight. Right?" The others nodded.

The boy said, "We couldn't miss the barrel. Just lying there. Filled with something, cement, I bet. And legs sticking out the top." He shuddered and rubbed both hands over his face. "Maybe it's a dummy from a store?"

I shook my head. "Afraid not."

He hugged himself. "That's sick," he said, his voice going all pitchy. "What a freaky, awful way to die."

I left them to their vigil and headed to the parking lot. I was halfway there when Dom shouted. "Olivia, wait."

As he jogged toward me, warmth blossomed in my belly. Sometimes my body refused to listen to my head. In motion, Dom sizzled. In truth, he exuded heat pretty much all the time. It was the Italian in him.

"I know you think it's Shauna in the barrel," he said. "But until we're sure you can't print her name."

"Everyone knows who wears those shoes." My voice caught when I pictured Shauna in her trademark fiery red stilettos. I shook my head to chase the threatening tears away and reminded myself she'd been dead to me the minute I learned about her deceit. No crying then, no crying now. I cleared my throat and said, "I won't need to mention her name. One look at the photos and people will figure it out."

"You can't use a picture either."

When I sucked in my breath, Dom raised his hands. "You know I'm right. It could be someone else."

"Those are her shoes, and that's her in the barrel, and you know it."

Dom shook his head.

"Designer stilettos with jeans?" I said. "That's pure Shauna."

Dom watched the coroner's van enter the lot. Then he dropped his gaze to my bandaged hand. "What happened?"

"I gouged it trying out my new hobby."

"You should pick different hobbies. Like reading." Dom ran his hand through his hair. Silver glinted in the dark waves —more of it than I remembered. "Here's the deal. If you use a picture, pick one without the shoes."

"Fine. Just promise to tell me the minute you identify her."

I checked my watch. I had five hours and a bit if I wanted to make the digital edition of the *Gazette*, Prospect's local newspaper. It would take ten minutes to sort through my pictures for one without the shoes and perhaps another ten to write what so far was a two-line story.

That left ample time to stop by Shauna's house before I sat down at the computer. Dom might be right—she *could* be alive. Of course she could. Politicians would stop lying; Nashville would stop singing about trucks; and I would wake up tomorrow thinking about Dom in bed with my former friend and not puke.

Chapter 3

WHEN I RETURNED TO PROSPECT, I drove to Ridgeline Plateau, a rarified neighborhood amid aspen and Jeffrey Pines, where several hundred thousand dollars got you two private acres and a knockout view of the rolls and folds of the Truckee River valley. Half a million more dollars bought you a nondescript two-bedroom bungalow to plunk in the middle of your rural piece of northern California.

The wrought-iron gates at the entrance to Shauna's thirty-acre ranch stood open. I followed the stamped concrete driveway around her soaring timber frame house and parked not far from her three-car garage. Two dandelions dared to poke their heads through the manicured lawn and glowed yellow in the afternoon sun. A few leaves from nearby quaking aspens floated in the competition-sized pool.

I turned off the engine and stared at Shauna's outdoor arena. The ground was raked smooth, ready for riders, and three faded two-toned barrels sat in the distinctive triangular arrangement for barrel racing. Just six weeks ago, before things all went to rat shit, Shauna and I had raced Rocketman and Sugarplum around those barrels, practicing for the Silver State Stampede in Elko.

No. That wasn't true. Shauna had raced, urging Rock-etman toward and around the barrels, leaning forward in the straight run to the finish and screeching with triumph as the big palomino cut two-tenths of a second off their time. Sugarplum and I had negotiated the course at a lope, turning the barrels cautiously. When I brought the appaloosa to a halt beside Shauna, she had said, "That wussy saunter won't even get you past the qualifying run. What's going on?"

"It seemed fast to me."

She removed her cowboy hat and finger-combed her auburn bob. Her gold and amethyst chandelier earrings swung and glinted in the sun. "I could have made pasta from scratch while you ran the route."

I laughed. "Like you've ever made anything from scratch. I was being careful, okay? Tipping a barrel means a five-second penalty."

"What have I been teaching you since May? Lean forward in the saddle, look ahead and not down at the barrel as you round it, signal her with your legs rather than the reins. She knows her stuff. You can let her run. She won't crash."

"Easy for you to say. You were on a horse before you were out of diapers."

"You'd have as much experience, if not for the thing with the Shetland pony." Shauna paused. Then she said, "Sugarplum's not a Shetland. You're not twelve anymore. You have a saddle, and a horn to grab. You won't fall."

She knew me so well—how could she not? We'd lived in each other's pockets since kindergarten. Of course, she'd zeroed in on what was holding me back. A humiliating and painful experience riding bareback on a Shetland pony and falling. Only to find my hand caught in the rein as the pony continued trotting along a rough path. By the time I freed myself, my back was scraped and bleeding.

I winced and smiled at Shauna. "Yeah. Remember how furious Mom was when she saw my back?"

"Gawd almighty, I thought she would kill us both. Or worse, quit working for my parents and then they would have grounded me for life."

"Instead, she just forbade me to even pet a horse until I was thirty."

Shauna smirked. "Little did she know how often you broke that rule. And look where you are today—thirty-three and soon we'll both be competing in Elko."

I had believed her that day.

But now? The Silver State Stampede was this coming weekend, and I definitely wouldn't be competing. Those plans, like so much else, had ended three weeks ago.

I shook the thoughts of what could have been from my head, took a deep breath, and stepped from my car. I walked to her back door and rang the doorbell. When no one answered, I tried the handle before walking ten steps along the deck to peer through the kitchen window. A single water glass sat on the island, a faint smudge from Shauna's Gypsy Red lipstick visible below its rim. I walked further along the deck to the den's French doors. Shauna's purple Gucci bag slouched on the hardwood floor next to a red leather club chair. Her laptop sat on the desk, its lid open but the screen dark.

I returned to the door and considered entering the house. I knew the four-digit combination as well as I knew my own. My finger hovered over the buttons while I debated about breaking and entering. Did possession of the combination make a difference? I pressed 3—2—9, and hesitated.

Who was I kidding? She wasn't here. She'd been trying to talk to me for three weeks now, leaving phone messages, sending email, and finally resorting to the U. S. Post Office. Her surveillance cameras would have picked up my hybrid the minute I turned off Panorama Drive onto her driveway. She'd know I was here. If she were home, she'd answer the door.

To be sure, I peered through the glass panels in the garage doors, looking for her Firenze Red Land Rover. I spotted her

Polaris snowmobile, her mountain bike, and her Harley. But no Land Rover.

I walked toward my car, glancing again at the dented green and yellow barrels in the arena.

My stomach flipped. The horses!

Chapter 4

I RAN to the stable and when I called their names, the horses stuck their heads over their stalls' gates. Rocketman snorted. I rushed over. "Big guy, you okay?" An acrid smell hit my nose and made my eyes water. His stall needed serious mucking. The water and alfalfa levels were low, his feedbag empty. No doubt Sugarplum's stall would be in the same condition.

I phoned Dom but was punted to voicemail. "I'm at Shauna's place. If you need more proof it's her body in the barrel, her horses haven't been tended to for a long time. Their stalls are a mess. Poor things. I'm going to put things right. But you might want to send someone out here."

I led both horses outside to the paddock, filled the water trough, and gave them fresh alfalfa. Then I tackled their stalls, trying to breathe through my mouth as I worked. My left hand ached and the bandage made grasping the pitchfork difficult. Twenty sweaty minutes of scraping and scooping proved I had no future as a stable hand. However, compared to the conditions I'd found originally, their stalls would win a good housekeeping award.

I let the horses stay in the paddock to enjoy the fresh air. It wouldn't take me long to return after dinner and re-stable them.

I put the pitchfork back with the other tools in the barrel by the stable door and brushed myself off as I trekked back to my car. A police cruiser sat in the driveway. A member of Dom's team, who'd been at Donner Lake earlier, climbed out. "Mrs. Bertucci, hello."

No matter how often Dom and I reminded his colleagues that I used my maiden name, they called me "Mrs. Bertucci." Five years since our wedding, five years telling his squad my name was Olivia Mercier, and they still did it. Or worse yet, called me "ma'am." Two years ago, I decided to give my blood pressure a break and pick other battles to fight. I put a polite smile on my face. "Corporal Clapton, glad you're here. How are you?"

"Surprised to see you here."

"Did Dom tell you I called? I hoped to find Shauna at home, but she's not answering her door. It looks like her horses haven't been tended to for ages, which is alarming. So, I took care of them."

He glanced toward the stable and then at the house. "I'll check things out."

"I can give you the lock's combination and the alarm code."

He wrote the numbers in a small notebook. "How did you come by this information?"

I felt my cheeks flush. "We were friends."

He clicked his ballpoint twice and wrote in his book. "Not anymore? Or because she's dead?"

When I stared at him in confusion, he said, "You said 'were friends.' Past tense. Because you know Ms. Wylie's dead, or because you aren't friends anymore?"

I gawked at him. How much did he know about my private life? I cleared my throat. "Not friends. Not so much anymore."

Clapton raised his eyebrows. "But you came here and went into her house today?"

Talking to cops was one thing when I was the person doing the interviewing. It was a whole other thing when Clapton turned the spotlight on me. Much like the heart racing, breath-shortening experience of being thirteen and on the hot seat in the principal's office explaining how I became trapped in the storage cabinets above the biology lab sink.

"Yes. I mean no. I mean yes, I came here. After the thing at the lake, I thought perhaps it wasn't her in the barrel, so I came here. But I didn't go in. I rang the bell and looked in the windows. Then I went to take care of Rocketman and Sugarplum."

"Uh huh. Those are the horses?"

"Yeah. I knew about them because Shauna and I used to ride together. Practiced barrel racing in that arena. Before … So, I looked in on them."

He clicked his pen again and made another note.

Many women would have left it there and made a gracious exit. But I burned to know. "Can I ask something technical? How long will it take to remove the body from the barrel? I mean, they can't simply take a jackhammer to it, can they? That would be risky."

He stared at me like he wished he had a string of garlic to wrap around his neck.

A bubble of laughter formed in my gut. I swallowed it down. "Ahhh. I mean risky if you don't want to mess up evidence, right? That means a jackhammer's out. Unless they x-ray the barrel to see where she is in there? To figure out where to put the jackhammer? Or will they use a chisel?"

His ballpoint flew over the notebook. He clicked his pen closed. "I don't know, Mrs. Bertucci. You'd have to ask the M.E."

"Can he get her out? Or will he ship the whole shebang somewhere specialized?"

Unfortunately, I react to the surreal by allowing dark humor to slip past my teeth. If anything was surreal, it was the thought of Shauna encased in concrete. So, of course, I then said, "Where's Michelangelo when you need him, hey?"

I chuckled and then choked it down. But when I looked at Clapton's shell-shocked face and heard the rapid clickety-click-click of his pen, a cascade of giggles escaped.

Would Dom see any humor in this when Clapton reported in? In better days, yes. Now, maybe not. I took a deep breath and backed away. "The horses are in the paddock. Could you return them to their stalls before you leave? I'll be going."

He studied me for what felt like an hour, but was probably only half that. About the time I was ready to confess to every instance of jaywalking, speeding, and rolling through stop signs, he pocketed his notebook, and nodded at me. "Take care, Mrs. Bertucci."

I tried very hard not to run to my car.

Chapter 5

IT TOOK two and one-quarter hours for Dom to learn about my escapade and express his opinion. The time frame would have been much shorter, except I hid out at the *Gazette*.

Amanda Brammell, the owner and editor of the *Gazette*, wasn't in the office, so I sent her a quick text:

> Tipped to body at Donner Lake. Def suspicious. Will send you draft copy.

Immediately my phoned pinged with her response:

> K. Maybe this time we scoop our fave blogger?

The anonymous author of the *Cheat Sheet* blog had beat the *Gazette* to the more salacious news in Prospect ever since the blog first appeared online. If a prominent person was up to no good, the *Cheat Sheet* knew what it was and told the public about it. Some exposés the blogger published amounted to sordid gossip, but many of them revealed things voters or consumers needed to know.

Both Amanda and I wanted to identify the blogger. Amanda saw the *Cheat Sheet* as a threat to the *Gazette*'s position as the leading newspaper in the Prospect area. I resented the blogger because I had a reputation as the pre-eminent investigative reporter in town, and not a week went by without someone asking me, "Did you see the latest in the *Cheat Sheet?* Why didn't you report on that?"

I had tried everything I could think of to unearth the author of the *Cheat Sheet*, from hanging out in online chat rooms, to reading the blog for telltale clues, to trying to connect with victims of the blogger's exposés. All with no luck. I had even asked Shauna for help during one of our brunches at Dockside Restaurant. "Amanda and I want to identify the author of the *Cheat Sheet,* that silly tell-all blog," I'd said.

"Does the *Gazette* want to hire them?"

I snorted. "Only if Amanda wants tabloid trash instead of quality writing. No, just wanting to know the competition. Have you heard any scuttlebutt?"

Shauna shook her head. "No. But don't you agree there could be some value to the *Cheat Sheet?* I mean if, as you say, it's competition." Shauna sipped her mimosa. "Maybe the blogger has a nose for news."

"More like a nose for rumors and innuendo. Whatever. Can you keep an ear out?"

Shauna had smiled and raised her glass. "You mean, for rumor and innuendo?"

That brunch had been a couple of months ago, and even Shauna, with at least a gigabyte of contacts, had come up dry.

This time, however, I was fairly certain I would scoop the blogger, unless they also had a contact within the ranks of first responders. I wrote the bare-facts story, attached a picture that showed nothing of the victim's body, and sent it to Amanda.

Then I frittered away an hour or so tidying my desk and making to-do lists, before I plucked up the courage to head home. Perhaps I'd given Dom the slip.

A fairly useless hope, considering Homicide Captains don't reach that rank by being hoodwinked easily. He did what you'd expect—parked outside the house and waited for me to show up. A cop can out wait anyone.

Dom followed me along the walk to the front door of the house. Rather than punch in the entry code, I turned to face him. I didn't bother smiling. "What are you doing here?"

"We need to talk."

"No," I said. "We have nothing to talk about. You made sure of that when you cheated."

"What was this morning, then? You were happy to talk to me then."

"That's different. We were interacting in our professional capacities."

"Which is exactly why I'm here," Dom said. "To discuss what you did after you left Donner Lake."

I stood by the front door and glared at him. "Can't it wait?"

"No. You can let me in, or we can stand out here and let the neighbors watch the show. Either way, we have to discuss things now."

"Fine," I said, and punched in the entry code. I pushed the door open. "After you."

I affected nonchalance and ignored Dom's grim face as he entered the house. I swept by him, headed straight for the fridge, and poured a healthy slug of Pinot Grigio.

"What were you thinking?" Dom's clenched jaw contradicted his calm tone. "Going to Shauna's. Messing with a potential crime scene."

"Crime scene?"

"If the body is Shauna's, we'll be looking for evidence at her ranch." He paced in front of the kitchen island. "And you were there, screwing things up."

His tone had moved past pseudo-calm to genuine-edgy. I swallowed some wine and shrugged. "I fed the horses and cleaned their stalls. What's wrong with that? Plus, I left you a message about the situation."

"Did you take pictures?"

"No."

"All we have is your word for what you did at Shauna's, or what it looked like before you touched things. Corporal Clapton said you gave him the combination and alarm code. Please tell me you didn't go into the house."

I shook my head. "I didn't. Why isn't my word good enough?"

"Because you said Shauna wasn't your friend anymore. Yet you were out there." He lifted his hands, palms up. "And then, *then,* you ask about jackhammers and crack wise about Michelangelo. The entire department's talking about it. Honestly, Michelangelo?"

"It just slipped out. You know how I get when faced with bizarre situations." I raised my eyebrows and shrugged. "Admit it, Michelangelo had the right touch with a chisel."

Dom's lips ticked upward on the right side as he stared at me. "Clapton thinks you have an unacceptably dark sense of humor. Of course, he has none, so don't put much weight on his opinion."

The tension dissipated. After a moment, Dom said, "I have a question."

I tightened my grip on the wine glass until I thought the stem would snap, waiting for yet another "let's reconcile" plea from him.

"I met a landscaper," he said. "Can you hire him?"

I stood there gape-mouthed. "Pardon?"

"We attended the homeless camps along the river today on a wild goose chase. I met a couple with two young kids and a little dog. Last spring, the guy lost his job. Then they lost their house. About all they have is an old truck, a tent, and a Coleman stove. His wife works at Sierra Bistro. Meanwhile, he's taking care of the kids and looking for work."

I thought about the lawn that hadn't been cut since Dom moved out and now looked like a barley field. "I'll talk to him. Can you show me where their camp is?"

Dom shook his head. "They've moved to the Riverbend Motel for now." He tilted his head as he smiled.

As sure as I knew my name, I knew what he'd done. "You paid for their room."

"Just until the end of the month. Children shouldn't live in a homeless camp. What d'you think? I'll cover the costs of the landscaping."

"Sure, why not?"

"Great." Dom took a step toward the doorway and then paused. "Chief Gavric said you're interviewing him tomorrow?"

"Yes, about his rescue of a kidnapped boy twenty-five years ago. It's part of our Local Heroes series."

"He may be testy. He heard about Michelangelo and suggested I do more to keep you under control."

"Really?"

Dom's eyes glinted as he flashed a grin. "His exact words were 'rein in that little filly.' I said I'd get right on it, but sarcasm is lost on him."

"Rein in that filly."

"*Little* filly. Yep. Go easy on him tomorrow."

Chapter 6

I HAD no idea what little fillies wore to meetings with throwbacks, so Tuesday morning I donned my usual jeans and a T-shirt. I'd interviewed many people with whom I disagreed and didn't plan on confronting Chief Gavric about his comment. The story was more important. Still, his words irked me and, in an up-yours gesture, I pulled on cowboy boots.

I refreshed my knowledge of Gavric's background by reading his bio and archived stories about the kidnapping. Then I checked a few details online and found only one wrong note, an oversight on his alma mater's website.

If Gavric was feeling testy (as Dom had suggested yesterday), he hid it well as he ushered me into his office. When I suggested photos to accompany the article, he gestured at a wall bearing framed pictures. "How about by my wall of honor?" After I snapped a few shots, he pointed out his favorite items: arriving from Poland as a kid with his parents; receiving a wrestler-of-the-year-award in college; swearing the citizenship oath; his graduation certificate from First Responders Advanced Training; and last, a snapshot with six-year-old kidnap victim Clipper Milliken who Gavric had rescued twenty-five years ago.

I raised my phone. "May I record the interview?"

He settled into his desk chair. "Certainly. Sit, Olivia, relax. Let me express my condolences."

"Pardon?"

"The body at the lake? They say it could be Shauna Wylie. I understand she's a dear family friend. Was she Dom's friend first, or yours? Sad affair, isn't it?"

My stomach tightened, and my cheeks burned. A nice touch that, telling me he knew about Dom and Shauna, while spouting social niceties. When I didn't respond, he said, "She's a member of the Police Advisory Committee, so the department would suffer a loss as well if the body is in fact hers." He clapped his palms on his desktop. "Shall we begin?"

"Sure thing," I said. I opened my notebook and tapped the phone's record button. "Tell me about the kidnapping and rescue."

He leaned back and stared at the ceiling. "A low-level hood named Jasper Cruikshank grabbed little Clipper Milliken on his way home from school in the middle of winter. He demanded a million bucks for ransom. Long story short, I got a tip about unusual activity at a cabin a few miles from Donner Memorial State Park. I took a snowmobile most of the way and then hiked in. Cruikshank was in the cabin. Clipper too, tied up."

"How'd you get Cruikshank away from Clipper?"

Gavric laughed. "I banged around making like a lost elk and Cruikshank came outside toting a rifle. When he realized I wasn't an elk, he shot at me. I returned fire, hitting his leg and incapacitating him. I handcuffed him, untied Clipper, and loaded them into Cruikshank's piece-of-junk vehicle. Which wouldn't turn over."

"Of course."

"Yeah," Gavric said. "Nothing's simple. I tried to call in, but you know the mountains. No reception. I hotfooted it to my snowmobile, and got back to the cabin barely in front of a record-sized blizzard. Fortunately, there was an ancient toboggan in the cabin, so I secured Cruikshank to it. Clipper rode behind me on the snowmobile and held onto the rope from the toboggan so we could tow Cruikshank. Good plan, I thought. Right until the snowmobile conked out about five miles from town."

"Didn't I read in the archives you carried them to town?"

He shrugged. "Not both of them. Clipper was a tough little guy and walked more than halfway. I pulled the toboggan with Cruikshank because he couldn't walk. Hard slogging, I don't mind saying. About two miles from town, Clipper fell and just lay there, saying he'd wait for his mom. I knew that spelled disaster, so I hefted Clipper onto my back. I carried Clipper and dragged the toboggan and Cruikshank the rest of the way."

"Impressive." I smiled. So did Gavric.

I said, "Give me a moment to rein in my emotions so I don't gallop past something important." Gavric's smile didn't falter.

I flicked through my notebook. "Do you think wrestling in college contributed to your ability to bring Clipper and Cruikshank back safely?"

"Wrestling made me a fitness addict. The answer's yes, of course."

"I looked at your alma mater's website. You were wrestler-of-the-year twice?

"Twice in four years."

"Doubly impressive. I noticed in your bio that Poland, your home country, invited you to compete for them in the '84 Olympics."

He glanced toward the citizenship picture on the wall. "That was just before I was gonna become an American citizen, so I turned it down." He shrugged. "Anyway, Poland ended up boycotting the Games."

"Weirdly, your college website mentions other athletes who received offers to compete, but omits your invitation from Poland."

He jerked his head toward me. "Seriously? That's strange."

"Mistakes happen, I guess." I stashed my recorder and notebook in my bag. "Thanks for your time, Chief. I'm not sure when the article will run. I need to talk with Clipper Milliken if I can find him."

"I heard they moved east," Gavric said. "Probably to get Clipper away from terrible memories. He apparently had issues after the kidnapping. What kid wouldn't? His mother said he had trouble differentiating dreams and reality. If you find him, please tell me how he's doing."

As Gavric escorted me from the building, he said, "I'll call my college and have them rectify that error. I'd hate for you, or anyone else, to think I lied."

Chapter 7

AT HOME, I drafted my Local Heroes piece about Gavric.
Even if I used the wrestling angle, I had little that made my
article more than a rehash of previous stories. Then I remembered Gavric's comment about the Police Advisory
Committee and thought back to the independent audit the
committee had undertaken two years ago.

The review had been unfavorable and Gavric vowed to
ensure negative reviews of the Prospect Police Department
became a thing of the past. It would be interesting to know
whether he had, in fact, improved things. It was no use asking
Dom because he never shared anything with me that he didn't
want to see in a newspaper. If Shauna was alive (and I was
positive she definitely was not) and if we'd been on speaking
terms (which we definitely were not), I could have wormed the
information out of her.

I opened my contacts on my phone to hunt for other
members of the advisory committee who I could call for an
update, but then thought better of it. The paper's Local
Heroes series featured stories about people in the area who
had done extraordinary things. Cluttering a laudatory piece
with details about the hero's possible past failures seemed

contrary to the spirit of the series. I omitted the departmental audit and saved the draft article to my computer. Then I sent a note to Amanda, my editor, saying as soon as I obtained comments from Clipper Milliken, I would submit the final version.

Just before four o'clock, I glanced out my living room window and spotted Mrs. Bagnovicz weeding her garden gnomes. She was nothing if not dependable. She fussed with those little ceramic guys every day, no matter the weather, spring, summer, and fall. I didn't need to look at the calendar to know today was Tuesday, because Tuesday was "weed the gnomes" day. Tomorrow would be "polish the gnomes" day, a.k.a. Wednesday.

I suspected Mrs. Bagnovicz used the gnomes and other miniature garden props as a convenient cover for the real reason she lingered in her garden. Every neighborhood has someone who takes the phrase "keeping an eye out" to heart, and Baggie was ours. Her oversight of our street had skyrocketed in the last few weeks, ever since an otherwise serene June day when Dom dodged and ducked the hailstorm of clothing and footwear descending on him from our upstairs bedroom window. Baggie's house was directly across the street from my next-door neighbor Pierre, so she saw it all. Now she practically lived in her front garden, keeping an eye on me— whether to protect me or herself, I wasn't sure.

On the upside, I told myself as I walked outside and opened the garage door, if I ever needed an alibi, Baggie might come in handy.

Theoretically, since Dom had moved out, and this was a two-car garage, my small Ford hybrid should fit easily. However, lately I had filled much of the space with the necessities for my new metal lawn art hobby. Which meant I had to park in the driveway. Which meant everyone knew when I was home.

I set about rearranging things to clear space for the car.

Hidden behind some old metal farm implements that I'd bought at a yard sale were two boxes from Prospect Wine Cellar. I stared at them while I tried to decide what to do with the contents. Save the wine or trash it? Only one way to find out if soul-destroying memories affected the taste, I decided. I unscrewed the cap on a bottle of Cabernet Sauvignon and took a sip.

The wine was smooth and delicious. Shauna and I had done well when we had selected that wine for our crowd's annual camping trip. I took another sip and corrected myself. Although the wine was to be Dom's and my contribution to the trip, Shauna had been the connoisseur. She had chosen the wine, and I had paid for it. The wine-purchasing excursion was three and a half weeks ago. I saw Shauna only once after that. If the planned camping trip took place, it happened without me, because I opted out of all events with Shauna after I discovered her betrayal.

I set the wine down, blinked back tears, and surveyed the mess in the garage. There was still not enough room to park my car inside. My shoulders slumped. Tomorrow. Collecting the bottle of wine, I returned to the house. I would finish clearing the space tomorrow. Tonight I just wanted to forget.

Chapter 8

MY HEAD WAS foggy Wednesday morning. I probably should have stopped drinking when the wine bottle was half empty. Or sooner.

After a quick shower and two cups of coffee, most of the mist had cleared from my brain. I checked my calendar and discovered I had nothing scheduled until Thursday's interview with Maggie Shillingford, chair of the Prospect Garden Show.

The blank space for today was initially inviting. Rather than finish clearing the garage, I elected to fashion a piece of garden art. I threw on old jeans and a sweatshirt and then opened the overhead garage door to invite the sunshine and fresh air in. My first idea was to make a metal bird out of some rebar and old gardening tools. When I approached the barrel where I'd stashed the rebar, I immediately envisioned another barrel swaying from the police boat's winch.

I shook that thought from my head and tried to come up with another design. Perhaps a windmill? A turtle? Half an hour later, I admitted defeat. Visions of the concrete-filled barrel kept interrupting my attempts to plan the sculpture. Obviously, a solitary activity would not keep those images at bay. It would be better to seek human company.

I gave Maggie Shillingford a call. "Excellent and very civilized idea, Olivia," she said, when I asked if we could move the interview ahead. "Tomorrow will be panic stations because it's opening day for the Garden Show. Today I have lots of time. Shall we say noon-ish at the Exhibition Grounds?"

Shauna had introduced me to Maggie six months ago. We had been sitting near the fireplace at the Dockside restaurant when Shauna glanced over my shoulder and waved at someone. "Margaret Shillingford's making her way over here," she said. "She's on the board of the hospital foundation with me. Also, a master gardener and head of this year's Garden Show."

Since my exposure to the manure-is-more-than-a-bad-smell-set began and ended with the clerk at Prospect Posies who sold me hanging baskets each summer, I expected to shake an American Gothic's calloused hand.

Margaret Shillingford's hand, however, was callous-free and smooth. She was tall and trim, and looked like she spent hours every day in her private spa. She clasped my hand. "Olivia, how nice to meet you. You're with the newspaper, aren't you? Excellent."

When Shauna invited her to join us for dessert, she claimed the extra chair and said, "It's always a good day for sweets, isn't it?"

I caught a hint of Britain in her word choice and nodded. "Do I hear a British accent, Margaret?"

She laughed and pushed a stray lock of perfectly streaked hair away from her forehead, her chunky silver and turquoise bracelet catching the midday sun. "Please, it's Maggie. I've been in this country for two decades, even so, traces of Britain remain. Interesting isn't it, how parts of your past never leave you?"

"Like some ex-husbands," Shauna said.

"Speaking from experience?" Maggie said.

Shauna grinned. "Three trips to the altar, three trips to divorce court. Two exes I'd rather not see again, and one—well, you can't have everything you wish for, right?" She tapped the menu. "However, we *can* have any dessert we want."

"*You* can," I said.

When Maggie stared at me with a question on her face, Shauna said, "Olivia claims the devil uses desserts to entice humans down the slippery slope to hell."

"Not all humans," I said. "Not Shauna certainly. The word 'diet' has never crossed her lips. But for me? Yes, the devil's tools. And it doesn't help—"

Shauna interrupted. "When her best friend makes a point of telling her what she's missing." She grinned. "Like scones that are unbelievably jam-worthy, croissants loaded with butter, or Black Forest Cake—the dessert I'm about to order."

I laughed. "Yes, exactly."

Maggie patted my hand. "Never mind, Olivia. Karma always finds some other way to punish those who don't need to diet."

Later, as Shauna and I walked to our cars, I asked whether Maggie worked.

"God no," Shauna said. "She's loaded. A place in town, a mega-cabin here at the lake. Certainly, more money than the rest of us peasants."

Now, as I changed into clean jeans and a T-shirt, I nodded at Shauna's comment. Over the last months, I'd learned enough about Maggie to know she had big bucks. And if Shauna, who was in fact screaming rich, believed she was a peasant in comparison, then Maggie's wealth had to be stratospheric.

I jumped in the car and waved at Mrs. Bagnovicz, who was outside giving her gnomes a spit-polish (it being Wednesday), as I passed her house. Since the Exhibition Grounds were on the outskirts of town, I stopped by a few secondhand dealers and yard sales on the way and bought items I could transform into quirky garden art.

Just before noon, I arrived at the Exhibition Grounds and found Maggie supervising a crew unloading boxes. "Our programs," she said. "Should have been here a week ago. Too late to worry about typos, so I won't."

She linked her arm through mine. "It's so good to see you, Olivia. We must make time for lunch after the show is over. Now, come with me."

She walked me through the Garden Show exhibits while I snapped pictures. Maggie deftly highlighted items that were beneficial to wildlife and pollinators and which she believed deserved prominence in my article. In the garden décor section, I stood still for a moment, checking out the items on display. "Something interests you?" Maggie said.

"I've begun making sculptures from reclaimed metal and need sturdy bases. I tried putting concrete in buckets, but it's impossible to unmold, so that's a bust." I pointed at a round steppingstone. "Do you think I could cut a base out of that?"

Instead of answering, Maggie lifted a circular metal mold and eyed its depth. "Depending on your sculpture's weight, you could pour concrete into this and before it sets, insert the sculpture."

"Worth a shot," I said. I found the stall vendor and paid him for a mold, said goodbye to Maggie, and lugged my treasure to the car.

Chapter 9

It was mid-afternoon by the time I returned from the Exhibition Grounds, parked in my driveway, and opened the garage door. I had just wrestled an old iron garden gate from my car's trunk when Dom's cruiser pulled up out front. Clapton climbed from the passenger seat and said, "Good afternoon, Mrs. Bertucci."

I nodded at him and silently lectured myself about not running off at the mouth like someone on amphetamines.

Dom's expression was somber as they approached me. He reached out as if to touch my shoulder, but seemed to think better of it and drew his hand back. "They removed the body from the barrel today. It *is* Shauna. Bashed on the head."

The wrought-iron gate slipped from my grip and clattered to the driveway. From the moment I'd seen the vivid flame-colored stilettos on the body's feet, I'd told myself Shauna was dead. I hadn't dwelt on the how. Now, however, Dom's words filled my head with thoughts of being forced headfirst into a barrel of wet concrete and held there until I suffocated. Revulsion made my stomach clench. I swallowed several times against the urge to vomit.

Dom spoke again, his voice pulling me away from the

horrid images and allowing me to focus on something else. "The forensics guys are at her ranch. We need to know what you touched when you were there."

I cleared my throat. "Sure. Um, the stall gates; a bucket; the faucet; feed bags; pitchfork."

"Her doorbell?"

I nodded.

"Anything else?" Dom said. Clapton's pen clicked.

I said, "The door handle and the lock. Not the whole combination. The first three digits."

Dom picked up the wrought iron piece I'd dropped. "What's this?"

"Yard sale goodie. Can you put it against the far wall in the garage?"

He wove his way through the shambles in the garage and set the iron gate down beside my workmate bench. "Sheesh, you've turned our garage into a scrap metal joint."

"This may look like junk at the moment, but when I weld things together, it will be art."

Dom ran his hand through his hair. "Ohhh-kay. Sure."

"Been making concrete?" Clapton said. He stood beside a partly used bag of Portland Cement and the old green and yellow oil drum full of rebar. His eyes were on the remains of my latest batch of concrete in the wheelbarrow about three feet away from him.

I'd been married to Dom long enough to know how cops do math: body encased in a concrete-filled barrel, plus evidence of a person recently mixing concrete, equals a possible killer. I blushed and stammered. "I've been trying to make bases for my sculptures. I tried putting the concrete into metal buckets, but that flopped. So now I'm trying molds for steppingstones."

Clapton eyed me for a long moment and then jerked his head in a quick nod. "I see."

Dom put his hand on my shoulder. "You gonna be okay?"

I nodded and blinked quickly to clear my eyes of the tears threatening to leak out. "Yeah. I was going to reorganize the garage, but probably I'll just go inside and make tea."

Dom and Clapton left. I closed my garage door, went into the house, and put the kettle on. "Geez, Shauna," I said out loud. "Look at me, making tea. Mom always said tea soothes the aching heart." The tears began then, and my hand shook as I poured the water into the teapot. "Not sure it's gonna work this time, Shauna."

I sat in the living room and alternated between sipping my tea and crying. I liked it better when Shauna was alive, and I could be righteously angry. Sure, I said I never wanted to talk to her again. But this was different. Now I never would. Why the hell did she have to go and die?

I took a shaky breath and walked to my bathroom, where I stood at the sink and splashed some cool water on my face. My phone rang when I had my face buried in a towel. I quickly dried off and checked my phone's display. Amanda Brammell.

When I answered, Amanda said, "Oh good, glad I caught you, Olivia. I wondered if there was any update we could run on the body at Donner Lake?"

"Um, hi Amanda. Yes, I suppose."

"Have you come down with a cold? You sound all stuffed up."

"No. Not a cold. Dom was just here to tell me. It's Shauna, Amanda. The body."

Amanda's voice rose. "Shauna Wylie? Are you kidding me?"

"I wish I was."

"Omigod. How horrid for you. She's your friend. Or was." Amanda was quiet for a few seconds and then said, "You know this means you can't write the story, right? You've got a conflict."

I pushed back. "Surely the fact we were friends doesn't stop me reporting on her death?"

After a moment's hesitation, Amanda sighed. "If you update the obit we have on file for her, we can run that. But without your by-line. As for the rest of the story about her death and the probable police investigation, I'm assigning it to Owen. No doubt you'll be a suspect. I don't know a bigger conflict than that."

That floored me. "A suspect? Don't be ridiculous. We were friends."

"I can't believe you don't see it, Olivia. I didn't say anything to you before, because it's your private life. But it's no secret Shauna slept with Dom. Everyone knows you kicked him out of the house, and why. If I can see your motive, so can the cops."

I snorted in disbelief. "I'd need a much bigger motive than their romp in the sheets to kill Shauna. She was my best friend, for heaven's sake."

"Exactly," Amanda said. "And she did you wrong. You can bet the minute they identified the body, one of the cops jotted down 'best friend plus betrayal equals motive' and put your name beside the note."

"Maybe. But that person would be a dumb rookie. The others, the ones who work on homicide with Dom, will recognize that as a stupid motive."

"Let's hope so. Send me the updated obit tomorrow once you have it finished."

———

It took ages for me to fall asleep that night. Amanda's words had shaken me. Every time I closed my eyes, I envisioned the speculative expression on Clapton's face as his eyes had taken in the rebar in the barrel, sitting in my garage near the wheelbarrow and its dregs of concrete.

Chapter 10

By Thursday morning I had regained my senses. Cop or not, Clapton wouldn't suspect me of killing Shauna. I'd never had a speeding ticket; I chaired the police gala three consecutive years; I brought homemade cannoli to the department's staff parties. Cannoli-makers do not kill people, unless you count death by calories.

Shortly after eight, I was standing in my kitchen watching the coffee brew when I heard children's high-pitched voices telling someone named Charlie to behave. I wandered to the living room, peeked out the window and saw a small white dog streak along the driveway and leap into the barley field my lawn had become. I tracked his progress by the swaying of the seed heads. He exited the grass and skidded to a stop beside a small boy and girl. The dog's five-inch tail flashed back and forth like the pendulum on a maniacal metronome, before he once more repeated his race around the yard. I opened my door and stepped onto the porch. The dog stopped mid-stride, checked me out, and launched himself toward me.

"Charlie, no!" This from a brawny red-headed man

standing on the sidewalk beside a truck that had seen years and years of better days. The dog immediately stopped and was still. Except for his metronome tail, which evidently listened to no one.

Undoubtedly, this was the landscaper guy Dom met at the river. The freckled and gap-toothed boy and girl belonged to him. And the white speed demon with the possessed tail was Charlie.

The man tossed a leash to the boy. "Mind the pooch, Ben." He waded through the grass to me. "You must be Olivia Mercier? I'm Duncan McAdams. I'm very sorry Charlie's being a bother, but as we have no babysitter, I had to bring the entire clan along."

"Not a problem. Cute dog. What is he?"

McAdams said, "A mini schnauzer. We couldn't bring ourselves to crop his ears or tail."

"I'm with you." I gave the McAdams family and dog a tour of the yard, front and back. When Duncan McAdams asked me what work I needed done, I fumbled around for a bit, rambling on about pruning and trimming and edging and mowing and planting until I finally threw up my hands and said, "Beats me. Let's agree the garden's an ugly duckling. What will it take to make it a swan?"

He squinted his eyes and studied the landscape, or lack thereof. "Swans can run upwards of ten thousand dollars."

"Oh."

"The thing is," McAdams said, "this place doesn't want to be a swan. Its feathers are a tad ruffled, but it likes it that way. Nope, this place wants to be a goosander." He held his hand above the crown of his head and splayed his fingers. "You ever see one? It has reddish spikey feathers on its head. A duck with personality."

"Uh-huh." I steeled myself for the sales pitch. Personality-rich goosander ducks no doubt ran upwards of fifty thousand.

McAdams went on. "I'm thinking we can coax the unique

36

quirkiness out of this fledgling goosander for two, maybe three thousand. Or we can just smooth its feathers, make it look neighborly, for twenty-five bucks an hour."

I relaxed. "Let me talk to Dom about the scope of the job. Meanwhile, can you start making the place look like it belongs in the neighborhood? I can pay you at the end of each day if you like."

He shook my hand and grinned. "That'd be great. I can have it neatened up in two, three days, tops. I hope it's okay to bring the kiddos and Charlie along. My wife works days, so I'm in charge of Ben and Claire. And, god help me, Charlie."

We agreed McAdams would start the next day to give me time to talk to Dom about how much he wanted to spend.

After I said goodbye to the McAdams clan, I sat at the kitchen island to update the *Gazette*'s tribute to Shauna. Like most newspapers, the *Gazette* kept a file of obituaries for prominent people so that, when the person died, a tribute could be published quickly. The one for Shauna mentioned her education, the boards and committees of which she was a member, and the charities she supported.

I contemplated what I could add to the tribute. Even though I had cried for Shauna yesterday, the anger and hurt I felt because of her shoddy behavior still existed. That side of me was tempted to write that concrete looked good on Shauna. The adult side of me (which sounded an awful lot like my Aunt Gaye) said, "Get over it. You're a professional, act like one."

I reread the file copy. Although it was accurate and respectful, it was dry. It contained nothing about the real Shauna. Nothing that spoke of her flamboyance, or her love of animals.

I added a paragraph:

"Shauna Wylie's zest for life was evident in her exquisite and yet often quirky fashion sense, and her belief that stilettos, the more colorful the better, were the perfect accessory for everything from evening wear to jeans. Her love of animals was never more present than when she spent time with her horses. Rocketman, her Palomino, and Sugarplum, her Appaloosa, will miss their favorite groomer terribly."

I stopped typing long enough to text Dom:

Pls check on Shauna's horses

I reread the tribute and realized it had also overlooked another of Shauna's characteristics. When Shauna and I had been in grade school, a snotty rich kid with ringlets had picked on me because my mother was the Wylie's housekeeper and, in the girl's words, "an ignorant servant." She also told me my favorite pink socks were proof I had no class. When Shauna learned about the episode, she wore pink socks to school. "Just because you're rich doesn't mean you have class. Pink rocks," she told everyone. Soon all the snotty kid's clique were wearing pink socks.

I expanded my paragraph in Shauna's tribute:

"Her love of animals extended to the underdog. She believed wrongs needed to be righted and would fiercely defend your right to wear pink socks (or none, if that was your choice)."

The more I eulogized her, the more I missed Shauna, her sardonic grin, and her wicked sense of humor. I blinked back tears, wondering if I was mourning the loss of Shauna, who I had loved more than a sister, or the loss of our almost thirty-year friendship, which I had believed to be indestructible.

I sent the revised tribute to Amanda. She'd look it over and then publish it without a by-line. Fine by me. Most of the article was a file piece in any event. And I agreed I had a conflict because Shauna and I had been friends.

I wasn't worried about Amanda's assertion that I'd be a suspect. Corporal Clapton was smarter than that, surely. However, I was worried about the other comment Amanda had made.

Chapter 11

"SHAUNA AND DOM," Amanda had said. "Everyone knows why you kicked Dom out of the house."

Yesterday, visions of the concrete-filled barrel swinging from the winch had taken up residence in my head and forced me to seek human company. Today, the thought I was the talk of the town (and not in a good way) infiltrated my brain. "Everyone knows. Everyone knows. Everyone knows."

I jumped in my car and drove to the Altitude Mall outside of town, hoping some mindless window shopping would push thoughts of Shauna and Dom from my head. Not a chance.

Sixty-five hundred people, give or take, lived in Prospect and when Amanda had said "everyone knows," she probably didn't mean every single one of them. Still, as I wandered through the mall, I studied shoppers' faces, searching for clues they knew Dom had slept with Shauna.

I finally entered a grocery store and purchased kibbles for Charlie and cookies for the McAdams kids. When I carried my purchases to my car, I spotted an ice cream vendor near the parking lot. My mouth watered at the thought of a choco-late-dipped cone.

Yes, ice cream contained mountains of calories. But when things got tough, like they seemed to be doing lately, the calorie mountain was a hill worth climbing. I bought the cone and sat on a bench in the plaza while I calculated how many people might have an inkling why Dom's car was rarely in our driveway lately.

Chief Gavric knew we were separated, I was certain. Dom's squad might have guessed, but he wouldn't have talked about it. My doctor knew, but she was all about privacy. My hairstylist might have clued in when he said, "How about a bob, à la Shauna?" and I casually mentioned I'd rather stick pins in my eyes. Still, Zipper-Lips Jared didn't get to be the hottest stylist in town by blabbing.

I had worked my way through half the cone before I finally focused on what no doubt had made Shauna and me the topic-of-the-day around town. Three weeks ago, I'd gone to Dom's and my tiny cabin near the Truckee River to get it ready for a cook-out with Dom's team from the Police Department. I noticed the duvet was off center and began to remake the bed. Imagine my surprise when I found two earrings wedged between the sheet and duvet, one at the bottom of my side of the bed and the other mid-bed.

Not my earrings. And not just any earrings. Shauna's signature chandelier earrings, handcrafted for her by a jeweler on Pont de Vecchio. Which I'd noticed she hadn't worn for a while. Shauna, those chandelier earrings, and those vibrant stilettos. Inseparable.

I had phoned Dom. "Why are Shauna's earrings in *our* bed at *our* cabin?"

Dom sputtered. "Huh? What are you talking about?"

"Her prize earrings. In our bed."

"It's gotta be a joke."

"Really? Who has keys to the cabin besides you and me? No one, right? Is it you playing this joke?"

"No, Livvie, no."

He sounded strange. Not vehement enough. Almost afraid. "Oh shit. You slept with Shauna? My best friend?"

"Livvie. Olivia. It … no, nothing happened at the cabin. She wasn't there. I wasn't there. No."

I screamed into the phone. "It happened somewhere else, didn't it? I don't believe this. My husband tom catting around with my best friend? How long have you been doing this?"

"Livvie, no. It's not what you think. I'm not screwing around. There's nothing going on. It was … it was a huge mistake. I only want to be with you."

I was stuck back at "was a huge mistake." I disconnected the call. Dom had slept with Shauna. Mistake or not, he had admitted it. Where did that leave me?

After I spent several hours driving around, ignoring Dom's psycho-dialing, and rehashing the entire conversation in my head, I knew where it left me: pissed off.

At seven that same evening, I had driven to Chez Patrice. I knew Shauna would be there. Just that morning, she had told me her brother Noel was coming in from L.A. for a brief visit and invited me to join them for dinner. I had begged off, but she'd said, "Come by, even for coffee."

I marched into the restaurant, clutching the offending earrings. When I spotted Shauna and Noel at a table by the windows, I waved off the *maître de* and stormed over to their table. Shauna looked up from her meal and smiled at me. I threw the earrings into her *boeuf bourguignon*. "You are a man-eating bitch, Shauna Wylie. If you want any more Italian meat, look for it in a trattoria. And stay out of my life."

God, at the time it felt so *good* to throw those earrings and to say those words. Now, however, three weeks later, I had to admit the whole thing could have been ill-advised. Poetic? Yep. Circumspect? Nope.

My appetite vanished. I tossed the ice cream into the trash and trudged to my car. I had no one but myself to blame for whatever gossip was making the rounds. Sure, Shauna and

Dom shared the blame, but I'd made the story worth spreading.

Fine. I could deal with it. I had a freezer full of frozen dinners, a fully stocked wine fridge, the Food Network, two unopened jigsaw puzzles, and a computer. I could survive months without venturing outdoors.

And wouldn't that be ironic as hell? That Dom and Shauna could cavort on my sheets, and I was the one to hang my head and hide out. If not for them, there'd be no scandal. I wouldn't be popping anti-anxiety meds, buying hair-thickening shampoo, and eating food that added pounds I didn't want. I wrenched open my driver's door, flung myself onto the seat, turned on the ignition, slammed a ZZ Top CD into the player, and cranked up the volume. I peeled out of the lot. Every emotion I felt at Chez Patrice three weeks ago came back, high test, and extra hot. I could happily kill both of them and didn't care who knew it.

Chapter 12

ZZ TOP POUNDED from the stereo. I took the long way back to town and stamped the beat out on the steering wheel as I detoured along the pine-edged route that led me to Donner Memorial State Park. I pulled into the Park and lingered in the public lot, breathing in the fresh mountain air, and watching tourists pose for pictures by the Pioneer Monument. When I finally felt calm, I left and drove back to town.

It was late afternoon by the time I hit Main Street. I craved a coffee and stopped at my friend Harlow Hammer's Sierra Bistro. While I waited for my Americano, I received a call from Ronald Malkins, Shauna's lawyer. I stared at the neon palm trees of Oasis Auto Detail across the street while Malkins droned on about condolences and the shock of her death, and about her will and how I was mentioned in it. "If you could attend a meeting at my office Saturday at eleven, I would be grateful. Shauna's brother Noel will be there as well."

Spending my Saturday morning in a lawyer's office was not on my list of fun things to do in Prospect. Especially with bit-player Noel, who no doubt was still squandering his share of the Wylie family wealth on private acting classes with anyone who could spell Stanislavski. Shauna, who was the reluctant trustee of Noel's inheritance, had once told me, "I wish our parents had appointed someone else. My brother can spend money faster than a government official hoping to be re-elected, and he hates I don't fill his coffers whenever he's broke."

Now, as I considered the lawyer's request to meet, I was tempted to tell him no, but manners won out. "Tomorrow would be better. Or sometime next week."

"Noel's tied up in L.A. and won't arrive until late tomorrow night. We want to start the probate ASAP, so I'm afraid Saturday is it."

"Must I be there? Can't you simply mail it to me?"

"Pardon?"

"Her mother's cameo. Shauna told me she'd put my name on it."

"There is a bit more than the brooch. I'd rather we talked about this in person. Eleven on Saturday?"

I relented.

A bit more than the cameo, he'd said. Shauna knew I wasn't a big fan of jewelry, so why would she leave me more of it? If it was her chandelier earrings, I would grind them to bits.

I shrugged off my foul mood when the barista put my order on the bar. Coffee in hand, I strolled across Main Street to the car wash. "How much?" I asked the attendant.

"Your basic wash and vacuum, twenty-five. The full deal —wash, wax and shampoo—forty-five."

"How long does the full job take?"

"About an hour and a half. But we're closing early today. Soonest we can get you in is tomorrow morning."

I booked an appointment for the next day, thanked the kid, and jaywalked toward Sierra Bistro's lot. I noticed the police cruiser about the same time my left foot hit the center-line of the street. Clapton was behind the wheel, and I hoped he'd cut me some slack, but he turned into the lot, parked, and climbed out. My heart dropped.

"Hello, Mrs. Bertucci," he said.

"Hi. I usually use crosswalks even when it's a longer trek, but it's hot out today, isn't it? And there wasn't any traffic. Except you, of course." I took a deep breath. "Can I ask you not to ticket me?"

"I never write tickets when I'm off duty and right now it's my coffee break." Clapton touched his finger to his forehead in a small salute and turned toward the coffee shop.

I had my driver's door open and one foot in the vehicle, when he said, "Oh, one thing. Yesterday in your garage I noticed all that rebar in a barrel. I think the barrel's green and yellow?"

I slid into the driver's seat and nodded at him. "It's kinda faded, but yeah."

"Same as those out at Ms. Wylie's ranch? Did you get yours from her?"

I concentrated on placing my coffee in the cup holder and hoped he didn't see my hand shake. "Actually, Shauna and I bought a bunch from a local recycler last year."

"How many did you buy? All the same colors?"

"Six. The guy had maybe thirty, but they were all green and yellow. So, yeah, all the same colors." I checked my watch. "Look at that, I'm late."

"You have one, and there would be five at her place?"

I thought about lying for a second, but then said, "No. I took two. She kept four." I started the car. "I should go, Offi-cer. If that's it?"

"Thanks for your time, Mrs. Bertucci." He closed my door, and I pulled away.

AT HOME, my Americano grew cold while I sat at the table, stared at the pictures I'd taken of the concrete-filled green and yellow barrel hanging from the winch over Donner Lake, and thought about how two barrels had become one.

Chapter 13

THE DOORBELL RANG Friday morning only moments after I stepped from the shower and poured my first coffee of the day. Expecting Duncan McAdams, eager to start on the weed-infested half-acre masquerading as my garden, I put my eye to the peephole. Corporal Clapton stood beside an unfamiliar female officer.

Clutching the collar of my comfortable grungy robe, I cracked the door and peered out.

"Good morning Ms. Mercier," Clapton said. Today he seemed to know my proper surname. "I have a search warrant for your premises and vehicle. Please allow us to enter."

Externally, nothing moved. Not my feet, not my hand on the door, not my face. Internally, all systems were in overdrive. My heart rate approached tachycardia, my stomach bounced like it was on a trampoline, and in my head little voices screamed, "Incoming. Close the door. Incoming."

Finally, I broke eye contact with Clapton. I looked down at my slippers. Two Hello Kitties stared back at me, eyes oval and blank. "Give me a moment to change clothes."

"Sorry. Can't allow that." He held the warrant out to me and when I reached to take it, he pushed the door open and stepped smoothly inside. The female officer nodded at me and said, "Constable Jackson." She pushed by me and disappeared down the hallway.

I heard kitchen drawers opening and closing as I tried to focus on the document. The words shimmered and shifted. "What's going on?" I said.

Clapton's face was expressionless when he replied. "That's a warrant to search and seize evidence relating to the death of Shauna Victoria Wylie. It pertains to your house and outbuildings, your grounds, your vehicle."

"Are you kidding me? I'm calling Dom."

When I moved toward the hallway, he followed. "Corporal Clapton, please. Some privacy?"

"No can do. I have to keep you in sight."

This couldn't be happening. I phoned Dom's cell and when he answered, I said, "Corporal Clapton is here along with a Constable Jackson. It's not even eight and I'm standing in my Hello Kitties feeling violated, and I can't believe you would do this to me."

"What are you talking about?"

"Don't play innocent, Dom. These are your officers. Clapton gave me a search warrant. If this is a joke, it's a bad one. You better damn well fix this."

"Livvie, I swear I know nothing about this. Put Clapton on."

I handed Clapton my phone.

"Yes, sir?" Clapton said into the phone. I heard Dom's deep rumble.

"It's legit," Clapton said. "Issued by Judge McMillan late last night. To do with the Wylie case. Premises and vehicle. My affidavit in support should be on the file by now." He listened for a moment and said, "Sure, will do," before handing me the phone.

I put the phone to my ear. "So?"

"I'm on my way over there," Dom said. "Clapton has agreed to hold off the search until I arrive. Just stay calm."

"Are you serious? He won't let me get dressed and I've got my old robe on and my hair's wet and my coffee's cold."

"Make a fresh pot. I'm sure the officers will enjoy a cup. I'm on my way."

I drew in a shaky breath. "Okay."

"And Livvie? Do *not* say anything to them. About anything other than how they like their coffee. Got it?"

Chapter 14

THE TWO COPS and I sat in the living room after I made fresh coffee. Clapton studied his phone. Jackson examined her fingernails. To fill the silence, I switched on the local morning show. "Oh goody. Amish quilt making. Sit back, officers. Enjoy."

Twenty minutes later, Dom and another female officer arrived. Any more visitors and I'd be forced to bust out the folding chairs. Clapton raised his eyes from his phone and stared at the female cop with Dom. She ignored him.

Dom said, "How are you doing, Olivia?"

"Peachy. Except for the fact you arrived before we finished learning about the Three-Part Harmony Quilt, which I'm sure these officers agree was perfectly *à propos*."

Dom gestured at his colleague. "Corporal Cassidy will go with you while you change your clothes."

"Gee, and here I was hoping I could stash weapons of mass destruction in my Victoria's Secret underpants."

Cassidy's eyes crinkled, and her lips twitched. As she crossed the room to me, Clapton's gaze followed her.

Dom frowned. "Olivia, just change."

I turned on my heel and flounced down the hall with as

much hauteur as any woman in oatmeal-stained terry cloth and purple cat slippers could.

Behind me, Cassidy whispered. "Last time I tried to cram a weapon in my underwear, the thong ran far enough up my ass to make my eyes bug out."

My shoulders relaxed and I unclenched my fists. I entered the bedroom with a grin on my face. "You're saying wear granny briefs instead?"

"That would work." Cassidy leaned against the door and folded her arms. "Ms. Mercier, I know the situation sucks. But my presence protects you, as well as any possible evidence."

Shrugging, I changed into jeans and a T-shirt and tossed my robe into the hamper. I heard children's voices outside. Seconds later, my doorbell chimed. Cassidy watched me fold my nightshirt. "You didn't get Wonder Woman at Victoria's Secret," she said.

I smoothed the image on the folded garment. "Reno's Save-All. $11.99. Wide choice of colors."

"Thanks for the tip. Every woman needs her Lasso of Truth. Especially reporters and police."

"You know I'm a reporter? Did Dom tell you?"

She shook her head. "I recognized your name. I read your stuff in the *Gazette* all the time. Thorough and balanced. You seem to do your homework."

"Thanks. The day just got less crummy."

When we returned to the living room, Dom was alone. He rose from the sofa. "Corporal Cassidy, please wait in the car. I need a moment with Olivia."

After she left the house, I said, "I like her. How long has she been on your team?"

"Cassidy? A few months. She moved here from the Bay Area. While you were changing clothes, Duncan McAdams showed up, so I sent him away for a couple of hours. He asked about the landscaping, and I okayed something he called the personality makeover, whatever that is."

"Thanks." I listened to the silence in the house. "Where are the others?"

"Clapton's in the garage; his partner Jackson's out back."

"I can't believe this. What are they looking for? Why?"

"Apparently, Clapton put a few things together and asked the Chief to okay a warrant."

"Without checking with you?"

"Do you blame him? The woman he thinks possesses evidence about a murder is married to his immediate superior. I wouldn't have checked either. He says it was only after he talked to the lawyer and then saw you at the car wash that he decided to pursue things."

"Huh?"

"Shauna's lawyer. Clapton talked to him yesterday and found out you are in her will."

I shrugged. Some jewelry, the lawyer had said. Big deal.

"Then Clapton sees you coming from the car wash and when he checks with the attendant, he learns you've booked your car for a full detailing."

"So what?"

"Let's see. You have a barrel like the one in the lake; you've been making concrete; you had words with Shauna at Chez Patrice; she's the reason I don't live in this house anymore; she was struck with a narrow object; and there's rebar in the garage."

"I'm a suspect? For real?" I wanted to laugh. Or maybe cry. Or maybe go back to bed and pull the quilt over my head.

"You're a person of interest. For now."

"Oh, come on. I'm making yard art. And so what if Shauna and I argued? Lots of people argue."

"I agree. Most of it is weak."

"What do you mean, most of it?"

Dom said, "Did you know you were a beneficiary?"

"Sure. Her mom's cameo. And probably also her chandelier earrings, which, as you well know, she forgot in *our bed in our cabin.*"

Dom blew out an exasperated sigh.

I said, "Anyway, Shauna told me she was giving everything else to Noel, against her better judgment."

"Hmmm. She must have changed her mind. The lawyer said Noel inherits the ranch. But you get the rest."

That made no sense. Of course, Noel inherited it all. Unless Dom meant her personal belongings.

"What?" I said. "Like her horses and car and stuff?"

"Yeah." Dom cleared his throat. "And some cash."

"Huh?"

"At last count, about seventeen point five million. Dollars."

The floor became liquid. My vision swirled down, down, down through the narrowing eddy. I followed it, and Dom's voice became muffled. "Livvie? Livvie?"

Chapter 15

I WASN'T OUT LONG, but when I came to, I felt like I'd run a marathon in those few seconds. "I feel like crap."

"You don't look so good either," Dom said, his face hovering over mine as I lay on the floor. "You fainted."

Most of my brain seemed to float just out of reach. The small bit that could still reason registered Dom's comments once more: a wrecked marriage, a public spat, and a major inheritance. Circumstantial perhaps. My stomach lurched and my heart began pumping double time when I again focused on what they added up to. I pushed myself to a sitting position and the room tilted to the left. I clutched at the carpet to stop myself sliding off the floor. The room tilted to the right and a small acidic ball bumped against the top of my gut. "Gonna be sick."

"Uh oh." Dom lifted my right arm around his neck, hoisted me upright and sprinted, dragging me to the bathroom. "Want me to stay?" he said, as I collapsed and wrapped my arms around the toilet seat.

"Nooooo." I barfed. Ugly, putrid streams of coffee and bile. I heard the bathroom door close as vomit caught in my throat, its acidic taste triggering more gagging. My stomach clenched and released in sharp spasms, pushing more puke up my gullet and into the toilet bowl. I gasped between retches, trying to catch my breath. Even after it was empty, my stomach continued to heave and wrench for what seemed hours until it declared a shaky truce.

I sat on the floor for several minutes, soaking wet and spent, and then struggled upright. The face that met my eyes in the mirror was my grandmother in hospice. I splashed water on my face, brushed my teeth, gargled, and combed my hair. Now the face that met my eyes in the mirror was my mother on a chemo day.

Corporal Cassidy stood in the hallway with a glass of water when I exited the bathroom. "Drink. Captain B's making you something to eat."

"Oh gawd. Food."

She took my elbow and guided me to the kitchen. "Nothing exotic. Toast." She followed me into the kitchen and put the water glass on the counter. "Drink the water. I'll get you more."

Dom brought over a plate of toast and set it down. "You okay, bella?" He smoothed my hair away from my face. "You look better than before. Your color's coming back. Want to eat?"

I shuddered.

"Okay. Well, it's there for whenever."

We sat there, me drinking water, Dom watching me drink the water, and Cassidy alternating between refilling my glass and checking her email. I finally tired of being treated like an invalid and made myself some tea. "What's happening with Shauna's horses?" I said.

"They're good," Dom said. "Same as I told you the fifteen other times you asked. Noel is on his way, and in the meantime, her lawyer made arrangements."

"I hope whoever he hired is giving them some exercise,

not just throwing food at them and leaving them alone. Poor things. They won't know what's going on."

Cassidy said, "I was out there yesterday. That lawyer Malkins hired a couple grooms from the Reno racetrack. They're taking great care of the horses. It's fine."

"Maybe I'll go out there and check them over. To make sure."

"That's not a good idea, Livvie," Dom said. "Relax. They're in excellent hands."

"Maybe for now," I said. "When Noel gets here, though, I can't see him looking after them. He doesn't care about animals like Shauna did."

"Relax," Dom said again, at the same time as Corporal Clapton appeared in the kitchen doorway with a clipboard.

"Captain, we have the inventory."

Dom glanced at the form on the clipboard and handed it to me. "You need to review this and sign it, Livvie. It's a list of what they're seizing."

I scanned the inventory: One green and yellow barrel containing thirteen pieces of rebar, one opened bag of Portland Cement, one quart-size bag of gravel samples and another of sand, one MacBook, one mobile phone, one 2015 Ford CMAX.

"They're taking my computer and phone? And the car? How am I supposed to work?"

"You'll have to buy a burner. I'll lend you my laptop," Dom said. "You've backed stuff up, right?"

"Yeah. But I need my contacts. And my calendar and email files. This sucks. When can I have my computer back?" I paced the kitchen. "Crap. This is crap."

"Calm down. Give me a flash drive and I'll get the okay to copy that data. We'll do it at the station this afternoon."

"And my car?"

"I'll lend you my Jeep until your vehicle's released."

"How long will that be?"

"Couple days. They'll examine it for trace evidence and then release it." He smoothed my hair again, his touch warm and reassuring. I jerked my head away.

"And then," Dom went on, "perhaps a week to ten days to complete any tests or follow up on evidence they find."

"Meanwhile, the town gets to think of me as a suspect," I said. "This sucks."

Dom shook his head. "Person of interest."

Right. Everyone knew that the only difference between a person of interest and suspect was the perp walk.

Chapter 16

By eleven o'clock Friday morning, the cops had gone, Dom had dropped off his Jeep for me, and I was once more alone in a quiet house.

While I struggled not to hyperventilate as I assessed how much trouble I was in, I spied on Baggie Bagnovicz as she spied on my house through the aqua slats of her blinds.

The items the cops had seized added up to nothing as far as I could see. However, a niggling problem was the second green and yellow barrel I had admitted possessing. It was not the one they pulled from the lake, but to prove that I'd have to produce it, which meant unearthing things I'd rather leave buried.

But really, it was one missing barrel in the grand mess of what Clapton would surely realize was nothing more than circumstantial foofaraw. Still, suppose Clapton believed he had found his killer? Anxiety pushed adrenaline into my bloodstream, making my skin clammy and my vision narrow. I breathed in deeply, held it, breathed out slowly. Again. Again. And again, until the sensation eased.

I turned away from my window and strode to my bedroom. Anger had moved into the space vacated by the anxiety. First, I lost what would be a great story because of a conflict. Okay, yes, I understood. But nothing said I had to be ecstatic about it. Then Clapton shows up with a search warrant. And now I had no computer or phone, and I was expected to sit around meekly relying on Clapton to find the truth. Did I trust him to do that?

I remembered something Aunt Gaye, who was fond of Calamity Jane, often said: "If a woman wants to be a legend, she should just go out and be one." Well, I was an investigative reporter who needed to save her neck. Ergo, I should just go out and investigate Shauna's murder.

First step: find out what the cops thought they knew. Easy peasy. I didn't even have to ask Dom. All it demanded was a trip into town. A quick shower and blow-dry, a few passes of blusher and mascara, and a strategic selection from my closet transformed me outwardly into a woman even Attila wouldn't mess with. As testament to the power of Armani silk and Weitzman pumps, the more I assessed the in-charge woman reflected in my mirror, the more I believed she was me.

A few minutes before I was ready to leave, the doorbell rang and when I checked the peephole, I saw Duncan McAdams on the porch. I opened the door and he said, "Is now a good time? If not, we can come back."

"Now is perfect," I said. "I'm sorry things were a little crazy earlier."

"It's all good. Ben and Claire got to see inside a police car, and Charlie got to pee on its tires. All three were ecstatic. Your husband explained the police were running an exercise."

"Really?"

McAdams laughed. "Yes. Exercise in stupidity, I think he called it." He looked over his shoulder at his truck. "Shall I let the horde out, then?"

"Before you do, can the children have cookies? Any allergies?"

"No allergies. And yes, to the cookies, but only one or you'll have to answer to my wife Samantha."

After McAdams fetched his children and Charlie, I led them to the kitchen. I set Charlie up with a small bowl of kibbles and handed the bag of cookies to Ben. "I hope you and Claire like chocolate chip cookies? There's one for each of you."

Ben peeked in the bag and then looked at his father. When McAdams nodded at Ben, Claire did a little jig.

Before ushering his clan outdoors, McAdams told me he'd be at the house for several hours. When I offered to pay him in advance, he said, "No need. Dom and I made arrangements."

That few minutes with the McAdams family had relaxed me, uplifted my heart, and made me feel normal again. I tidied up, grabbed my bag, breezed out the door and down the driveway to Dom's Jeep. Baggie was outside now, watering her wooden tulips and plastic bunnies. It being Friday, her gnomes had repositioned themselves closer to the ceramic farmers' market under her hydrangea. I waved at her as I drove by. She ignored me.

I dug in my bag for my phone so I could access my music. When I remembered the cops had seized my phone, I smacked the steering wheel and then drove on, accompanied only by silence and the slow burn in my gut.

My first stop was the Clerk's Office at the Courthouse, where I asked for a copy of the information filed to support the search warrant Clapton had served on me. Accessing public files was something I routinely did as part of my job, but it felt bizarre to request something about myself. The clerk blushed and said, "I'm sorry, Olivia. I can't release that except to a lawyer or when a court file is opened. And so far, there's no formal file."

"By court file, you mean a criminal case file?"

"Or a civil lawsuit."

"Like the one I'm going to bring against the police department for malfeasance?"

She grinned. "Gawd, I hope you do it."

The funny thing about throwaway comments was they often planted a seed as you tossed them about. Why shouldn't I sue? Surely the inconvenience of being without my vehicle and computer and being expected to rely on my estranged husband for replacements was worth something? Not to mention the indignity of using a burner phone. Give me a break.

Next stop on my outing was Marshal's Electronics in Altitude Mall. "I need a pay-as-you-go phone, please. And I'd like to rent a MacBook Pro," I told Marshal. "Loaded."

Just over an hour later, Marshal had set me up with a loaner computer. I sat in Dom's Jeep and looked at the burner phone. Sheesh. Enough was enough. I could put up with the loaner laptop and this basic phone, but no way could I accept having to use Dom's Jeep.

I phoned Ritzy Car Rentals and placed my order. They asked when I wanted to pick up the vehicle. I said, "I have to stop by the police station. Could someone deliver it to me there, say, in half an hour?"

By the time I parked Dom's Jeep in the police lot, it was one in the afternoon, and I was starving. "USB drive, car, lunch, in that order," I told myself. I grabbed my belongings, locked his Jeep, and entered the building.

The civilian clerk at reception adjusted his red and green polka-dot bow tie as he smiled at me, his brown eyes cheerful. "Hey, Olivia. How's by you? I'll let him know you're here."

"Thanks, Clarence."

After he called Dom's office, Clarence said, "Say, Olivia, the missus and I are wondering." I steeled myself for the first of many questions from many people about why the cops searched my house. Clarence leaned closer to me and whispered, "Are the twins still living in your suite?"

His question took me by surprise until I remembered his wife taught English at Prospect High School. Clarence was referring to two of her students, teenaged twins who had run from a rotten home life and hunkered down in our garden outbuildings last winter. When we discovered them and Dom heard their story, he said, "Family services be damned," and arranged for them to live in our basement suite. They'd graduated from high school in June.

"Connor and McKenna?" I said. "No, they're working in a vineyard in Washington, earning money for college."

He grinned at me. "Good, good. It was a real nice thing you and Captain Bertucci did, taking them in. The missus had been worrying about them for some time before you rescued them, but you know kids, every time she tried to find out how things were at home, they said things were hunky dory."

"I think their favorite class was English. I'm sure it was because of your wife."

Either Clarence didn't know I was a person of interest in Shauna's death, or he should have been on stage. While we waited for Dom, he chitchatted with me about his wife's opinions on funding for education and then moved on to the upcoming Open Water Swim meet at Donner Lake.

Dom strolled into the lobby area, tossing a USB drive in his hand. "You look fabulous, Livvie. I've got the flash drive for you—contacts and emails, right?"

"And my calendar."

"Oops." He grimaced at Clarence. "Could you take this USB to Corporal Cassidy, tell her to load Olivia's calendar on it, and then bring it back? I'll watch the desk for you."

While Clarence ran the errand, Dom leaned on the reception counter. His face looked drawn. Maybe he hadn't been sleeping well either these last few weeks.

"The forensics team will be done with your vehicle Tuesday or so," he said. "The guys don't work weekends."

I shrugged and handed him the Jeep key. "No problem. I

rented a car and left your Jeep in the lot. I won't need your computer either." I swung the cardboard box with its distinctive Apple symbol onto the counter.

"You bought a new computer?"

"It's a rental from Marshal. Not cheap, but my lawsuit's gonna get it all back for me and more."

"What lawsuit?"

"The one I'm bringing against the Prospect Police Department. Maybe Clapton too."

"For god's sake, Livvie. That's ridiculous. You don't have any basis to sue."

I squared off with him and glared. "Try harassment. Try interfering with enjoyment of life. Try subjecting me to Mrs. Bagnovicz's spying."

"None of that will stand up."

I shrugged. "Perhaps not. But I don't like people thinking I'm a criminal, and this is one thing I can do about it." I paused and met his gaze. "I know it might make things tough for you here."

"Least of my worries," he said. I glimpsed something in his eyes then. Fleeting, but there. Before I could ask about it, a guy in overalls strolled into the lobby, flicking a key fob in his hand.

At the same time, Clarence reappeared. He passed the flash drive to me. "Here you go, Olivia." Then he turned to the newcomer. "Help you?"

"Yah. Looking for Ms. Mercier. Got her rental car here."

"That's me," I said. When I turned to say goodbye to Dom, he was staring out the glass door to the street and the robin's egg blue Thunderbird sitting there, top down.

"You rented a T-Bird?" Dom said.

"Crazy, hey?" the guy in overalls said. "I told her 'we got a Porsche in stock,' but nope, she wanted the T-Bird. Go figure."

Chapter 17

ON FRIDAYS DURING THE SUMMER, the Dockside Restaurant on the north shore of Donner Lake was usually jammed with people getting a head start on the weekend. There were two main reasons: first, the view, and second, affordable casual dining.

Luckily, when I arrived about one-thirty, I snagged the only open table, a premium spot by the window. Looking out at the water that only a few days ago had hidden Shauna's body was unsettling, but I told myself if I hoped to solve her murder it made sense to start here, close to what probably was the scene of the crime. Perhaps a staff member had seen or overheard something that could lead to the killer.

I opened the menu and was happy to see it still offered a seared Ahi tuna salad. I ordered that, and a glass of California Pinot Grigio.

When the server returned with the wine, I told her I was doing a feature article on the life and death of Shauna Wylie. "I imagine the police have interviewed all the staff about the days before the body was found."

She tucked an errant strand of violet hair behind her ear. "For sure. We all gave statements. But basically no one knows anything. Except that Ms. Wylie was a real good tipper, and she loved the Ahi salad too."

I grinned and nodded. "I know. She and I discovered it together several years ago. Unfortunately, I'd lost touch with her over the last while. She still dined here often?"

The girl shrugged. "Now and then with ladies from the country club, or the hospital foundation. And I saw her once with a man not long ago." She raised her eyebrows and leaned in closer. "*That* was an intense happening. They both were like really serious, and she started crying halfway through the meal."

"Who was he?"

Another shrug. "Beats me. Tall. Good looking for an old guy."

Before I could ask more questions, Maggie Shillingford approached the table, trailing the hostess behind her like a pull-along toy. "Olivia, how fortunate to see you here. The restaurant is full, and here I am, positively famished and without a reservation. Might I join you?"

I'd barely nodded in response when she told the server to bring her the special. "Whatever it is, I'm sure it will be spectacular, as usual. And wine, of course. Your California Merlot." She slid onto the chair across from me and flicked the napkin with a flourish. The chandelier lights bounced off the chunky silver and turquoise bracelet on her right wrist. "A good Merlot is the new black, don't you think?"

In my book, a passable Pinot Grigio went with everything. I fought the urge to cover my possibly gauche wine choice with my napkin. "Are you at the lake for the weekend, Maggie? I remember Shauna telling me you have a cabin here."

"I'm here for most of the summer, actually. My cabin is the one on that knoll." She pointed to a massive log home perched on a rise along the south shore of the lake. Its copper roof glinted in the sun. A wooden staircase zigzagged down the steep bank to a small boathouse and dock, where a bright red Sea-Doo and a dazzling white powerboat about twenty-five feet long were tethered.

She brought her gaze back to me. "When I'm at the lake, I usually eat here rather than drive into town. Or, heaven forbid, cook for myself."

"You don't enjoy cooking?"

Her smile faded. "It's a lonely pastime when it's just for one."

I'd learned exactly how accurate her comment was when Dom moved out.

Maggie settled more comfortably in her seat. "I read the *Gazette*'s tribute to Shauna. It's so unfortunate, isn't it? And the two of you being such good friends—I remember that lunch when I first met you, Olivia. It was obvious that you and Shauna have—had—a long and close friendship. Did you write it?"

I shook my head. "No, it was an editorial piece."

"Well, I've read many of your stories in the paper," Maggie said. "I think your reporting is superb. I admire young women with your talent."

The server delivered our meals and poured the Merlot. After Maggie tasted her wine and, with a courtly nod of her head, declared it acceptable, she said, "I knew Shauna more from a business perspective. We sat on a few boards together. She had a good head for finances, an excellent trait if you want to protect your assets."

I had my mouth full of Ahi tuna, so merely nodded.

Maggie went on. "Plus, there was the country club and a few other social circles, but nothing like your relationship with her. I don't mean to sound crass, but even though we traveled in the same circles, Shauna never mentioned how she accumulated her wealth."

"It's family money," I said.

"Ahh, so only one of the three."

"Pardon?"

Maggie swallowed a sip of wine. "There are three ways to become wealthy. You are born to it, you marry it, or you work for it."

She knocked back the last of her Merlot. "*I* have never worked a day in my life."

I giggled. "So, you lay claim to two of the three?"

"Yes, only two of the three, alas. I simply wasn't ambitious enough to go for the trifecta."

It was so exactly the outrageous type of remark Aunt Gaye would make that I snorted into my wineglass. A wicked grin creased Maggie's face.

We fell quiet then as we both ate our meals. It was a comfortable silence, one you might share with a great friend, or your spouse when all is going well.

I swallowed the last morsel of tuna and asked Maggie, "Were you here at the lake the day they discovered Shauna's body? Or perhaps the days before?"

She set her cutlery down and dabbed at her mouth with her napkin. "The police asked me those exact questions. On the Monday they found her I wasn't at the lake. But you know, I saw Shauna a few days before then. She dropped by my cabin the previous Thursday in the early evening to discuss a few board matters, and we shared a glass of wine. Now she's dead. I can't believe it." She shrugged. "Isn't that trite? People always say, 'she can't be dead, I just spoke to her.' As if that could somehow reverse things."

Maggie sipped her wine and poked at her special with her fork. "Even though I was here the week before they found her, I'm a useless witness. I putter in the garden behind the cabin, so I wouldn't have seen anything happening on the water."

"My guess is they didn't drop her into the lake in daylight. Did you hear any sounds at night that were out of place? Like a boat, or splashing?"

She shook her head. "It's summer, and the lake is busy.

There are always boats out, and I've grown so accustomed to hearing outboards the sound doesn't register."

Why did I think this would be as simple as asking a few questions? If that were the way it worked, the cops would have their killer by now.

Chapter 18

SATURDAY MORNING, I once more donned my Armani suit. Not only was it appropriate for a visit to Shauna's lawyer, it was one of only two alternatives I had to jeans and a T-shirt. As I assessed my image in the mirror, I remembered a free-lance article I'd written about fashion among the wannabe-gentry-set. My research included a well-known sorority's *Fashion Handbook for Pledges* that advised, *"One does not wear the same outfit more than twice in two weeks, and absolutely never on consecutive days."* The word "absolutely" was underscored. I stepped into my elegant Weitzman pumps, feeling fortunate I had never pledged a sorority.

I was searching for the keys to the rental T-bird when Amanda phoned. "Hope I'm not interrupting," she said when I answered the call. "I'm reassigning a few things and would like you to take on the food column. Temporarily. Just until, you know, they solve Shauna's murder. And until I can find a permanent food critic. What do you say?"

"Umm."

She hurried on. "I know you're an investigative reporter and this may not be in your wheelhouse, but it would really help me out. Owen's going to take over the Shauna story, so I need to move him off the food column. And between you and me, he's a good kid, but he tends to review too many burger and pizza joints. I'm hoping you can target a few more upscale places."

"Umm."

"Maybe think of it as investigating restaurants. Plus, all expenses paid."

The food column. Great. Just when I was trying to lose weight, she wanted me to visit upscale restaurants. Where everything on the menu was cooked in butter. "I'm just running out the door to an appointment," I said. "Can I think about it?"

"Absolutely. Are you going somewhere fun?"

"Hardly. Shauna's lawyer wants to talk about her will."

"Oh. That reminds me, did you hear the latest on the investigation?"

"What latest?"

"I thought Dom would have told you. They apparently found a bloodstain in the trunk of your car and sent a sample off for DNA testing."

I had stopped breathing when she said "bloodstain."

When she said, "Olivia, are you there?" I exhaled and said, "Yeah, sorry, I was watching a squirrel outside. About the stain. I cut my hand hauling scrap metal out of my trunk a while ago."

"Oh great, so then it's not an issue."

"No," I said. "Not an issue at all."

But it was.

———

It happened last month when Shauna and I bought the wine for the annual camping trip. We had carted the two cases of wine back to my house. I backed into the garage and raised the hatch. I must have left the hatch open too long because when Shauna moved forward to remove the second case, the trunk lid suddenly lowered, and she smacked her forehead against the latch.

"Ouch! Whoa, that smarts," she said.

She swayed slightly and braced her hands on the trunk's carpeted base. Blood trickled from a cut on her forehead. She swiped at it and then once more rested her hands on the carpet. I grabbed some tissues and handed them to her. "Are you okay?"

She pressed the tissues against her forehead. "I will be. Some ice and some wine, not necessarily in that order."

In my kitchen I dabbed at the cut with a wet cloth and then fashioned an icepack for her. While she held the ice to her head, I poured her a glass of Pinot Grigio. "I'm not sure about drinking when you've got a head injury," I said.

She laughed. "Gimme that. This is just a little nick. You know how they say your head always bleeds a lot. And so what if it bruises? It's not like I have any romantic plans." Then she looked at me and her face crumpled. "I'm sorry, so sorry," she said, and burst into tears.

"What for? It was my trunk lid. I'm the one who's sorry."

"No, it's not that. It's ..." She cried silently for several seconds while I stared at her, flummoxed. Finally, she sniffled and said, "Never mind. I'm being silly."

"Told you," I said. "Head injury. Makes a person silly."

That was three and a half weeks ago. I saw Shauna only once after that.

At the time, the last thing that concerned me was a spot of blood in the trunk of my car. I forgot all about it. Now the police had noticed it. They would test the sample. When it turned out to be Shauna's blood, the evidence against me would take a turn toward the danger zone.

Sure, I could tell them the story of how Shauna's blood ended up in my trunk. For what that would be worth. When Clapton added the bloodstain to the scene I made in Chez

Patrice, the inheritance, the concrete and rebar in my garage, and the missing barrel, he would only need the DNA results to seek an arrest warrant.

How long did I have before those results came back? After sorting through several online articles, I learned forensic testing could be completed in seven to fourteen days. There was also rapid DNA testing, which made my heart pound because police could test a sample in less than two hours. I calmed myself down when I realized that if the Prospect police had access to the rapid test, Clapton would already have results and would have knocked on my door first thing today. Besides, Amanda had said the police sent the sample away for testing.

I'd be a fool to think I had two weeks to find Shauna's killer. Better to assume Clapton would push for early results. Conservatively, then, I probably had up to seven days to solve the mystery. Six, more likely, if the sample was sent away yesterday.

Shauna was the athlete, not me. Shauna loved races, loved sprinting to the finish line. She would love this challenge. "Six days to solve the case?" she'd say. "Count me in!"

I wasn't Shauna. I hated races. But like it or not, I was in this one.

Chapter 19

WHEN THE RECEPTIONIST AT MALKINS' office announced my arrival, the lawyer came into the foyer to greet me. Mid-forties, dressed neatly in khaki slacks and a casual shirt, he looked like he'd rather be on a sailboat or golf course than in an office. His gray eyes lit up when he smiled, and his handshake was efficient and firm. "I'm sorry to meet you under these circumstances, Ms. Mercier. Shauna spoke highly of you, and I know you were close." I didn't bother telling him his information was more than a month out of date.

Shauna's brother, Noel, was waiting in Malkins' private office when the lawyer ushered me in. Noel's handshake—if that was what you'd call the touching-you-because-social-graces-demand-it-grip—was noticeably cooler than the lawyer's had been.

I said, "I'm sorry about Shauna."

He flicked his head dismissively. His mouth curled, but not in a smile. He hissed. "Really? Forgive me if I don't believe you." Noel returned to his chair, slouching and stretching his long legs before him. "The heir apparent has arrived. Shall we proceed?" he said.

The lawyer pointed me to the other client chair and took

his place behind his desk. He opened a file and summarized Shauna's will. "Two one-million-dollar bequests to charities, the ranch land and house to Noel, and the balance to Olivia. I'm sure a realtor can tell you the value of the real property, but it's probably near ten million. As for the bequest to Olivia, I've estimated its value at around seventeen and a half million. We will file the documents on Monday to start the process, and there will be the usual canvassing for creditors and so on."

Even though Malkins spoke softly, and his tone was measured, it didn't negate the harshness of the realization we were now dealing with the business of Shauna's death—appraisals and debts and payouts. Part of me—the bit that missed my former friend—didn't want to be there, with my hand out for a share of the spoils. That part of me wanted to be back where I was mid-June, sitting in the sun on the patio of the Dockside Restaurant at Donner Lake, sharing a glass of wine and Ahi tuna salad with Shauna.

My thoughts returned to the day she'd hit her head on my trunk lid. I remembered her bursting into tears. "I'm so sorry," she'd said. Now I wondered if she had wanted to own up then, to confess she'd slept with Dom, to make things right.

As if that would be possible. As if we could ever go back to the way things had been. I swallowed the urge to scream.

Noel said, "How long will all that take, searching for creditors, processing the will?"

Malkins closed the file and folded his hands on his desk. He cleared his throat. "In normal circumstances, and unless someone contests the will . . ." Malkins paused and looked at us. I gave him a weak smile. Noel's shoulders tightened, but he said nothing, his gaze remaining on the lawyer's face.

"The process usually takes several months," Malkins said. "But because Shauna's death is suspicious, the Court will not allow any distribution of your inheritances until her case is resolved."

"Why not?" Noel said.

Malkins shifted in his chair, looking uncomfortable. "There's no easy way to say this. Not that I think either of you is responsible, you understand. In legal terms, it's called the slayer rule. To put it bluntly, California law prohibits Shauna's killer from inheriting. So, we must wait for the case to be solved."

Noel's laugh was sharp. He looked at me for the first time since I'd taken my seat. "Perfect. I'd hate to see my sister's killer get rich."

I flushed and gasped. Malkins said, "Pardon?"

"Don't you know?" Noel said. "Yesterday, the cops raided Olivia's house. They think she killed Shauna. So do I."

I shook my head and concentrated on keeping my voice even and calm. "I didn't kill her. That's ridiculous. We were friends."

"Maybe once upon a time." Noel turned to face Malkins. "Only a couple weeks ago, Shauna told me Olivia was ghosting her. She never told me why, but rumor has it Shauna and Olivia's husband played hide-the-Genoa-salami, if you get my drift. Surely you heard about Olivia seasoning Shauna's stew with earrings at Chez Patrice a while back?"

My cheeks burned. I wanted to leave and slink away home. I cast a glance at Malkins, who sat motionless, mouth open, obviously reeling from too much information. I took a deep breath and said, "I was hurt and angry. I still am. I kicked him to the curb and cut her out of my life. But I didn't kill her."

"Yeah?" Noel said. "Well, she also said someone was harassing her. The cops have her computer, and I gave them her passwords. So if you sent her any flaming stuff, if you threatened her, it will be there. Just like in the movies, they'll get you."

Noel hadn't changed. Everything was all about the movies. I ignored him and did a quick mental inventory of communications from Shauna over the last few weeks. Daily voicemail messages and emails. I had ignored all her voicemail. I had read her first email plea of "meet me, let me explain," responded, "F.O.A.D. bitch," and relegated all others to the junk folder. She'd also sent several letters. I had opened the first one, skimmed its variation on the "it-wasn't-what-you-think" theme, and then shredded it. The rest of her letters I had shredded unopened.

Now, I considered whether my FOAD response to her first email would move me from a person of interest to a suspect. Noel's words broke into my thoughts. "Surprised I knew her passwords, Olivia? I set up her system, put in extra layers of security for the *Cheat Sheet*, so of course I knew the passwords. And now the cops do too."

"The *Cheat Sheet*?" I said.

"Her blog."

I sat numb with shock as Noel rambled on to the lawyer about how the blog was really his idea. "It bothered Shauna that some prominent people were living lies, conning, or hurting others. She was always a do-gooder, so I told her she could do good by exposing the liars and cheats. And voilà, the *Cheat Sheet* was born."

Chapter 20

THE MEETING with Malkins didn't last much longer—what's left after someone is accused of murder but to verify contact information and send the parties on their respective ways? I hurried out, eager to be away from Noel and his accusations, and wanting quiet and privacy to process his information. The T-bird offered both, so I drove in the general direction of the Aspen Heights Country Club and mulled things over.

I would never have pegged Shauna as the anonymous blogger. In school, she had gravitated to drama, sciences, and sports, shuddering at English assignments and begging me to do them for her. Now it appeared she had not only been the competition for my husband's affections, she'd been my professional rival. Not that I'd call the *Cheat Sheet*, or the writing that went into it, professional. In fact, I'd expressed that very opinion to Shauna several months ago when I had asked her to help me identify the blogger. "Tabloid trash, not quality writing," I'd called the blog. I winced now. I hoped I would have been much less cutting had I known Shauna was the blogger.

Rather than try to analyze myself, I focused on a more important meaning of Noel's revelation. Suspects. The blog had trashed several lives, and surely among them would be one or two vindictive people. The tight band I'd felt around my chest all morning loosened with the realization that all I had to do was point the cops to the blog and its targets, and I'd no longer be a person of interest. Life would be normal again, or as normal as it got these days.

Although I was anxious to phone Dom with the news about Shauna being the anonymous blogger, I resisted speeding as I neared the country club because of the road's tight curves that had resulted in several accidents. When I passed by the sign warning "high crash zone," I wondered how many drivers even registered the presence of the camera mounted above the sign as they blew by. We all knew about it, but it had been there so long its existence faded from consciousness.

I slowed and pulled into a viewpoint above the country club to place my call. When I glanced down the hill at the club's grounds, I noticed two police cars in the parking lot and uniformed officers inspecting a red vehicle parked in a slot by the Clubhouse. From where I sat, the vehicle looked like a Land Rover, and if so, the odds were it was Shauna's. There were maybe four Land Rovers in Prospect, but the only person who owned a Firenze Red one was Shauna.

Instantly, I wanted to know what was going on. The call to Dom could wait. I drove down the hill, parked in the club lot well away from the police, entered the Clubhouse, and approached the reception desk. While I waited for the young receptionist to end her telephone conversation, I studied the club's lavish interior. Rich and glossy wood paneling, brass balustrades on the soaring staircase leading to the Members' Library, enormous leaded glass doors guarding the entrance to the dining room, which was fronted by a sign announcing, "Members and Guests only." The exclusiveness of the very rich.

When the receptionist ended her call, I said, "Is Captain

Bertucci of the Prospect Police in the building?" I knew full well he wasn't, but I wanted to get her talking.

"Nope. All the cops are outside except one who's in the loo." She quivered a bit as she said it. This must have been the most excitement she'd had in her job in years.

"I imagine it's been quite the morning?"

She shuffled from foot to foot and glanced around the lobby.

I said, "Don't worry, I'm not trying to pump you for information. Captain Bertucci's my husband, so I'll get the scoop at home tonight." Liar, liar, pants not quite on fire. I smiled at her, leaned forward and whispered, "That's Ms. Wylie's car they're looking at, isn't it?"

The dam burst. "Yah, for sure. The manager called them this morning."

"What a break for my husband's team. Maybe the video-tapes of the lot will show what happened to her."

My hopes were skewered by her answer. "Nope. The camera only records twenty-four hours, and we don't save the tapes."

"So, no way to know when the car arrived?"

She shook her head. "It could have been here for ages. No one ever pays attention to cars in the lot. Except the manager 'cause it was in his spot." She put air quotes around the words "his spot."

"Why'd he take so long to report it?

"He was on sick leave all week." Her eyes sparkled. "Had a little snip job. Guess he couldn't walk without screaming." She rolled her eyes. "Men are such babies."

Corporal Cassidy came out of the women's washroom then and headed for the exit. I said goodbye to the receptionist and hurried after her.

"Officer," I said, when I caught up to her. "I was driving by and saw the cars. I was hoping Dom was here. I wanted to tell him Shauna's brother said she was the blogger behind the

Cheat Sheet. I thought it might open up some avenues for you all."

"Captain B's probably still at the station," Cassidy said. "Last I saw him, he was meeting with Chief Gavric. Thanks for the tip about the blog, I'll pass it on to Clapton. He's in charge of the case."

That was odd. Dom was head of homicide. He should be in charge.

Chapter 21

IT WAS late afternoon by the time I returned home. Duncan McAdams had performed magic and made the lawn reappear. It preened and called out, "I'm back and I belong in this neighborhood. Miss me?" I had to say yes. It was a much better accessory for my rental T-bird than its predecessor barley field. McAdams might restore balance to my life, one blade of grass at a time.

My renewed lawn reminded me I owed the *Gazette* a report on the Garden Show. I hurried inside and filed a report online.

"From earthmovers to garden forks, the Prospect Garden Show has it all. For the DIYers in the crowd, check out the nifty bee watering system. It's an ingenious yet simple thing: put a few stones and marbles in a dish, add a mister and voilà, bees can drink without drowning."

Fifteen minutes later, before I'd even had time to change out of my going-to-town duds, Carling Alamo, the owner of a local bar, phoned. "Hey Olivia, come on by the bar, okay? Dom could use a lift."

"Huh?"

"He came in an hour ago," she said. "Knocked several stiff ones back. I've taken his keys away."

Thirty minutes later, I swung by The Other Alamo and found Dom slumped on a stool at the end of the long mahogany bar, a coffee cup in front of him. When Carling handed me the key to Dom's Jeep, he smiled sheepishly at me. "Hey, Livvie. Carling won't let me go home."

I slid onto the next stool. "What's going on?"

"I like that suit. You wore it yesterday."

"I know. What's going on?"

He sighed and slurped his coffee. "Had a meeting with Chief Gavric. He took me off the case. Shauna's case. 'Cause, you know, you might be involved." He raised his hands, palms out. "Don't get me wrong, sweetheart. I don't think you killed her."

"Okay. So? You have lots of other cases."

"Ahhh, well. Yeah. I expressed my concerns about the conclusions so far in Shauna's case. And Gavric objected."

"Your concerns being?"

"That anyone who believed you could kill anybody, stuff them in a barrel of concrete, *and* dump them in a lake had his head up his ass so far, he'd need night vision goggles to find his way out. Unless of course he liked the smell of the shit in there so much he just decided to stay put."

"You always express your concerns so eloquently."

"Yep. At that point, he gave me a choice of a transfer to the marine unit until you're cleared or an indefinite unpaid leave."

Really, Dom had no choice. During the happier days of our marriage, it usually took at least two glasses of Italian red and the suggestion of wild and abandoned sex to convince Dom to join me in our hot tub. And even fortified by wine, he clung to the edge of the tub. The marine unit probably ventured into much deeper waters. I hoped his savings account was healthy.

Chapter 22

As soon as he was settled in the passenger seat of the T-bird Dom said, "It's dinnertime. You're all dressed up. We got your classy T-bird wheels, so let's head to Reno. It's less than an hour away. We'll go to Dusty's, that new steak house. No expense is too big for my beautiful lady."

I was working my way around to feeling flattered when he said, "Besides, I gotta eat and the cupboards in my pitiful *bachelor* pad are bare."

"Oh yeah?" I fired back. "Whose fault is it that you're alone? Shoulda thought about how much you hate cooking before you slid under the sheets with Shauna."

Dom threw himself against the passenger door and raised his hands in mock self-defense. "Don't hurt me, Livvie. I was just going to say I've been so distraught at being without you I haven't had the energy to buy groceries."

I glared at him. He raised his eyebrows and risked a smile.

I started the car. "Not a bad recovery, Dom. Next time you can leave out the poor imitation of a scaredy-cat."

"Okay. Or better yet, I can get the comments right the first time," he said.

"That too."

I should have taken Dom back to his bachelor pad, pitiful as it may be. But as he so aptly put it, a girl's gotta eat. And perhaps he'd give me investigation tips.

Before we drove away from The Other Alamo bar, I typed "Dusty's Reno" into the GPS and seconds later the app offered me a choice of Dusty's Housecleaning, Dusty's Trail Riding and B&B, and Dusty's Steaks. I accepted the third option and a map to the restaurant popped up.

When Dom nodded off ten minutes into the trip to Reno, I found a radio station playing smooth jazz and let the warm sounds of an alto sax waft over us. In the middle of a George Benson tune, Dom said, "set up." I glanced over, about to ask what he meant, and realized he was still asleep.

Rather than shake Dom awake, I increased the stereo volume, hoping the sound would interrupt his dream, which I surmised was an anxious one because Dom never talked in his sleep unless something weighed on him. When he sighed and began snoring lightly, I congratulated myself for my ploy.

A couple minutes after I exited the highway and began weaving through Reno's streets, heading for the city center, Dom said, "Back off." Before I could reach over to shake him, he jerked awake, rubbed his face, and said, "I nodded off."

"Yes. You must have needed the rest. We're almost at the restaurant."

"Did I talk in my sleep?"

"Nope. The only person talking was the bot on the GPS."

Dusty's Steaks was still new enough on the restaurant scene in Reno that we didn't have to wait long for a table. The enticing smell of the wood-fired grill told me that in a month or less, the wait for a table would be measured in weeks instead of minutes.

After we ordered our meals, I told Dom about Shauna being the author of the *Cheat Sheet*. "There could be viable suspects among her targets, right?"

"Sure. But you told me that blog kept on scooping you?"

"Yeah, so?"

"So, it's another reason for you to get rid of Shauna."

"Give me a flipping break. How shallow do you think I am?"

"Not me. But cops like Gavric and Clapton love a multitude of motives. You have three now in their book—the inheritance, a professional rival, and me."

I didn't react to his mention of his role in all of this. What could I say that I hadn't said already? Instead, I changed topics and told him Amanda asked me to handle the food column.

"Really?"

I nodded. "Temporarily. Until the case is solved. To hurry that along, I intend to find the killer. Where should I start?"

"That's not a good idea," Dom said.

I bristled. "Sure, it is. I'm smart. I investigate stories for the paper. This is just another story."

"Nope. It's a murder investigation. Murderers get nasty when someone tries to nail them. Leave it to the police. We'll solve it. We're equipped to do the job."

I shook my head. "Not *we*, Dom. You're off the case. It's *they*. And *they* think I did it. They won't look any further because they think they've already solved it."

"Stay out of it. The officers won't take kindly to you poking around in their business. And as I said, the killer could strike back. You could get hurt, or worse."

I folded my arms and jutted my chin at him. "I'm investigating. End of story. You can help me or not."

He blew out a breath. "Jesus." He put his knife and fork down and sat back in his chair. After a few seconds, he said, "I still don't have to like it."

"Where should I start?"

"Start with what you know and go from there. Ask questions. Find things that don't add up and ask more questions until you come up with the only answer that fits." He paused and frowned at me. "And if you get to that point, call me. Or call one of my officers."

"When. Not if. I'm going to solve it."

I was ready for Dom to make a comment about the odds of success. It must have killed him to bite back the words, but he did. He raised his wineglass. "I hope you do, bella. This is a great steak, don't you think? Maybe your first food critique should be this place."

Dom didn't mention the bloodstain in my car. I considered filling him in, but then I would have to admit it was Shauna's blood. Asking him not to divulge that to Clapton would put Dom in a terrible position. Withholding evidence was not a thing homicide detectives did. Especially when that detective was Dom.

The other topic that didn't come up was the status of our relationship. Dom was attentive, charming, and relaxed. He seemed to accept our separation. Contented, even, to be moving on. A frisson of concern rippled in my stomach. Which ticked me off, but I pushed my emotions down and presented an unruffled exterior to him.

Dom deflected the server's suggestion of after-dinner coffees. "Let's go back to the house, bella. I'll make you my famous cappuccino."

That comment immediately started a war in my head.

Chapter 23

IT WAS A FEROCIOUS BATTLE.

In one corner, The Protector, who knew exactly how I responded to Dom and his cappuccino. She said, "They have coffee in the restaurant. If you want a cup, have it here. Then, drive him straight back to his pitiful bachelor pad."

In the other corner, The Lover of the Chase, who had awoken earlier when I speculated that Dom might have adjusted to being separated, might have given up the pursuit. She told me to allow Dom to make that cappuccino. With its splash of Grand Marnier. And chocolate flakes on the froth. "Remember?" she said. "The lovemaking that usually follows that cappuccino?"

We ended up back at the house.

Dom ground the espresso beans while I sat at the kitchen island and calculated whether I could surreptitiously make the bed, perhaps even change the sheets. He frothed the milk while I asked myself when I last shaved my legs. He grated unsweetened chocolate and opened the Grand Marnier while I fretted about the chipped polish on my toenails.

Very aware that the Italian in him was revving up my

engine, I sought a topic to diffuse the heat. "Really, Dom, how can Clapton think I'd kill someone?"

"He doesn't know you. He knows only you have more than one motive, like money, and Shauna being a man-stealer."

My engine sputtered. When I shot him a look, he said, "Your term, not mine."

"Actually, the term I used was man-eater."

"I stand corrected," Dom said, as he set the finished cappuccino on the island in front of me. Mounds of glossy froth, a light dusting of chocolate, a heady aroma of orange liqueur and espresso. He played with the hair at the nape of my neck, curled it around his index finger. My engine hummed.

He leaned down and whispered in my ear. "Livvie-licious." His breath was as warm as his tone and made the tiny hairs on my neck stand up. The turbo booster kicked in.

Once more, the battle began.

My libido presented its case to my head. "You are adults. You can be separated but still share an evening of intimacy. It doesn't mean you have forgiven him or that you would have to get back together."

My head retorted. "Dom will never see it that way. You know how persistent he can be. He'll be twenty times more persistent if you let down your guard. He's Italian, for heaven's sake."

"Yes," my libido said. "He's Italian. I end my case."

My libido was the clear winner of the debate.

Dom said, "You know she never could have taken me away."

And my engine stalled out. The emotions I'd pushed under the surface in the restaurant had festered there, biding their time like a bomb. Dom's words hit the detonator. I pushed the cup away, sloshing the contents across the countertop. I batted his hand away. "You never should have given her a chance."

He expelled a breath and ran his hand through his hair. "Sweetheart. Can we be adult about this, move on, get past it?"

"You really mean can *I* be adult about it." I lurched out of my chair. "If being adult is pretending I'm not shattered, then no, I can't be adult. You showed me how little I matter to you. And you used my *best friend* to do it."

Dom followed me as I ran down the hall to the bedroom. "Olivia please, you mean everything to me."

I stepped into the bedroom, turned and pushed him back before he could cross the threshold. "I don't believe you. I don't trust you anymore." I closed the door.

"What can I say other than I'm sorry?"

"You can say good night. Then you can call a cab. Or you can sleep in the guest room. Suit yourself."

I took a shower and cried under the spray until the water ran cool.

Chapter 24

SUNDAY MORNING, I heard the front door close a few seconds before the church bells began calling people to early Mass. When I peeked through my bedroom blinds, I saw Dom, unshaven and rumpled, sliding into the back seat of a taxi. As the cab gathered speed, Dom shot his left arm out the cab's window and gave a jaunty wave toward Mrs. Bagnovicz's house. Her aqua blinds snapped shut in response.

Even though last night had ended horribly, I giggled through my shower. If I owned a negligée, I could have thrown it on and charged out onto the lawn to stare longingly after the taxi. Baggie would never believe Dom had spent the night in the guest room anyway, so why not give her a tad more fuel?

Dom's note sat beside the coffeemaker. As I read it, my mood deflated.

> Olivia, bella, I miss you. I miss us. I want to come home. I
> will spend the rest of my life making it up to you, if only
> you let me.

We had been over this several times in the past month. I

fought the urge to break down once more. It would get me nothing except puffy eyes. Instead, I made coffee, opened the rental computer, and inserted the flash drive Dom had given me at the police station. I let out a relieved breath when my files and folders appeared on the screen. My email messages seemed complete, as did my contacts.

I updated my calendar to add Shauna's funeral on Tuesday and noticed an entry for a Police Advisory Committee meeting that evening. The stress of the last week had obviously messed with routine memories because I couldn't remember adding the Advisory Committee meeting to my calendar. I studied the calendar for the upcoming week in case I had forgotten other appointments, but there were no entries after Tuesday. For once I was glad to see an almost-empty calendar because it gave me most of the week to investigate Shauna's murder and, if the heavens were with me, solve it before the DNA results on the bloodstain in my car arrived.

I poured a second cup of coffee and focused on how to investigate Shauna's murder. Dom had said to start with what I knew.

I thought about people who might have killed her.

First: Noel. Because if my inheritance was a motive, so was his.

Second: the wife of some other man Shauna slept with, or for that matter, the paramour himself if he wanted to keep his dalliance a secret.

Third: her blog targets.

Last: Dom. I put him in the "weak suspect" category. Keeping his romp on the extramarital sheets a secret was a powerful motive. But once I found out about his infidelity, his motive to kill Shauna disappeared. And I had found out about the treachery at least three weeks before Shauna died.

Who to investigate first? I doubted Noel would want to talk to me about whether he killed his sister, and at the moment I had no idea who else Shauna had slept with. She never kissed and blabbed.

I decided to start with the victims of the *Cheat Sheet*. I logged on to the internet and found the blog. A quick scan revealed there were at least twenty blog posts that exposed misdeeds scandalous enough to ruin the subject's life. I compiled a list of the blog's victims.

All I needed to do was call them and convince them to talk to me. A few months ago, when I'd been trying to identify the mysterious blogger, I'd called several of the people mentioned in *Cheat Sheet* articles. My questions about whether they knew the name of the blogger were met with abrupt, and sometimes snarky, negative responses. I expected I would get the same type of response now if I opened my conversation with, "So, did you kill Shauna Wylie?"

It would be better to use something that would encourage them to open up, like a feature story on the impact that tabloid-style reporting had on the victims. I felt confident most of them would want to tell their side of things, or to rant about how the blog got things wrong and ruined their lives. I hoped they'd also divulge whether they knew Shauna was the *Cheat Sheet* blogger.

I was about to place the first call to Quayle Jonasberg, a bull semen magnate Shauna had accused of selling blanks, when my doorbell chimed. I checked the peephole and saw Pierre Roche, my next-door neighbor, standing on the porch clutching a handful of envelopes. I opened the door wide. "Hey, Pierre, welcome home. How was London?"

"Absolutely out of sight. Eight days wasn't long enough. I've got your mail. I don't know why our carrier can't tell the difference between our house numbers."

"Do you think we've offended her?"

"Beats me." Pierre gestured at the T-bird. "Your car in the shop?"

"For a while."

"Well, if you gotta drive a loaner, that's a good one to go with." He scanned the lawn and said, "I see you did a bit of haying."

I laughed. "Not me. Duncan McAdams, a landscaper Dom found. He's going to tackle the back garden next week."

Pierre yawned. "Sorry, jet lag. Time for a nap. I need to be fresh for the movie tonight. I missed last Thursday, gonna make up for it today."

When Pierre was in town, he went to the late showing of *Rocky Horror Picture Show* every Thursday. I winked at him. "Is it the movie hall you missed, or Darlene?"

"What can I say? I love her popcorn."

After Pierre left, I sorted through the envelopes. Three bills, a bank statement, and an envelope from Shauna. I thought about shredding it. But the fact she was now dead made me hesitate. I felt conflicted. Was disposing of the last communication from a person disrespectful? Was hanging on to it masochistic?

I hated to think I might be a masochist. I shredded the envelope unopened, returned to the kitchen, checked my list of *Cheat Sheet* victims, and looked up the contact information for the first one. Then I placed the call.

Chapter 25

My call to Quayle Jonasberg, the king of bull semen, was immediately bumped to voice mail. I introduced myself, mentioned I'd like to interview him for a feature story, and asked for a call back at his earliest opportunity.

Next on the list was Lionel Hardy, who, according to the *Cheat Sheet*, was also known as The Nose. He was a Reno city councilor who, during his campaign in a municipal election, had trouble keeping his love of recreational drugs off the internet. Despite his extracurricular drug use, he won the election handily because of his platform of balanced budgets. My call to the snorting yet fiscally responsible councilor also went to voicemail.

Where the heck was everyone on a Sunday? In church? Judging from the things Shauna's blog accused them of, they could go to church, sit on the hard pews, kneel in the confessional, and light candles every day for the next fifteen years, and still be denied cleansing.

I left a message on Hardy's phone, asking for an interview to discuss the effect of exposé journalism on public life, and went to the next name on the list: Followers of the Thrilling Holistic and Ecstatic Way, aka THE Way.

According to Shauna's blog, THE Way preyed on the vulnerable. Their website listed "shepherds" and "healers", which Shauna's blog had defined as dogma drill sergeants and pseudo-counselors. The "Pastor Who Lights Your Way" was Floyd Nash.

Seeing his name triggered a memory of a spring day when Shauna and I had visited the Prospect Book Store at the Altitude Mall. While I debated whether to buy the latest hard cover Michael Connelly book, Shauna made two trips to the cashier with teetering stacks of romance novels. "How many did you buy?" I asked as we exited the shop, me clutching one book, Shauna lugging two shopping bags full.

"Twenty-one. Guaranteeing me at least three weeks of cozy evenings at home, in front of the fire, wine in hand, losing myself in a story."

"Why do you read that stuff? Why not a thrilling adventure, or even a mystery?"

"Because romance novels end with a promise of lasting love. What else?" Her shoulders slumped then, and she added, "I keep hoping I'll learn how to find it."

Shauna had blinked rapidly and turned her face away from me. Before I could comment, she pointed down the sidewalk at Abel's Table, a small diner. "See that restaurant? There's something fishy in there, and I don't mean just on the menu."

My jaw dropped. "What were you doing in Abel's Table? Isn't it a greasy spoon?"

Shauna laughed. "Hey, I love me some greasy spoon. The truth is, I discovered it because I saw Floyd Nash—you know, the pastor at THE Way church? He went in, so I thought I'd tag along and see what I could learn about the dietary preferences of preachers who fleece their flock."

I raised my eyebrows. "Seriously?"

She laughed again. "Yeah, okay. I was bored and felt like snooping."

Now, as I placed my call to THE Way I realized Shauna's agenda in following Nash into Abel's Table was more than wanting to study his menu choices. She was gathering information for her blog. And I had been clueless. Some investigative reporter I was.

To my surprise, an actual human person answered my phone call. "The Followers wish you a morning of grace and light. How can I help you?"

"Floyd Nash, please."

When Nash answered his line, I introduced myself and said, "I'm doing a feature on the effect of exposé journalism and would like to interview you because your organization was a *victim* of exactly that type of underhanded journalism recently. I'm referring to the *Cheat Sheet*, of course."

The line was quiet. I imagined Nash consulting his list of Appropriate and Approved Responses to Requests for Interviews.

He said, "The Followers welcome legitimate opportunities to interact with the press. Regrettably, we are not in a position to comment on this matter. Thank you for your call. Our next service is Friday evening at seven o'clock. If you wish to follow THE Way, please join us."

"Really, Mr. Nash, wouldn't you like to share your views on the *Cheat Sheet's* practice of exposing nefarious organizations and people?"

"Let me put this in plain English, Ms. Mercier. Find sordid material for your misbegotten, illegitimate, stinky afterbirth of a feature article somewhere else. Like a cesspool."

"Can I quote you?"

The line went dead. Hmmm. Why did he not want to give me their side of the story? Was there something about Shauna's allegations that made him nervous? Angry? Willing to kill? I circled his name on my list.

Next, I phoned Hannah Scrimshaw, a prominent socialite recently involved in a costly divorce, thanks to the *Cheat Sheet*. I expected her calls would be screened by her private assistant or social coordinator or whatever front office staff the Give-me-Prada-or-Give-me-Death set employed these days.

"This is Hannah," she said. If ever a voice could sound like it belonged on a rich woman, this was it. Slow, deep, creamy like Häagen-Dazs, but much warmer. There perhaps a hint of the finishing school penchant for marbles in the mouth, but hers were subtle, expensive marbles.

I gave her my shtick about the feature article and dastardly exposé journalists.

There are many ways to tell a person to kiss off and die, but Hannah's approach left me wishing I had recorded the call.

Chapter 26

A NANOSECOND after I asked for an interview about the *Cheat Sheet*, Hannah Scrimshaw's voice lost its cultured tones and became the voice of a working stiff, with a vocabulary to match.

"Reporters. You effing leeches, you can kiss my rich ass till cowboys don't effing ride the range or anything else anymore and I still won't talk to you. You can quote me on that too. How's that grab ya, Miss two-bit-gas-bag-of-a-gazette that I wouldn't read on a bet reporter?"

She broke off the call. I'd obviously caught Ms. Scrimshaw at an inopportune moment.

When my stomach signaled it was time for lunch, I took a break from the phone calls. I didn't need to look in my fridge to know that the contents would be minimal. Salad makings, eggs (probably stale) and cheese (also probably stale). Since Dom moved out, I hadn't had the desire to do more than reheat leftover pizza.

I could shop for groceries, order in, or dine out. It would be good to use lunch to gather more information for my upcoming food column at the *Gazette*. It would be excellent if I could combine lunch with a food column and my investigation of Shauna's death. A three-bagger.

When I glanced again at my list of Shauna's blog victims, I focused on the circle around Nash's name. Shauna said he went to Abel's Table. Not only that, she said there was something fishy about the place. How much worse could the food at Abel's Table be than what I had in the fridge? Abel's Table it would be.

I dressed in what I imagined food critics wore on the job—a white shirt and black slacks. Comfy black loafers.

I wondered if the owner of Abel's Table had chosen the Altitude Mall location because it was near, but not too near, several churches, including the expansive glass monstrosity that housed THE Way and Floyd Nash. The restaurant's location allowed it to cater to the church-going crowd, offering them a place to gather and gossip, safely away from the touchy ears of their pastor. Perhaps Nash went into the café for the totally innocent reason of surveilling his flock.

When I entered the restaurant, a tired-looking server handed me a menu and told me to sit wherever I wanted. I chose a booth by the window and studied the menu, hoping for something healthy. When the server came by, I said, "What do you recommend that is both tasty and healthy?"

She brushed her hair away from her brow and said, "Chicken curry; corn tostada stack; grilled salmon. I'd go for the barbecued chicken thighs. Chef's sauce is to die for. I can give you a crunchy salad for the side dish."

A man and woman entered the restaurant, walked past us to a door at the back of the room, and punched in a code on a screen near the door. Staples secured the hem on one of her pant legs; red-eyed skulls adorned the backs of their greasy denim jackets; dirt rimmed the bitten fingernails on the hand he used to wipe his nose. If there's a look to the church-going crowd, they didn't have it. A quick click sounded, the door opened, and they slid through.

The server watched them go through the door, glanced around the quarter-full restaurant at the tables, some occupied, some needing clearing, and once more pushed her hair back. "I'll have the barbecued thighs and salad," I said.

While I waited for my order, I watched the server whiz through her job, bussing tables, picking up and delivering orders, refilling coffee cups, cashing out patrons. Other than the guy in the kitchen, she was the only staff. A slim man wearing a dark blue suit and carrying a briefcase left the room behind the unmarked door at the back, walked past me and outside, where he climbed into a waiting Mercedes. He could have been a lawyer, an accountant, or the owner of Abel's Table. Even a churchgoer.

When the server brought my meal, I said, "Can you tell me if Floyd Nash has been in here recently? I wanted to talk to him about playing the piano at his church."

She nodded. "He was in yesterday. He just got back from a two-week trip to Europe on an evangelical mission. Looked like he hadn't eaten for the entire trip. I guess European missionaries don't eat meatloaf and gravy."

Floyd had an alibi. I mentally drew a line through his name on my suspect list. I looked around the diner. "Are you the only one on today?" I asked the server.

She blew out a breath. "Usually there are two of us. But the other server quit yesterday. Hey, you want a job?"

I snorted. "Trust me, I am *so* not capable of working in a restaurant."

"Shoot, all it takes is good shoes and a brain quick enough to stay one step ahead of the Neanderthals. And that don't take a ton of gray cells. Enjoy your meal."

The food was as tasty as she promised, but what interested me more was the activity at the back of the room. I counted twenty people in and out of the door in the time it took me to finish lunch. Some were frayed at the edges, some could have been the crowd from the college down the road, and others would fit right in at a PTA meeting.

On the drive home, I dictated thoughts about the restaurant into my phone.

"Sparely staffed, Abel's Table offers a basic homey menu to diners interested in reasonably priced meals. The barbecue sauce has as zesty a personality as the staff does. The layout is conducive to privacy yet offers easy access to the highly popular room at the back. During my visit, more people entered the mysterious room than sought lunch. What is behind that door? Stay tuned folks, as your intrepid food critic investigates whether something other than barbecue sauce smells at Abel's Table."

At home, I checked the *Cheat Sheet* archives but found nothing about Abel's Table. I suspected that the unmarked door, and the traffic through it, was what made Shauna say something was fishy. Perhaps she hadn't finished her research, or the exposé she planned was somewhere on her computer in a draft form. Good luck to me accessing her computer, since it was currently in the Prospect Police evidence locker.

I tucked the questions about what was happening behind the unmarked door away for the moment and resumed telephoning Shauna's blog victims. After five calls I had collected three more kiss off and die invitations and two assertions of "I'm over it, yeah I was pissed when the blog first came out, but that was then and this is now and things are fine again and my wife's talking to me once more (or my wife left me) and really it was the best thing that coulda happened so you know, I should be thanking that blogger."

Disheartened, I went online and read a few more items on the *Cheat Sheet* blog. Stories of embezzlers, cheaters, scammers —all based on rumor and innuendo from what I could see. I shook my head in dismay. How could Shauna stoop to sliming people merely for the rush of having a large online following?

My phone rang just as I read the blog's sly hint about a public official sleeping his way to the top. Glad to leave the ugly exposés behind, I shut down my computer and answered the call.

"Ms. Mercier, this is Lionel Hardy returning your call."

It took me a moment, but when I remembered the Reno politician, I responded enthusiastically. "*Thank you*, sir, for calling back." I winced at my gushing tone.

"I'd be happy to talk with you," he said. "I read your articles regularly and follow you online. Nice headshot, by the way! So, listen—suppose I treat you to lunch on Tuesday? We can discuss sensationalist reporting and other disreputable things."

I didn't need to check my calendar to know I had at least one event Tuesday: Shauna's funeral. "Can we make it a late lunch? I'm tied up most of the morning."

"No problem. How's one o'clock sound? I'll reserve a private dining room at the Nevadan Resort."

The Nevadan was one of the newest high-end hotel and casino complexes in Reno. I quickly agreed, thanked Hardy for his generosity, and hung up the phone feeling optimistic. Here was a double score for me—I could interview the blog victim and size up the restaurant for a review in the paper's food column.

So long as I didn't get ptomaine, I figured I'd come out ahead.

Chapter 27

MONDAY MORNING, when I heard Ben and Claire McAdams' high-pitched voices telling Charlie to get down and behave, I went onto my porch. My next-door neighbor, Pierre, stood on the sidewalk as Charlie circled his legs like a dervish and then streaked through the perennial bed and back across the lawn to the sidewalk. He whirled around Pierre once more and stopped, his metronome tail flashing back and forth. The calm was short-lived however, because Charlie spotted me and let loose a series of bark-yelp-whine-growls before racing over and joining me on the porch. I figured he knew who, out of the five of us, might have treats.

Pierre introduced himself to the McAdamses and when Duncan apologized for Charlie's behavior, Pierre said, "It was my fault. I made the mistake of greeting the dog."

"Hah," McAdams said. "Greet Charlie, don't greet Charlie, it makes no never mind to him. People equal high excitement."

Pierre laughed. "Olivia, could I borrow Mr. McAdams for a moment?"

When I nodded, McAdams directed the children to mind Charlie, and followed Pierre through his garden gate. Ben ran to the truck and retrieved a small brown bag before he and Claire climbed the steps to the porch. He held the bag out to me. "Mom sent this for you." Claire nodded.

We went inside to the kitchen, where they watched intently as I peeked inside the bag. "Ahh, a muffin. Just what I wanted today." I told the children to dig out some kibbles for Charlie from the pantry. Claire tended to the dog, who did a short-ened rendition of his whine-howl-yelp that I imagined was dog talk for "yippee." I heard Ben gasp and turned to see him standing inside the pantry, staring at two pears on a shelf. They each bore a tag. "These have our names on them," he said.

"Really? I wonder how they found their way into my pantry?"

He faced me, one pear in each hand. "I think you put them there."

"You'd make a great investigative reporter. You caught me, but let's keep it our secret, okay?"

I gave Ben an extra pear for his father before we traipsed outside where we found Pierre and McAdams standing by the decrepit truck. Both of them were grinning, so I assumed McAdams had secured a second job.

"Tell your wife thanks for the muffin," I said to McAdams. "I'm taking it with me for a morning snack."

"Samantha appreciated your gesture with the cookies for the kiddos the other day. And she's doubly grateful because my makeover of your garden means she doesn't need two jobs. So, she quit working at Abel's Table."

"She worked at Abel's? I was there yesterday. I might review it for the paper. Interesting place. Lots of activity, and I'm thinking not all of it is related to meals."

McAdams raised his eyebrows. "Oh yeah. Sam's glad to be gone."

That raising of his eyebrows made me think Shauna had been on to something when she said the restaurant was fishy.

"Really? Do you think she would talk to me? It could be off the record."

"Why don't you phone her at Sierra Bistro today? I'll give her a heads up."

Thirty minutes later at the *Gazette*'s offices, I told Amanda I'd take on the food column. She said, "Excellent. As I said, all expenses covered, so feel free to take a companion along."

As I turned to leave, she went on. "You're going to Shauna's funeral tomorrow, I assume?"

"Of course." I remembered the calendar notation about the meeting scheduled for Tuesday evening, and said, "I see you want me to cover tomorrow's Police Advisory Committee meeting. Any specific agenda item?"

She looked at me blankly.

To fill the silence, I explained. "I noticed an item on my calendar about the committee meeting tomorrow evening and presumed you'd inserted it as a nudge to attend."

"For heaven's sake, Olivia, why would I bother to put things in your calendar when I can text or email you with instructions? But yes, cover that, and any other town events."

I made a copy of my notes about the discovery of Shauna's body at Donner Lake and handed the package to Owen Starshult. "Here's a copy of my notes on Shauna's death, but they are probably old news to you. If I hear anything pertinent, I'll pass it on."

"Thanks Olivia," Owen said. "That's big of you. I was worried you'd be upset that Amanda took the story away from you."

"No, she's correct. I have a conflict. If you want to run things by me, just ask."

"There is one thing," he said. "What's the normal time for DNA results to come back?"

"I think between one to two weeks. I figure the earliest they'll arrive is Friday."

"Hmmm."

My stomach flipped. "What?" I said.

"I heard the DNA results could come back Wednesday."

My stomach went into free fall. This was Monday. I couldn't figure out who killed Shauna by Wednesday. I had many people to talk to and many wheels to spin. The familiar sense of narrowing vision—the precursor to a panic attack—began teasing me.

"Where'd you hear that?" I said.

"Noel Wylie. We go back a way."

How would Noel know about DNA testing? "You should check with the crime lab in Sacramento," I said.

"Okay. By the way, I heard you're in the will. I think Noel expected to inherit everything."

"I thought he would too."

I left Owen with a few words of encouragement, sat at my desk, and accessed the paper's archives of restaurant reviews to learn which restaurants had already been covered. Fortunately, neither Dusty's Steaks in Reno nor Abel's Table had been reviewed. When I searched further, I found three more places I could visit: "Sierra Bistro," my friend Harlow's bistro and the place where Samantha McAdams worked, "Vlad's Curry," a Hungarian Indian fusion experience, and "High Drifts," the restaurant at the Aspen Heights country club.

I noted down the names and then bashed out a review of Dusty's.

"For those who love riding the range and chowing down by the campfire, get yourself on over to Dusty's Steaks in Reno, where the wood-fired grill delivers authentic western style steaks (that is, enormous, juicy and packed with flavor) and the seating is a lot comfier than the pesky tree stumps that seem to be the rage at every campfire. Highly recommended dining experience for carnivores. Not so much for anyone following a vegetarian regime."

My review of Abel's Table would wait until I figured out what exactly was going on behind the mystery door. Based on my brief exchange with Duncan McAdams, I hoped his wife could help me. Thinking I could meet her for lunch, I was about to call Sierra Bistro when Maggie Shillingford phoned me.

"Olivia, thank you so much for your article about the Garden Show. Attendance really picked up after it was published, and we've had lots of interest in tricks to make gardens helpful to birds and bees."

"Great."

"As an added thank you, would you care to join me for lunch today at High Drifts?"

I could have put her off, but High Drifts was on the list of restaurants yet to be reviewed, and Maggie might be my only hope to gain access to the members-and-guests-only venue. I accepted.

"Wonderful," Maggie said. "Shall we say noon?"

She said goodbye and ended the call before I thought to ask if the country club had a dress code. I assessed my black slacks and white shirt and sighed.

Chapter 28

WOULD other diners at High Drifts mistake me for a server? Were slacks gauche?

I thought back to the day I'd chatted with the receptionist. I was certain she'd worn slacks. I shrugged. I had three choices: my food critic outfit that I currently wore, my Armani suit, or a trip to the trendy dress shops along Main Street.

Before I could decide on wardrobe, the *Gazette's* front counter clerk phoned me and said, "Hannah Scrimshaw is here to see you. Are you available?"

I hesitated. Either the socialite with the extensive trucker vocabulary was here because she had decided to talk to me, or she wanted to shoot me for being a member of the league of effing leeches, as she fondly called reporters.

"Is she armed?"

"I don't see how she could be."

"Be right out." I grabbed a notepad and my phone. Before I opened the door to the front office, I peeked through the glass sidelight and saw a tall, lithe woman with skin the color of honey and long black hair with deep red highlights. I agreed with the clerk. I didn't see how Hannah Scrimshaw could be armed, either. The sleeveless dress she wore had room only for her body, no accessories. Her hands clutched her phone and a key fob. I supposed she could hide a teeny gun or poisonous dart in the key fob, but decided to risk it.

"Ms. Mercier," Hannah said, when I introduced myself to her. Her voice had regained the sultry, syrupy tones and proper language of finishing school. "I'm so glad you could see me. Forgive me for not phoning ahead, and I must apologize for my crass comments yesterday. You caught me at a terrible moment."

"No worries. Can I ask if this means you're willing to talk about the *Cheat Sheet* and the article they wrote about you?"

"Well, yes, why else would I be here?" She glanced at the clerk. "Can we speak privately?"

I led the way outside the building and around the corner to a tiny open space with a bench shaded by two trees.

"How's this?" I said.

Hannah scrutinized the bench seat, flicked at a fallen leaf with a perfectly manicured finger, and then sat. "Fine. Now, I don't want you to print any of this conversation without my prior approval. I want to retract my suggestion yesterday that you could quote my comments about . . . well, the whole unfortunate conversation. Agreed?"

Our mouth-off-first-then-consult-adviser socialite had evidently chatted with her lawyer. Part of me wanted to make her sweat a bit and even beg me not to run the quote. The other part of me, the save-myself-from-arrest part, needed to discover whether Hannah had known Shauna was the blogger, and perhaps killed her.

Normally I'd never agree to give the person I interviewed the power to nix a story, but in this case, I had no intention of running a story about Hannah and her affairs. "You got it," I said.

"Good." Hannah breathed out and relaxed against the back of the bench. "That makes me feel better."

When Hannah agreed I could record our conversation, I

pressed the record button on my phone and set it on the bench. Then I opened my notepad, pen poised, and nodded at her.

"Really," Hannah said, "the blog had the story correct. I *was* having an affair. Extracurricular field trips, if you will, with my son's soccer coach while my husband was overseas on his trade missions. Who knows what *he* was doing on those little jaunts of his? The story was accurate, but not welcome, because it embarrassed my husband, and that translated into a divorce suit."

"How did the divorce impact your life?"

"My husband claimed alimony. Big alimony. To keep him in the style he was accustomed to." She frowned at me. "I don't understand why I should pay him when really, he contributed nothing of value to our marriage, unless you count his hoohaw if you get my drift, which I suppose wasn't insignificant. Fortunately, my lawyer had the foresight to insist we sign something before our marriage, so dear Ferdinand will get his alimony, which isn't chump change, but not as much as he could have got."

"Ahh. That's good."

She nodded and smoothed non-existent creases on her dress. "On the positive side, I discovered yoga is excellent for combatting the excruciating *stress* one feels when facing a day in court. And I learned life goes on. I have enough of daddy's money that Ferdy's payments won't really make a difference."

"Do you know who the blogger is?"

"No. I'd love to give them a piece of my mind. In fact, when I find out who the blogger is, I will sue in a heartbeat. Daddy's money means I can hire a top lawyer. Do you know who it is?"

"If I knew, would I ask you?" I said.

"I see your point," Hannah said. She was silent and stared at the tree's canopy for a moment. "If I had to guess, I'd say it's someone with links to Ferocious Bodies. The gym? That's where my closest friends hang out, and if anyone is going to hear about my naughtiness, that's where they'd hear it. Because my friends love to gossip about who's getting it and who isn't. Don't we all?"

"Mmmm," I said.

Ferocious Bodies was Shauna's gym too. Odds were it was the locker room where Shauna had learned about Hannah's liaison with the soccer coach.

I consulted my notes. There was only one more thing I needed to find out.

"Thanks for speaking with me, Hannah," I said. "Before you go, one other thing. Were you in town last week?"

"Why?"

Thinking fast, I said, "I'm also doing an article on air quality around town and last week we had some unusual emissions floating up the valley. I'm trying to speak with people who might have suffered negative effects."

"No, I was at a retreat in Canada. If you can believe it, at an actual nuns' convent where they took this vow of silence. I mean, no talking." She shot me a look of pure disbelief. "At all. I froze my patootie off and spoke to myself for seven of the longest days *ever*. Plus, it cost me mega house sitter fees."

"Oh! I'm looking for a house sitter," I said. "Do you mind giving me their contact information?"

———

AFTER SAYING GOODBYE TO HANNAH, I went back to my cubicle. Five minutes later, I had contacted the house sitter and verified Hannah's information. All I had to do was inquire about her services, and mention Hannah had told me the sitter had just done a week-long job for her. "Oh yes," the sitter said. "Ms. Scrimshaw has such a lovely house. It was a perfect way to spend last week."

Scratch another suspect. I tried to convince myself that

taking suspects off the list was progress and perhaps better than adding suspects. That would be an excellent theory if I actually could find someone to put on the Coulda-Done-It list. So far, all I'd done was populate the Didn't-Do-It list.

It was almost time to leave for my lunch with Maggie at High Drifts in the Aspen Heights country club. Again, the question of wardrobe arose. But when I remembered Maggie's wealth, I decided she probably had enough sway to get me into High Drifts even if I wore raggedy jeans and flip-flops.

Before I left the office, I phoned Sierra Bistro. When Samantha McAdams came on the line, I introduced myself, thanked her for the muffin, and asked if she had time to meet later in the afternoon.

"Duncan told me you would call," she said. "What do you want to talk about?"

"Abel's Table. I understand you used to work there."

"Yes."

"I'd like your impressions of the restaurant. Could we meet? I want to do a review of Sierra Bistro for my food column so I can drop by anytime."

"You're welcome to come by, but I have nothing to say about the restaurant. I was tired from holding down two jobs, so I quit. If Duncan made it appear there was anything more to it, he's wrong."

Her resistance surprised me, but I knew the more I pushed, the more she would dig her heels in, and I would risk losing the chance to talk to her at all. I put a cheery note to my voice and said, "By mid-afternoon, I am going to need coffee, anyway. I'll stop by, and at a minimum, I can have another of your fabulous muffins. Maybe we can chat."

"I'm not sure how late I'm working today. I might not be here when you arrive. Sorry, there's a customer waving at me. I must go." She ended the call.

There was something about Abel's Table that made Samantha McAdams nervous. And that made my antennae ping with excitement. Had Shauna discovered something worth killing for?

Chapter 29

I PUT the top down on my rental T-bird for the trip to the country club. Dom had estimated the forensics team would need until Tuesday to go over my hybrid. While I waited for its release, I vowed to enjoy every moment I spent in the gorgeous energy-inefficient convertible. That meant sun on my head, wind in my hair. And bluesy rock music on the stereo.

I replayed the conversation with Samantha McAdams. The vibe her husband gave off made me believe he thought the restaurant was hinky. How would he come to that conclusion unless his wife had mentioned things that worried her?

I wondered who owned Abel's. To find out, I could go back to the office and run a few searches. Or I could try a shortcut. I made a quick detour to the municipal hall and popped into the Town Clerk's office. I asked the woman behind the counter to access the business license of Abel's Table restaurant. "It's for a story," I said. "One of many local interest pieces."

She punched a few keys and studied the screen. "Abel's Table. Business license is current, no outstanding work orders."

"Does it say who owns the restaurant?"

"Yes. AB Restaurants Inc. A California company."

"Does it show who owns that company?"

She shook her head. "Nope."

"How about officers?"

She peered at the screen again. "I have a fellow who signed the application for the business license. Ronald Malkins. Signed as secretary of the company."

Ronald Malkins was Shauna's lawyer. I didn't believe for a second that Malkins actually owned the restaurant. There was nothing suspicious about him acting as secretary of AB Restaurants Inc. The number of lawyers who served as secretary of companies was astronomical. It made doing routine business easier if the company lawyer could sign documents on its behalf. To find out who actually owned the company, I'd have to wait until I could get to my computer and search government records. There was no time to do it now because Maggie and lunch were waiting.

When I arrived at Aspen Heights country club just before noon, the parking lot was two-thirds full—nothing but Mercedes, Beamers and a smattering of high-end imported SUVs. If I'd been driving my domestic hybrid, I would have parked a distance away from its ritzier cousins so as not to give my little car a complex. But today my racy ride fit right in, so I claimed a spot next to a BMW.

On my way into the restaurant, I noticed a customer with a wonderful head of Nordic blond hair sitting at the bar. He turned his head as I neared, and I recognized the man's dangerously blue eyes and full lips. The last of Shauna's three exes, Josh Lehbout, looking very buff as usual.

He slid from his bar stool and towered over me, grinning a ridiculously sensuous grin. "Olivia, is that you?"

My neck cricked as I looked up at him. "Hi Josh, what a surprise to see you here."

"Here, as in the club, or here as in Prospect?"

"Both I suppose."

"I could say the same about seeing you in the club, Olivia. Neither of us strikes me as the type. If it hadn't been for my marriage to Shauna, I'd never have discovered the Rusty Nails they make at the bar. It's the only reason I hung on to the membership." His grin faded. "That's why I'm in town. For Shauna's service tomorrow."

"How did you hear?"

"The cops phoned. Wanted to know if I knew anyone with a grudge. I think they were also checking me out. You know their first rule is to look at family when there's a violent death."

"Well, that's ridiculous in your case," I said. "You and Shauna had the most amicable split I've ever heard of. And what, it's been two years?"

He crossed his arms, and I watched his biceps ripple and the fabric of his denim shirt strain across his chest. Ah, geez.

"Yeah," Josh said. "We are, were, better apart than as a couple."

I smiled up at him.

"How about you, Olivia? Things going well?"

Before I could do more than nod, Maggie swirled through the entrance. "Oh, Olivia, I hope I haven't kept you waiting long. I was on a telephone call I couldn't end politely, and it did go on and on."

"Not at all Maggie, I just arrived." I introduced Josh to her, saying he was a former resident of the town, back for a brief visit.

Josh shook Maggie's hand and then kissed my cheek. "Nice catching up with you, Olivia. See you tomorrow."

Maggie took my arm and guided me to the dining room. "My, oh my, he's a dish," she said. "Quite a lot to him, isn't there?"

I grinned. One of Aunt Gaye's mantras was that age had nothing to do with sensuality. "A woman hits her fifties," she said in exasperation, "and people think her hormones have packed their bags and left town. Hah. Age means nothing. We're all still thirty-something, appreciating the hell out of another well-put-together human body." Maggie was probably in her late fifties and her comment underscored my aunt's words.

My conscience pricked me. I hadn't phoned my aunt since the day I found Shauna's earrings where they had no business being. Aunt Gaye, Mom's only sister, was my second mother. She took me in when I was fourteen, after Mom died. Aunt Gaye was as fierce a supporter of me as Mom had been. Without her love, I never would have survived the broken hearts and angst of my teens. After I graduated from university, Aunt Gaye decided I didn't need her to be more than a phone call away and moved to Sacramento. Since then, we kept in touch through occasional weekend visits and long telephone conversations.

I owed Aunt Gaye a phone call, but I couldn't bring myself to tell her my marriage was a disaster, or that I was actually a suspect in Shauna's murder. "You should call her," my conscience said. "Stop bugging me," I retorted.

As Maggie and I took our seats at the table and picked up the menus, I reflected on Maggie's reference to Josh's size. He had the strength to go with it too. I realized then that he wouldn't have any problem maneuvering a concrete-filled barrel into a boat.

The server had barely finished his spiel about the daily specials when a short man in his mid-forties hustled to our table. "Mrs. Shillingford," he said, "a word." He pushed upward on the nosepiece of his wire-rim glasses. When he removed his finger, the glasses slid back to their original spot halfway down his nose.

Maggie said, "Dear James, how nice to see you. Have you met Olivia Mercier? She's with the *Gazette*. Olivia, this is James Cupressis, the manager of the club." I smiled at him.

He gave me a quick jerky nod and turned his attention back to Maggie.

"Your car seems to be in my spot." His finger once more adjusted his glasses. "Again."

"Oh, silly me," Maggie said. She rooted through the contents of her bag. "It's force of habit." She extracted a key fob from the bag and offered it to the manager. "Be a dear, James, and move the car? And I promise to try harder to remember that's no longer my spot."

The manager snatched the key from her hand, nodded once, and scurried out of the restaurant. "He is quite territorial," Maggie said. "A shame, really, when a parking spot is that important." She waved her hand dismissively, her heavy silver bracelet, with one brilliant turquoise stone hanging from a chain, gleaming in the warm lighting of the dining room.

"That's a striking bracelet," I said.

Her eyes misted as she played with the turquoise stone. "Thank you. It was a gift from my late husband." She studied her menu. "I can recommend the roast chicken or, if you prefer a lighter lunch, the chef makes excellent salads."

I felt I'd stuck my foot in my mouth when I'd commented on her bracelet. After we placed our lunch orders, I said, "I'm sorry if my comment brought sad memories to mind."

She smiled warmly at me and fingered the bracelet again. "Don't be silly. And my memories are not the least bit sad." She leaned forward, a mischievous glint in her eyes, and with a conspiratorial tone in her voice said, "I know you're married, but I'm sure I detected sparks between you and lovely Josh. Is he an admirer?"

I laughed. "Friendly sparks only. I've known Josh for ages, and he knows all my flaws. He used to be married to Shauna."

"Ahh. I recall her hinting once that there was one divorce she regretted. Do you think Josh is the one who got away?"

"Yes. I think Shauna only realized he was *the one* for her after they'd split."

"What a shame," Maggie said. "Love is wonderful, but it can also cause so much suffering."

When I looked across the table at Maggie, I saw the same expression of warm interest that I'd seen so many times on Aunt Gaye's face—one of genuine caring, wanting nothing but good things for me; hoping against hope that life would turn out exactly the way I wanted.

I felt warmth blossoming on my cheeks and a tightness form in my throat. I took a sip of water to push the emotions down. My hand shook as I set the water glass back on the table. When I again looked at Maggie, her face showed concern. I buried my face in my napkin and sobbed.

Chapter 30

WAS it because Dom had cheated? Or because Shauna had betrayed our friendship? Was I feeling sorry for myself? Whatever the reason, and probably it was all of them, I blurted out the whole sordid and soggy mess to Maggie's sympathetic ear. Our lunches arrived about the same time as I grabbed a tissue, blew my nose, and offered her a weak smile. "The upshot is that Dom and I are separated, but being civilized and pragmatic about it, and I'm a suspect in Shauna's murder."

At the look of shock on Maggie's face, I said, "I promise you I did not kill her. Although I admit there were moments I wanted to."

"I believe you," she said, "on both points. How awful to be under police scrutiny. I'm not sure what I'd do in your shoes."

"I'm investigating the case."

"Oh, heavens. You want to be careful poking around a murder, in case whoever did it turns their eye on you."

I shrugged the comment away. "I have to do something. It's better than focusing on my shambles of a marriage."

Maggie said, "My husband and I had our moments of darkness too. We even separated for a brief time. I won't say I hope you and Dom get back together, because perhaps that's not what you want. So, I hope things work themselves out in the best way for both of you."

I steered the conversation away from emotional topics then and asked Maggie how long she'd lived in Britain. "Ages," she said. "I was born in Dorset and spent a few wonderful years at Cambridge, studying horticulture. Then I grew roses and dabbled in amateur theater until my marriage."

Before I could ask when she'd moved to the United States, Miles Kenworth, a local public relations guru, approached our table. I'd never met him, but you couldn't live in Prospect without knowing who he was. He arrived at Maggie's side, all smiles and charm. "Forgive me for interrupting, ladies." He turned to Maggie. "Margaret, I heard you've decided not to support our mayor in his bid for re-election."

She raised her hand in a "hold it there" motion, gestured at me and said, "Miles, do you know Olivia Mercier? She's a very talented reporter with the *Gazette*."

My news nose tingled. It didn't take a psychic to realize she was warning him to zip his lips unless he wanted things in the next edition. Kenworth nodded at me. "My pleasure. I'm a fan. Excellent work, a joy to read. The paper is lucky to have you. I must say they need to hire a new photographer, because the photo above your byline doesn't do you justice."

In his Public Relations school, they obviously offered Smarm 101. As well as Disarming by Cliché 301.

Kenworth backed away a step. "I'll call you later, Margaret. My candidate is an excellent alternative to the incumbent. We would welcome your support."

Maggie inclined her head in the manner I imagined a queen would convey her agreement to supplicants seeking favors. Kenworth almost bowed in return.

Once Kenworth was out of earshot, I said, "I wouldn't be doing my job if I didn't ask whether you've withdrawn your support of the mayor. And if you know who the mystery candidate is."

"Can we keep it off the record for a few days? I have a good idea who his candidate is. Perhaps you can be the first to get the news."

When I agreed, Maggie said, "I haven't formally withdrawn support, but I'm not pleased with the job our current mayor is doing. Stayed tuned."

The rest of our lunch passed quickly. Maggie asked if I would report on the investigation of Shauna's murder for the *Gazette*.

"No, someone else is. Instead, I've taken on the food column."

"Won't that hamper your ability to investigate the murder like you wanted to do?" she asked.

"Not really. The bigger challenge is that Dom has been removed from the police team investigating the murder. Not that I expect him to share details of an investigation with me, but it makes me nervous that there's no one working the case I trust as much as him."

"You can say that? Even though he betrayed you?"

"Trusting him as a police officer is different than trusting him with my emotions. If he was running the file, I know they would find Shauna's killer. And quickly."

"Of course. Well, onward with the food column. Will you review our lunch?"

"I thought I might."

Maggie laughed and raised her wineglass. "Oooh, what fun. I won't tell the chef."

After lunch, Maggie had to attend a meeting of the club's membership committee, so I said goodbye and drove downtown to Sierra Bistro. I cranked up the stereo and sang along with Adele, feeling upbeat despite the concern that Owen Starshult could be correct, and the DNA results could come back as early as Wednesday. It was Maggie who had lifted my spirits. She was warm and interested and supportive. It felt good and right to unburden myself to her. I liked her. When I phoned Aunt Gaye, I'd have to tell her Shauna wasn't the only richer-than-god-but-no-airs woman in Prospect. I grinned— Aunt Gaye would probably refuse to believe it.

Chapter 31

PARKING WAS at a premium in Sierra's lot, so I left the T-bird a block away and enjoyed a short walk in the afternoon sun. Harlow, my friend and the owner of Sierra Bistro, was no dummy when it came to operating a business. She'd picked the perfect location for her coffee shop, on the sunny corner of a busy intersection, close to several shops designed to attract both locals and tourists. Bright red sun umbrellas welcomed customers to the outdoor patio tables, while bar-height counters lined the floor to ceiling windows inside the bistro to encourage people-watching. It was more than location and seating that drew customers in, however. It was the coffee and the menu, along with friendly and knowledgeable staff.

Harlow stood behind the service counter, talking to a slim, dark-haired woman about my age, and when she saw me, she broke off her conversation to wave me over. When I joined them, Harlow said, "Olivia, I hear you are the new food critic at the *Gazette*? No pressure, and of course I'll deny I said this, but speak ill of us and I swear I will cut you off for life." She laughed then and went on. "You know I'm joking, right? I have nothing to worry about because I've got Samantha here, who is the world's best baker."

I shook Samantha's hand. "I know. I've already tasted a sample." I stood there and smiled at them both. They smiled back at me. Samantha seemed much more relaxed than she'd sounded on the telephone. I took a breath and dove in. "I'm wondering if I could get an Americano and borrow a bit of Samantha's time? That is, if you are willing to talk with me, Samantha?"

Harlow said, "I mentioned you and I had gone to school together, and if I could trust you with all my secrets from high school, she could believe you if you said something would be kept off the record. Right?"

"For sure. What I want to know isn't for publication anyway."

Samantha told me to find a table. "I'll bring over your drink and perhaps a treat."

I picked a table in a quiet corner of the room and settled back, breathing in the heady aroma of freshly roasted coffee beans, cinnamon, and chocolate. Soon Samantha set two coffees on the table, and a small plate containing four coconut crusted sweets slightly smaller than golf balls. "These are called Deadly Balls," she said. "Coconut, dark chocolate, agave syrup and pecans."

I bit into one and chewed. "Oh, my gawd, that's unbelievable. A person could get hooked."

"Yes," she said. "Deadly."

I sipped my coffee. "Before I launch into other things, your husband is saving my yard from the neighborhood's shame register, and your children and Charlie brighten my mornings."

"Ben and Claire are quite taken with the treasures your pantry holds." She took a sip of coffee and smiled. "It's fine to give them a treat, but only one cookie each."

"Of course," I said. "Now, about Abel's Table. I dined

there yesterday, thinking I'd review it. The food was tasty, and I liked the server. But I noticed several people coming and going from a room at the back. Many more accessing that room than dining in the restaurant. Some of them looked like members of the PTA and others not so much."

Samantha nodded. Her face was set. She looked less relaxed than she'd been when I first arrived.

"What's going on there?" I said.

She shrugged. As she lifted her mug her hand shook, and coffee slopped over the rim.

"Samantha, are you okay?"

She shook her head and pushed her chair back. "I'm sorry. I can't do this. I don't work there anymore. I don't know anything."

"Wait, Samantha. Please. I won't print anything."

Samantha stood. Her face was set. "No. Sorry. I have to get back to work." She hurried away from the table and disappeared into the kitchen.

I popped another Deadly Ball into my mouth, intrigued. Samantha was obviously scared of something or someone. However, if she didn't want to talk about it, there wasn't much I could do.

In any event, what did possible shenanigans at Abel's Table have to do with my investigation of Shauna's murder? I was letting this little tangent interfere with the more important task of saving my skin. I mentally shoved Abel's Table to the far back burner and left.

I made a quick stop at the *Gazette* to collect my laptop and notes before going home. When I pulled into my driveway, Pierre came outside and told me he'd hired McAdams to take care of his yard. McAdams was a reassuring presence around my house lately. I was glad to hear he'd be working at Pierre's as well. His burly calm made me feel safe.

Chapter 32

AT NINE MONDAY EVENING, I sat at my kitchen island and submitted my review of the High Drifts restaurant to the *Gazette* online.

"You have to know a member of Aspen Heights Country Club to gain entrance to this fine dining spot, and if you do know such a person, I recommend you beg, cajole, or threaten your way into an invitation. Although short on items for vegetarians or diners with food sensitivities, High Drifts delivers on its promise of a memorable dining experience. Part of my enjoyment undoubtedly came from my charming dining companion, but this restaurant scores high in taste and presentation."

I opened my calendar to verify my appointments for Tuesday. First was Shauna's service at nine in the morning, which I was dreading.

I had seen her shoes on the body; Dom had confirmed it was her body in the barrel; there was a murder investigation underway—all things that told me Shauna was dead. Despite that, part of me didn't accept it. Tomorrow, however. Funerals make everything final. Tomorrow Shauna's death would be a reality.

I was still furious with Shauna. Yet, I grieved deeply for her. How could I be both angry and grieving? I probably would be a wreck after the funeral, perhaps in no shape to go to the other two appointments on Tuesday: lunch with Councilman Hardy in Reno at one, and the Police Advisory Committee meeting at seven in the evening. But I would go to them, because I hoped attending those events would keep my mind off Shauna.

The calendar entry for the committee meeting still niggled at me. I had no memory of inserting it. How did it get there? I scrolled through my calendar, feeling more comfortable as I recognized each item as being one I had entered. Perhaps I had simply forgotten about the committee meeting.

Then I reached September fourth and saw the item "Conduct Review Board." I definitely had not inserted that into my calendar. There was no mention of which conduct review board. Whether it was the Bar Association, the Medical Association, or the police, was a mystery. However, since the first calendar surprise was the Police Advisory Committee, odds were this second surprise referred to a police conduct review.

If that were so, someone wanted me to learn about things involving Prospect's police department. Who? Perhaps a *Gazette* employee who noticed my laptop unattended? Ridiculous—they could simply mention the upcoming events to me. More likely, the entries had been made while my computer was at the police department, and before Dom had arranged for my calendar to be downloaded onto the USB for me. Intriguing.

Perhaps a member of the advisory committee could give me a sense of upcoming agenda items. In the past, I would have called Shauna because she'd been on the committee for the last four years. Now, however, I needed other sources. I studied the list of members on the committee's website and found three names I knew. First was Ingrid Schmuller, who had gone to high school with me and was now a prominent realtor in town. Second was Dr. Norman Cigments, my dentist. Third was Miles Kenworth, the PR guru.

It was just before ten o'clock. That was probably too late to phone a committee member if I wanted them to welcome my call. Still, I was leaning toward risking a call to Ingrid when Dom phoned me. "Hey sweetheart," he said, "thought I'd check in and tell you about life in the Prospect Police marine unit."

"That's a shock. I was certain you'd opt for the unpaid leave."

"Aw, you know me, not a golfer, and you can watch only so much reality TV."

"And then there's the unpaid part."

"Yep, that was the clincher. I spent today investigating scum of the aqua variety. Six hours scraping crud off boat bottoms, washing down the decks and polishing woodwork. Don't get me wrong, I'm not complaining because all six hours were spent on solid land. How was your day?"

"Pierre mentioned he hired Duncan McAdams to do his yard."

"Good, it looks like it might work out for the McAdams family," Dom said.

I remembered Samantha McAdams' obvious anxiety about Abel's Table, and ran the name by Dom. "I planned to do a review of a diner called Abel's Table for the *Gazette*. Has it ever come up on your radar?"

"Abel's Table?"

"Yeah, in the Altitude Mall."

"Nope, doesn't ring any alarms."

"Good, thanks. Oh, I had lunch with Maggie Shillingford

and discovered some mystery person is set to challenge our mayor for his job."

Dom was silent.

"Dom? Hello?"

"Oh yeah, sorry, I was wondering who it might be."

"I'll find out in a couple of days. Maggie gave me first dibs on the story." I glanced at the calendar on my computer screen. "Did you put some items into the calendar on my computer Friday?

"Huh?"

I told him about the two items on my calendar that I hadn't entered. "You had my computer at the station, so I wondered if you put them there. Because they obviously have to do with the department."

"Not me. Sure you didn't forget entering them?"

"Absolutely. One maybe, but not two. What do you think? Is there something going on at the department?"

"There's always something going on. Listen, I have two tips for you. Corporal Cassidy is keeping me in the loop on Shauna's case. First, there's a pattern to the wound on Shauna's skull that makes Cassidy think the murder weapon wasn't rebar. Second, they found a spot of blood in your car and sent it off for testing. I bet it's from when you injured yourself with your new hobby."

For a second, I considered fessing up and telling Dom that the blood was Shauna's. But he was a police officer. If I asked him not to share what he knew with the investigating officers, he would be in a terrible position, forced to choose between me and his professional obligation not to withhold evidence. I elected to dummy up.

Dom continued. "It will be a while for the DNA results because there's a backup at the lab. But don't worry, bella. I'll keep tabs on it. If results aren't back by Friday, I'll spur them on."

I wanted to scream at him. No, no, no, leave it alone, stop helping, stop fixing things. Instead, I said, "Okay. Gotta run."

"I'll see you tomorrow at the funeral. Meanwhile bella, I love you. Always will."

I knew he wanted to hear something encouraging back, but I ended the call with a weak "sleep tight."

Chapter 33

IT TAKES twenty minutes to dress for a funeral. Plus another fifteen to take everything off and add something in honor of a woman who loved spicy things. On the outside, my Armani suit gave me the sedate, respectable image most people expected to see at a funeral. Underneath the suit, I wore a fiery red bra and thong—exactly what Shauna would have worn. In fact, she had always claimed she wore racy lingerie every day, even under her riding duds.

Most people might wonder why I'd want to honor the woman who destroyed my marriage and happiness. As usual these days, my emotions were all over the place. I alternated between anger at Shauna, grief, and warmth when I remembered better times with her. The good times far outnumbered the bad. In fact, we'd had thirty years of great times and four weeks or so of excruciating horribleness. More and more, I found it hard to stay angry with Shauna. However, I was still light years away from forgiveness.

Moments before I left the house, I received a call from the bull semen magnate I'd phoned on Sunday. "Ms. Mercier, this is Quayle Jonasberg. Y'all called me about the *Cheat Sheet.*"

This man sounded about like I figured a bull semen salesman would. From his voice I could picture him sitting on the back of an appaloosa, Stetson brim pulled low over eyes squinting into the red sunset as a bull calf moseyed on by. Maybe a bit of tumbleweed in there to complete the atmosphere.

I reprised my story about a feature on exposé journalism, and then asked if he could tell me about his run-in with the *Cheat Sheet,* hoping he'd drawl on and on and allow me to enjoy my dream man on the appaloosa in the sunset a while longer.

"It was a time ago, last fall," he said. "They did a story saying George was nothing more than prime rib on the hoof."

"George?"

"King George the Third. Of my prize Angus bulls, he's the gold medalist. A bull that loves his job and performs with gusto. A bull that earns thousands every time he wanders into a cow's paddock."

"Got it. And the blogger said George was, um, defective?"

"They said his tamales weren't hot anymore, not even lukewarm. They said he was shooting blanks."

"Did they offer you a chance to rebut the story?"

"Hell, they told me they'd kill the story for the right price," Jonasberg said.

"What? They blackmailed you?"

"They tried. I told them, 'Go ahead, hit me with your best shot.' So, they ran the story."

"Did the publicity cost you stud fees? Or impact sales of semen from other bulls?"

"I'll tell y'all what I did. I gave a money-back guarantee to every customer. I know bulls and I know George. And this year he's the proud pappy of a whole new crop of calves. Twenty-six. Business has never been better. Blanks, schmanx."

I thanked Jonasberg for his time and tucked his information about blackmail away. It seemed uncharacteristic of Shauna.

Or was it?

Shauna had resorted to blackmail at least once that I knew of. Before Noel had left for Los Angeles, Shauna had asked me to help her follow him around town. "I can't use my car because he'll spot it," she said. "You need to drive."

She tucked her auburn hair under a scruffy cap and donned cheap sunglasses before handing me a Yankees ball cap. "And wear this."

"Why are we disguising ourselves and following Noel?"

"To find out who's selling him drugs."

"Oh shit."

When Noel parked outside a diner, we parked half a block behind him. "Wait for me," Shauna said.

She was out of the car and walking down the sidewalk before I could object. She held her cell phone up to her face as if she was involved in a deep conversation and strolled by the diner. Then she leaned her back against a window and pretended to snap a few selfies.

As soon as Shauna got back into my car, I laid rubber out of there. "Are you crazy?" I said. "They could have figured out what you were doing!"

"Nah, they were too interested in Noel's money. I have a video. And I know who those guys are."

Noel had no idea why his supplier started ghosting him. Shauna never told Noel that she'd sent a copy of the video to the supplier. "If you or your pals have anything more to do with Noel Wylie or bother me," her message said, "the original is going to the cops."

Yes, that was blackmail. But she'd done it because of someone she loved, and she didn't ask for money.

Could Shauna blackmail for money? I'd have said it was impossible, however she had done at least one thing I never would have believed possible—she slept with Dom. So perhaps blackmail for money could be added to the list.

Still, in my heart, I knew that person was not the Shauna I knew.

Chapter 34

I PARKED a block away from the huge brick church that, before now, Shauna had attended perhaps four times in her life, all weddings. Three of them were hers. The fourth was mine.

Now she was here for a fifth and last time.

Owen Starshult from the *Gazette* caught up to me as I stepped from the sidewalk onto the cobbled path leading to the church steps. "Hey Olivia, I have some news." We moved off the path to let others pass by. He lowered his voice. "I called the crime lab like you suggested. About the DNA? They said usually seven to ten days."

"Noel was wrong about the faster turnaround? Where'd he get his information?"

"He worked on a movie where the expert advisor told them three days for DNA results."

"Movies," I said. "For Noel, it's all about movies." I glanced over Owen's shoulder and saw Dom get out of his cruiser. Corporal Cassidy exited the passenger side.

Owen said, "Yeah, well, the lab said *usually* seven to ten. 'It all depends,' they said. It could be less."

I watched Dom and Cassidy as they stood by the cruiser

talking, their eyes on the people walking toward the church. Making mental lists, I knew, of who showed up. Looking for the person who was noticeable by their attendance or by their absence. When Dom spotted me, he touched Cassidy on the arm and started toward Owen and me. My stomach clenched at that touch and spasmed when I registered the way Dom smiled at her before he walked away.

"Thanks Owen," I said. "I should go inside."

I hurried along the path and hustled up the steps and into the church, slid into the back pew, and sat in the aisle seat. Sending that usually easy-to-deliver message: "Find a seat somewhere else."

Dom didn't seem to get the delivery. He wasn't even bothered by the hassle of moving past me in the pew. He plopped down beside me. "Hey Livvie."

"Shouldn't you be out on a police boat?" I said.

"Shift starts at noon. Frankie had some things she wanted to kick around, so I tagged along."

"Frankie?"

"Cassidy, Francine Cassidy," Dom said. He surveyed the church. "Good crowd, don't you think?"

A familiar tightness took hold of my chest. Dom called every one of his officers by their last name. Except Corporal Cassidy, it seemed, and that picked at me. The fact it bothered me ticked me off even more. I jammed myself against the side of the pew, taking satisfaction in gaining another inch of personal space.

When the minister appeared at the front of the church, the crowd made the usual shuffling, settling down noises. After the minister's words of condolence, Noel rose and addressed the crowd. "Shauna was my big sister. The best sister a guy could have. She covered for me when I sneaked out after curfew, she scared all the boogeymen out from under my bed before I went to sleep, she helped me learn my lines for auditions. She looked after me when our mom and dad died and told me I'd never be alone. She fought dragons for me at school, in the park, and at home, and I loved her. I still do. And I will miss her every day of my life."

I squirmed in the pew, blinking back tears. Eulogies do that to me. Dom, who remained dry-eyed throughout, squeezed my hand. "It's okay," he whispered.

Nothing's okay, I thought, and wrenched my hand away. I became conscious of people glancing over at me. I wondered what they thought of my attending the funeral. By now the only people in town who hadn't heard I was the cops' favorite suspect were those already interred among the pines and aspens that graced Prospect's two cemeteries. Some would call me a hypocrite for mourning a woman I had publicly called a tramp. Some would believe my presence indicated the killer was among them. It was silly to think I could control their words or thoughts, so I decided not to try.

I kept my head down. During the minister's final words, I realized that my fury with Shauna had lost its heat. The energy it took to stay enraged was exhausting.

At the end of the service, as people stood and prepared to leave, my phone chimed, announcing a text message. It was from a number I didn't recognize:

What do u know about hazing. #thoseinblack.

The hashtag had to refer to first responders. Prospect's fire and police departments, even the ambulance service, wore black uniforms. I nudged Dom and whispered, "Look at this."

He took the phone and read the message. I noticed a quick widening of his eyes and a slight tightening of his jaw. He handed the phone back to me, his face expressionless. "Who's it from?" he asked.

"No idea. Is something going on at the department?"

He shrugged. "Beats me," he said, his face still expressionless.

Before he put the innocent, know-nothing mask on his face, Dom had been surprised and anxious. "Beats me?" Baloney.

Chapter 35

After the service, I exited through the huge, carved church doors and noticed Noel at the bottom of the church steps. I squinted at the bright sunlight and wondered if, like me, he felt the day more properly ought to have been gray and raining. It always shocked me that birds sang and the sun warmed the day despite a person's grief. Or fear. Or disappointment. Or loss.

When Noel saw me, he turned his back and walked away.

I spotted Josh, Shauna's ex, hovering nearby. He grinned and kissed me on the cheek. "Olivia, you look lovely."

"Cut the baloney, Josh. My mascara is probably on my chin."

He ran his thumb gently under my right eye. "Nope, just a bit there."

He stood back, folded his arms and scrutinized me, a wry smile on his face.

"I heard about Shauna and Dom," Josh said. "It stinks. How about you and I form a club for survivors of unfaithful lovers?"

I knew Shauna tended to stray. But when she met Josh, I thought things would be different. "He's all I need," she had told me. "I'm done being a loose woman." I had hopes that Josh was indeed the answer to her dreams.

"For what it's worth, Josh, Shauna always said you were the one who got away."

Josh shrugged. "Shauna needed to be desired and admired by everyone. Or she felt less than worthless."

The minute he spoke those words, I was back in high school, hiding behind the stage curtains in the school gym with Shauna. We had been working on the sets for the upcoming play when the cheerleading squad burst into the gym for their practice. From our secret vantage point, we watched them practice cheers for the basketball team.

When Amber, the head of the squad, asked Helen to give a cheer for Shauna, Helen twirled and, in a singsong voice, said, "I don't wanna. Cheer for Shauna."

The squad burst out in laughter.

"Cut it out, y'all," Amber said. "Helen, you're just pissed because Jeremy is sweet on her."

"No way," Helen shouted. "He called Shauna two raisins on an ironing board. No one's worse than a skinny girl with braces."

Shauna pretended their comments didn't bother her. But the next year, when she had matured into a stunner, Shauna embarked on a campaign to date every one of the cheer squads' beaus, cause the breakup of their romances, and then dump the fellows unceremoniously. If she'd had a pistol, she would have carved notches on the handle.

Even though braces eventually come off, and a skinny girl matures into a dynamic, gorgeous woman, the taunts, and the insecurities they cause, live on. They become part of that woman's psyche.

Now, I shook my head and said to Josh, "Weird, isn't it? She could do it all, had confidence to spare. Except..."

"When it came to love," Josh said. "Then she got all tied up with self-worth issues."

When I looked again at Josh and took in his physique, I remembered the question I wanted to ask. "You've been here, what, three days? Had enough of Prospect yet, or are you sticking around longer?" I hoped he'd tell me when he had arrived in town, on the chance he'd shown up more than a week ago and killed the woman who cheated on him.

Instead, he said, "I'm taking off this afternoon. I guess the cops checked me out and verified I was in New York about the time Shauna died, because they said I don't have to stay in touch."

Scratch another suspect.

As if Josh mentioning cops had some magical power, Corporal Clapton appeared at my elbow. "Mrs. Bertucci, how are you?" Today Clapton was back to using Bertucci as my surname. I gritted my teeth. He introduced himself to Josh and then turned back to me. "I'm glad I ran into you. I have another question about those barrels. You and Ms. Wylie bought six, and she kept four?"

I nodded, a sick feeling forming in my gut.

"All barrels present and accounted for at her ranch," Clapton said. "I remember seeing one in your garage."

I nodded, mute.

"Where's your other one?" he said.

"In pieces. I cut it up to use in yard art. That turned out as badly as my first attempts at making the concrete bases. I dumped the sorry lot in the landfill." I looked over his shoulder, spotted Maggie looking our way. I offered a prayer of thanks to my guardian angel. "Oh gee, you'll have to excuse me. I see someone I've been trying to talk to for days." A fib, but compared to the pants-on-fire story I'd just told about the second barrel, nothing I'd sweat over.

Without giving Clapton or Josh another glance, I almost ran over to Maggie. "Olivia, how nice to see you," she said. "Of course, the circumstances could be better." She leaned forward and whispered. "I noticed your husband beside you in church. He was very solicitous. Any chance things are looking brighter?"

When I shook my head, Maggie tsked. Then she asked, "How's your investigation coming along?"

"It's stalled a bit."

"Chin up," she said. "Perseverance will pay off. By the way, I have an appointment this afternoon. If it goes the way I think it will, I shall try to get you that story about the candidate for mayor."

"Wonderful." I checked the time and saw it was time to leave for my lunch with Councilman Hardy in Reno. I thanked Maggie again for Monday's lunch and made my goodbyes.

———

I ARRIVED at the Nevadan Resort in Reno a few minutes before one. There was no sign of Hardy in the lobby, so I went to the front desk. "I'm Olivia Mercier," I said to the clerk. "Councilman Hardy is expecting me. I believe he reserved a private dining room?"

A knowing smile appeared on the clerk's face. "Yes, Executive Suite 2501. Elevators are to the right."

As I rode the elevator to the 25th floor, I calculated the odds that the hotel's private dining rooms were called executive suites: abysmally tiny. Which probably accounted for the snide smirk the clerk had tossed my way.

My instinct was to return directly to the lobby. I wasn't some naïve baby who would wander trustingly into a man's hotel room. But I needed to interview The Nose. I needed to know how he felt about the story in the *Cheat Sheet* and whether he knew Shauna was the blogger.

The elevator arrived at the 25th floor. I exited and stood in the elevator lobby. I stared at the door to Suite 2501. Was there an eyeball on the other side of the peephole? Was the person who owned that eyeball clutching a bag of cocaine and hoping for a rip-snorting good time? Or was he checking table settings and preparing for a stellar luncheon?

Run or stay?

Bailing out meant safety. It also meant offending Hardy and blowing any chance of an interview. Staying meant slime, at best. Bodily harm at worst.

Slime or safety?

Chapter 36

I STOOD in front of the door to Executive Suite 2501 and coached myself. "You are not a naïve baby. You are a modern woman. You are armed with a smart phone." I set my phone to video record and pressed the doorbell.

After a respectable delay, Hardy opened the door and stared into my phone. "Hello, Councilor," I said. "I'm Olivia Mercier. I hope you don't mind my recording our interview. It makes for accuracy."

He touched the perfect knot in his tie, then smoothed his impeccably groomed hair, smiled a politician's smile at the phone, and bowed. "No problem at all, Ms. Mercier."

In reality, the suite was one room, plus ensuite bathroom, together measuring about seven hundred square feet. A set of stairs divided the main room into two tiers. The upper tier held the bathroom and a large freestanding screen that partially hid the king-sized bed. The lower tier held an L-shaped kitchen, a living-room arrangement of a couch and two tub chairs, a workstation, and a dining table that was set for two. A chef stood next to the dining table.

Hardy directed me to the table. "I apologize for not asking you in advance if meeting in this suite would be acceptable, but I only found out a few hours ago that there was some confusion over the booking, and all the private dining rooms were promised to other diners. However, when the hotel offered me this suite *and* a meal prepared by Chef Maurice as an apology, I couldn't turn it down. Once you taste Chef's food, you'll understand why."

I turned the phone's camera toward the chef, a tiny man of about seventy. "Wonderful to meet you, Chef." He nodded at me and whispered a hello. I relaxed. Chef Maurice's presence would surely discourage The Nose from offering any pre- or post-dinner snorts. And should they both turn on me, I was confident I could easily lift Chef and use his body to bust Hardy's nose before beating a retreat out the door.

The lunch was pleasant, my host gracious, and the food superb. Hardy and I exchanged getting-to-know-you information while we enjoyed the appetizer. I got to the meat of the interview during the rack of lamb entrée. I delivered my usual spiel about the fictional feature on exposé journalism and then launched in. "Did the *Cheat Sheet* offer you an opportunity to comment on the story before they ran it?"

"Not at all," Hardy said. "But I don't know what I could have said by way of explanation or comment. The blogger had the story right. I *did* have a cocaine problem."

The anger and resentment I'd expected to hear was missing.

"How did the story affect your life?"

He cut into his lamb and thought for a moment. "Ironically, things turned out for the better. My wife stuck by me, and I went into rehab. I got re-elected, perhaps because people wanted to give me another chance. Now I'm living a clean and productive life."

Oh, give me a break. First Hannah Scrimshaw, the hot tamale socialite, tells me she's mostly unconcerned about the exposure the blog gave her. Then my appaloosa-riding king of bull semen tells me his bull is blessed with mojo to spare and the blog post actually increased his business. And now Hardy. Yet another victim of the *Cheat Sheet* insisting Shauna's exposé had not ruined their life. I wanted to identify suspects, and this was not working at all.

Perhaps, being a politician, Hardy was spinning a tale. "You know who the blogger is, right?" I said.

He put down his cutlery and leaned forward, eyes sparkling. "Who? I'm dying to know. I could give them stories about people. You know, in the interests of bettering society."

"I was hoping *you* knew who it was," I said.

He shook his head. "No idea, and not for lack of trying. When the story first came out, back when I was angry, I tried to find out. Asked everyone if they'd heard anything. Nada. Zip. After a week, I thought about hiring a guy to dig into it but by then things were settling down. I went into rehab instead."

I had to find out where he was during the days around the discovery of Shauna's body. "This is totally off the topic," I said, "but I imagine you heard about the body they found in Donner Lake a week ago?"

"Yes, terrible thing. We have a place at the lake and were actually there that day."

"Really?"

"We'd been in San Francisco for our son's graduation from San Francisco State and drove back on the Monday. Never have I been so glad that my wife keeps everything because when the police asked us where we were that weekend, she produced our hotel receipt."

The interview was an unmitigated bust. If not for the meal, which as Hardy had promised was fabulous, the trip to Reno would have been a waste of gas.

After dessert (how did Chef know that piña colada gelato was my all-time fave?) I stopped the recording, thanked Hardy, and excused myself to visit the bathroom. I listened to the muted sounds of table clearing as I washed my hands and mentally composed my review of Chef Maurice's meal. Since I wasn't likely to be in such a luxurious bathroom again, I dallied there, flicking through the sixty-odd channels on the flat screen TV, inspecting the soaps and lotions, and wondering if guests used all twelve of the shower heads and jets at once.

Finally, I snapped a selfie to prove I'd once been in a bathroom with gold faucets. Then I slipped the small container of bath gel into my purse (but not before checking the ceiling for cameras) and re-entered the suite. Where I found The Nose stretched out on the bed, wearing nothing but his tighty-whities and a smile. "Chef had another engagement," he said. "Why not join me for an après-lunch-something? Grand Marnier? Courvoisier? Or *moi*?"

The Nose had both knobby knees and tighty-whities on offer. My laugh started as a bubble in my stomach, quickly morphed into chuckles, and then became gut-shaking guffaws. I doubled over, holding my stomach, tears streaming down my cheeks as I tried to stifle the laughter.

When I glanced at him, Hardy appeared embarrassed, moving toward angry. Self-preservation kicked in. I stifled the giggles and said, "You should write comedy because you've got a wicked sense of humor and great timing. That's the best joke anyone's pulled on me in months."

His face relaxed, and he grinned. "Yeah, I figured you'd get a kick out of my prank, or I never would have risked it."

I moved to the door. "Again, thanks for the lunch and interview, Councilor. I'll send you a copy of the article." Then I rushed out the door and pounded on the elevator call button like a maniac. When the elevator arrived, I dove inside.

Interesting lunch. I knew three things. First, Chef Maurice could seriously cook. Second, The Nose was not a suspect in Shauna's murder. Third, he should keep his day job because headlining the Chippendales show wasn't in his future.

Chapter 37

THE HOTEL's elevator bank was conveniently next to an entrance to the casino, so I hid out by a slot machine until I could be sure Hardy had left the Nevadan. I'd found the episode in the suite humorous, but it could have embarrassed him to the point he would seek revenge. Or perhaps he'd worry I had recorded his come-on. Better to be behind him on the return trip to Prospect.

I found a lone five-dollar bill in my wallet and fed it into a quarter video poker machine with a good view of the hotel lobby. I hadn't played poker since university, so I bet one quarter a hand, hoping to extend my stay at the spying post. The hotel's meeting rooms were located down a short corridor next to the elevator bank, but unless Hardy exited an elevator at the same time as conventioneers left the meeting rooms, I felt confident I would notice him.

I'd invested half an hour and $3.75 when Hardy exited an elevator and marched across the lobby to the valet stand. He studied his cell phone until his white Mercedes arrived. Then he tipped the valet and drove away. I celebrated my successful stakeout by playing my last $1.25 on a final hand. When four aces appeared on the screen, I did a little dance and hit the button for a cash-out ticket.

As I stood at the ticket redemption machine, waiting for it to deliver my mini fortune of $62.50, I caught sight of the Public Relations guru, Miles Kenworth, entering the hotel lobby from the meeting room corridor. Trailing a short distance behind him were Maggie Shillingford and Chief Gavric. I retrieved my winnings from the machine and watched as the trio shook hands and said their goodbyes. They looked pleased with themselves. Maggie had mentioned having an appointment this afternoon. If her appointment had been a meeting with Kenworth and the Chief of Police, it had evidently gone very well. Because Kenworth wanted Maggie to support his candidate for mayor, I was certain Gavric was Kenworth's candidate.

Kenworth gave them a small wave and turned toward the street entrance. Maggie and Gavric watched Kenworth leave the hotel and get into his car. I debated flagging Maggie down, but hung back, waiting for Gavric to leave. When he leaned forward to hug Maggie, I concluded he'd definitely secured her support for his candidacy. I just about dropped my cash on the casino floor in surprise when they turned and walked arm in arm to a waiting hotel elevator.

I pocketed my winnings and headed to the Nevadan parkade where I sat in my car for a few minutes and called my two contacts on the Police Advisory Committee. In both cases, I was bumped to their voice mail. Dr. Cigments was probably lecturing a patient about the benefits of flossing, and Ingrid Schmuller was no doubt busy selling a million-dollar log home overlooking the river. I left messages, saying that I wanted to talk to them about Shauna.

The drive back to Prospect was quick. Even with the obligatory stop at the agricultural check-stop at the California border to prove I wasn't bringing produce into the State, I was home by three. I'd have plenty of time to write a food column about private dining at The Nevadan and still make it to the evening meeting of the Police Advisory Committee. With luck, I could talk to Dr. Cigments or Ingrid before the meeting.

When I fished in my mailbox for the mail, I heard something clink against the metal of the box. I peered inside and saw two USB drives, one silver, one red. Who would give me USBs? And why? Trying to keep paranoia about bombs in check, I grabbed a plastic bag and tissues from the kitchen. Then I removed the USBs from the mailbox gingerly, using the tissues in the hope of not destroying any fingerprints, and placed the two drives inside the bag. When nothing exploded, I stopped holding my breath.

I went next door and rang Pierre's doorbell. "Hey Pierre," I said, when he opened the door. "Did you see anyone drop anything in my mailbox? I didn't check my box yesterday, so it could have been then or today."

"Sorry, no." Pierre jutted his chin toward Mrs. Bagnovicz's house across the street. "I bet she could tell you."

I glanced at her house just in time to see her aqua blinds snap shut. "Right, like I'm gonna ask her."

Inside my house, I dropped the mail and the USB drives next to my computer before changing into my working-at-home uniform of jeans and a t-shirt.

I was desperate to learn what was on the USBs. First, however, my job demanded I file a review with the *Gazette*. I wrote a short but positive review.

"I fell in love today. I had the opportunity to enjoy a lunch prepared by Chef Maurice of the Nevadan Resort. He stole my heart with inspired and thoughtful menu choices, an appetizing presentation and, above all, melt-in-your-mouth deliciousness. His piña colada gelato is a definite winner. Keep this resort, and particularly Chef Maurice, in mind for your next private dining event."

I didn't say, "Who knew the private dining room would be a hotel suite? Who knew my host would offer more than port as a post-dining digestif?"

As soon as I hit "submit" for the review, I picked up the silver USB by its edges with a tissue (still being conscious of any prints I might smudge) and inserted it into my computer. While my anti-virus program scanned the drive, I thought about the lunch and wondered whether private dining liaisons were commonplace to Chef Maurice. When Maggie and Gavric entered the elevator, were they heading to a suite? Were they enjoying Chef Maurice's food right now, perhaps a dinner of *châteaubriand*—the perfect romantic meal for two? The wicked part of me wondered what post-dining goodies the Chief would offer Maggie. I'd lay odds *his* knees weren't knobby.

It struck me then how preconceptions influence a person's opinions. Because Gavric was head of the police department, and because he was a tall, muscular man, I'd cast him in the role of a stern authority figure, devoid of the capacity for affection. Yet I'd seen him embrace a woman in the lobby of the Nevadan Resort. The Chief had wrapped his arms around Maggie and enveloped her. Maggie was not petite. His size made her appear fragile.

I wondered how long Maggie and Gavric had been keeping company, as Aunt Gaye would say. They appeared to be very comfortable with each other. Did Gavric share information about his colleagues with her? Did she know Dom had been demoted to the marine unit? Or were she and Gavric so enraptured with each other that there was no room for routine, day-to-day conversation?

I shook my head and chuckled. I could hear Shauna's lecture. "Honestly, Olivia, the world does not revolve around you. People do not spend all their time discussing you and your life."

My computer pinged to alert me that the silver USB had

passed its anti-virus scan. The drive's menu, nothing more than a series of meaningless letters and numbers, appeared on my screen. I dragged the drive's contents to my desktop, named it "silver" and ejected the drive. Then I ran the anti-virus program on its red-cased mate, again handling the USB with tissues.

When I checked my watch, I was surprised it was nearing dinner time and I'd soon need to leave for the police advisory committee meeting. I had eaten so much of Chef Maurice's wonderful lunch that preparing a full dinner for myself was out of the question. I could get by with veggies and dip.

Which was pretty much what I'd been surviving on since Dom moved out. Snacks, and order-in pizza. Wine to wash it down. Real home-cooked meals—ones with starters and luscious entrées complete with meat or fish and decadent sauces—were a thing of the past. Just like my marriage.

Chapter 38

MY PHONE RANG JUST as I dipped a carrot stick into hummus.

"Hello, Olivia," a male voice said when I answered the call. "It's Norm Cigments, returning your call."

"Dr. Cigments, thanks. As I said in my message, I'm doing background on Shauna Wylie for a story, and I know you were on the Police Advisory Committee with her. I'd love your insights."

"What a shocker about her death, hey? We are going to miss her. She was one of the most active members, took the role of the committee seriously."

"Did she have any pet issues or bug bears?"

"Shauna was all about accountability and transparency. She wanted more of both, and as you know, she could be outspoken. Meetings were lively, to say the least."

"Did that create any strain among members?"

He hesitated. I knew he was considering how smart it was to speak to a reporter about committee business, and I expected him to end the discussion. But he opted for anonymity. "You never heard any of this from me, okay?"

"Absolutely."

"No strain amongst members that I saw. Most of us

agreed with Shauna's opinions. Any angst was more on the part of the Department bigwigs."

"The Police?"

"Yeah. The committee let Shauna do the talking whenever we met with Chief Gavric and his staff. Some of us hid behind her, I guess."

"Can you give me an example of department angst?"

"The biggest blow up was a couple of years ago when our outside auditor delivered the performance review."

I'd written a report on that audit for the *Gazette*. Besides exposing significant budget overruns, the auditor cited poor or non-existent communication between rank and file, inadequate equipment, and lack of ongoing training opportunities for officers, all resulting in a totally demoralized force. The report also slammed a failure to offer candid and honest commentary about internal matters that mattered to the public.

"I remember that audit," I said. "I did an article on it for the *Gazette.*"

"Then you'll know it revealed a complete breakdown in community support of the department and was an indictment of leadership. When we met with the Chief, Shauna told him management sets the tone and when things go south, it's management's fault. She said if it were her decision alone, she'd replace management, starting with the guy at the top."

That sounded like Shauna. I wished I'd been a fly on the wall during that meeting. "How'd Gavric react?"

"He said he was as appalled as we were by the auditor's assessments, that he'd obviously misplaced his trust in his division heads and vowed to turn things around."

"He blamed it on others?"

"Yeah," Dr. Cigments said. "The Chair of the committee told him budget overruns had to stop immediately, and that we wanted to see improvements in performance. Shauna reminded him the performance audit was every two years and she, for one, would be very interested in the results of the next audit."

"When is that scheduled?" I said.

"Not until the end of September this year."

I was quiet as I thought about the upcoming audit. It could not be the reason someone had placed tonight's meeting on my calendar. The reason had to be something that was on the agenda for tonight.

Dr. Cigments interrupted my thoughts. "Olivia, if that's all? I need to get ready for the meeting."

"One last thing and then I'll let you go," I said. "What's on the agenda for tonight?"

"The usual. Nothing controversial. There's one item of new business that Shauna added to the agenda. But the notice of meeting doesn't indicate what it was about and now we'll never know." He sighed. "I imagine most of the meeting will be spent missing Shauna."

———

THE SCAN of the red USB was complete and without checking the drive's menu, I dragged the contents to my desktop, named it "red" and ejected the drive. Then I grabbed my computer and rushed to my car, hoping I could check out the two drives' contents during a break in the meeting.

Mrs. Bagnovicz was on her knees in her front garden and looked up as I drove past. I waved at her and said to myself, "Baggie's weeding her gnomes; it must be Tuesday."

I could feel myself relaxing, my nerves calming, as I drove into town. It was all because of the scenery around Prospect, something I never tired of—from the granite faces of nearby mountains to towering Jeffrey Pines that lined the route, their tufts of five-inch needles reminding me of cheerleaders' pompoms. I opened my window and breathed in deeply, hoping to catch a whiff of the vanilla scent the pines' bark gave off in hot weather. I convinced myself it was there, just a hint.

Not long after I entered Prospect's town center, I reached the Civic Building. It was five minutes before seven when I pulled into the parking lot. I congratulated myself for getting there on time and without speeding.

I hurried to the Civic Building, where I spotted Miles Kenworth, the PR guru who apparently was running Gavric's campaign for mayor, waiting for an elevator. Since he was a committee member, I wouldn't have to scan the building directory for the meeting room. I could just tag along with him.

We rode in silence to the third floor. He gave no sign he remembered meeting me at the country club. I said, "Mr. Kenworth, hello." He studied me. I could tell he was mentally flipping through his mind's index of faces. "Olivia Mercier," I said. "Margaret Shillingford introduced us yesterday."

"Ahh, yes. How are you?" He motioned for me to precede him from the elevator.

"I'm looking for the Police Advisory Committee meeting," I said.

His upper lip lifted ever so slightly. If I didn't know better, I'd swear it was the start of a sneer. "Is there a particular agenda item that brings you here?" he said.

"Nope. Just the meeting as a whole."

"You're not speaking to an agenda item?"

I shook my head and smiled.

"Committee meetings are in camera," he said. He seemed happy to give me that news. He took a few steps along the hallway, turned back to me and said, "That means private, no public."

I followed him. Kenworth's arrogant sneer and his assumption that a lowly reporter wouldn't know the definition of "in camera" made me want to leap on his back and stab

159

him with my ballpoint. Instead, I said, "I know for a fact they weren't a year ago."

He resumed walking and tossed words over his shoulder. "That was then, this is now. Things have changed. Bottom line, the meeting's off limits to you."

"But surely the press is allowed access?" I hated the slight whine in my voice.

By now, he'd reached the meeting room. "Nope." Kenworth opened the door and shouldered past me through the doorway. "Believe it or not, the press is part of the public." His tone signaled that both press and public were high on his list of undesirables. "If we have anything for you, we will put out a release. Nice chatting with you again."

The door clicked shut, but not before I noted his self-satisfied smirk as he pushed it closed. What happened to the smarm and charm he'd exhibited at the country club? Probably he'd flunked Sincerity 101 at his Public Relations school.

On my return trip home, the hypersensitive switch on my brain's anxiety center engaged. The simplest things could trigger it. Like being excluded from a meeting where I was sure something was happening that my unknown benefactor wanted me to hear. Like being sure the something in question had something to do with Shauna's death. And like the constant worry that this may be the one time DNA results came back from the lab sooner than usual. By the time I pulled into my driveway, my pulse rate had quickened. It wouldn't be long before I'd be breathing into a brown paper bag.

Chapter 39

OVER THE YEARS, I had developed a few techniques for dealing with anxiety. Fainting, exercise and listening to ZZ Top were three of the most effective. The method I employed depended on the situation. The twanging, gritty, and bluesy sounds of ZZ Top usually dispensed with minor upsets. Exercise or focusing on a creative task worked to eliminate more traumatic worries, for example whether Dom and I were definitively splits. Fainting was not a choice I consciously made —my body initiated it in the face of debilitating anxiety, such as having the cops search my house, or the realization I was their prime murder suspect.

When I parked my car in my driveway, I was wet-palms-fast-breath-cold-sweats anxious. Not yet at fainting level but exceeding the degree of worry usually calmed by ZZ Top. The situation called for exercise or tackling a creative task. Add a glass of Pinot Grigio and all would soon be mellow.

I had the wine. All that remained was to decide on the form of exercise. Perhaps the time to finish clearing out the garage had come. I changed clothes, poured the wine, and entered the garage.

When the cops had searched the place, they'd created a

mess. Even my once neat gravel pile was strewn about. Just contemplating restoring it to an orderly pile was exhausting. As I stared at the gravel, I remembered the bee-watering system I'd seen at the Garden Show. Aha! Exercise: out. Creativity: in. The bees would be happy.

There was an old pottery dish on the back porch that cried out to play a role in quenching a bee's thirst. Excited by my bit of inspiration, I grabbed a metal bucket and filled it with gravel. I hefted the pail and headed for the door. Not three steps into my trek, the metal tabs holding the handle broke away and the bucket and gravel crashed to the concrete.

Rage engulfed me.

"Stupid piece-of-crap A-One Brand Buckets." I threw the handle at the shelves of paint supplies and watched it glance off a can of Quaking Aspen Interior Latex before coming to rest next to the cases of wine Shauna and I had hauled into my garage a lifetime ago. Why couldn't people make stuff that actually held together? Why was everything so completely awful? Why was I a suspect? Why couldn't the cops focus on finding out who really killed Shauna?

I drew in a slow, deep breath and let it out. "Get a grip, Olivia. People make cruddy buckets."

I returned to the house, where I poured another glass of wine and opened my computer. The image of Dom touching Officer Cassidy's arm outside the church at Shauna's funeral still sat at the back of my brain. Picking at me. As did his use of her first name when he spoke about her. Not just her first name, a diminutive. Frankie.

I googled her.

I found three Francine Cassidys on the internet, but only one was a police officer from the Bay Area. Francine Amelia Cassidy was 29 years old and a graduate of Stanford. And a former member of the U.S. Olympic swim team. And the winner of several marksmanship trophies during her time on

San Francisco's police force. And an advocate for equal access to education for disadvantaged girls.

After I skimmed the fifth glowing article about Officer Cassidy's accomplishments and overall perfection, I shut down the internet and rinsed my empty wine glass under the kitchen tap. I stared at the moonlight glinting off McAdams' handiwork in the back garden and played the dangerous game of *How Do You Measure Up*. I lost in the first round. I might wear a Wonder Woman nightshirt, but Francine Cassidy lived the role.

My time would be better spent investigating Shauna's murder than a cop's background. I clicked on my desktop icon for the red USB drive. As I waited for it to open, I acknowledged to myself that not only had I lost the *Measure Up* game, I'd also failed to accomplish what I set out to do when I first googled Cassidy. I had been looking for something to dislike about her and I'd only discovered things I admired. Some days, a person just couldn't catch a break.

The contents of the red USB appeared on the computer screen and drew me away from my funk. Underneath a title "7/15" were several blue folders. I scanned their labels, trying to decide which to open first. A few folders bore standard labels such as "email," "calendar," and "documents" while others bore more cryptic labels, like "graceless." One thing was obvious. This USB contained contents of someone's computer. The best way to find out whose computer would be to open the email folder.

I hovered the cursor over "email" but before I could open the folder, Dom phoned.

"Hey Livvie," he said. "Got a minute?"

I turned away from the computer. "Sure, what's up?"

"Frankie says they've finished with your car. Call her tomorrow and she can arrange for you to collect it."

"Okay."

"One other thing, for what it's worth. A guy from the

homeless camp by the river, Stan someone, came forward and said Shauna was out there on Thursday, July 9, around 8:30 p.m., dropping off groceries. We know she was alive then. Can you remember what you did that evening? It might help."

Of course I remembered. Same as every night, I'd been sitting on my sofa, wrapped in a quilt, staring at nothing as a cooking show played on the television, thinking about the life I'd had until a month ago. Wondering if I was a dupe and an idiot for loving a man who cheated, for trusting a thirty-year friend not to screw up my life. It was more than trusting, it was the-idea-never-crossing-my-mind. It was having faith, believing that, even though every other man was fair game, my friend knew how much Dom meant to me and would never, even if it meant her life, consider doing or saying anything to destroy my happiness.

"Not really," I said. "Nothing stands out."

My shoulders slumped after I ended the call with Dom. Circumstantial evidence seemed to be piling up against me. It was frustrating because I knew I wasn't Shauna's killer. "Then prove it," I told myself.

I brewed fresh coffee and sat down at my computer. The screen still displayed the title "7/15" above a series of blue folders. I clicked on "email" and when that folder opened, I clicked on a sub-folder marked "sent." As I hoped, the sent emails that appeared all showed the name of the sender at the top, in boldface type.

Whoa.

Chapter 40

THE SENDER'S name was Shauna Wylie.

My heart rate picked up a notch.

I checked the calendar in the drive's contents. Definitely Shauna's.

Both of which convinced me the red USB must contain a copy of Shauna's computer. That gave me hope I could find evidence among the data on the USB that would help me find her killer. Surely the cops had combed the contents of her computer by now and found whatever evidence there was, but since I wasn't privy to their investigation, the only way I could know what they knew was to do my own research. Specifically, read her computer contents. And because I knew Shauna well, I might spot something that would mean something to me but not to an impartial investigator. A slim chance, I knew, but it was more than I'd had an hour ago.

Who was my benefactor? Who would have access to Shauna's computer to make a copy? Dom, perhaps. But surely, he would have told me. Noel? Hah, not likely he would go out of his way to help me. Someone working on the case or in charge of the evidence room at the police department? Clapton? Perhaps.

Discovering the identity of my benefactor was not a priority right now. Finding evidence was. I poked around Shauna's emails, including her sent and trash folders, and focusing on any email that mentioned "blog" or "Cheat Sheet" in the subject line. I found several, all between Shauna and her brother Noel. Initially, the messages dealt with the creation of the blog and the security features to ensure Shauna remained anonymous, including voice-altering software that would allow her to disguise her voice when she interviewed people.

In later emails, Noel had sent Shauna ideas he thought she should use for articles. I grinned as I read the first of these. Noel had attached a link to a theatrical website and said, "Check out this jerk from the theater scene in Reno. Says he's producing world-class plays but refuses to cast 'foreign' talent. Foreign, as in anyone from outside Reno. He's not serving the arts in Reno well. You should expose the arrogant idiot for the small-minded know-nothing he is."

Reading between the lines, I concluded Noel had auditioned and failed to win a role in one of the theater's productions. Shauna's response was perfect: "Reno doesn't deserve you. Focus on L.A. You'll be most comfortable among your own kind."

Next, Noel sent Shauna a newspaper clipping about Peter Bonaventure, a Florida money launderer. "Remember Giles, my college roomie from Miami?" Noel's email said. "Last winter he and I skied Heavenly together, and he saw a woman he claimed looked like Bonaventure's wife. I thought he was nuts, but he sent me this clipping." Attached was a brief article about a money laundering trial. The caption under the accompanying picture said, "Annabelle Bonaventure testifies against husband." The photo was a bad shot, taken from the side and capturing not so much her face as her bracelet as she hid behind her hand.

Noel's email went on with, "Might be a story for you, sis. I bet old Petey's sitting in jail in Miami wondering where his wife went, and whether all his money went with her. She could be living here." Shauna had responded with a curt "not for me." She told Noel her blog would only expose slimy things people did, and a woman testifying against a money launderer was laudatory rather than slimy.

On his third attempt, Noel gave Shauna a lead she could use. "Ran in to Clipper Milliken in Vegas. Remember? The kidnapped kid that cop Gavric rescued? He goes by his formal name now. Clive. He was with a soccer coach named Patrick O'Hagen, who mentioned the sweet gig he's got in Reno with the mother of one of the kids he coaches. She's got megabucks. Hannah Scrimshaw."

I made a note to talk to Noel about Clipper, or Clive, Milliken in the hope Noel had contact information. Chief Gavric had said the family moved east, but Clive might have come back west once he finished school.

It was well past midnight, and all I had to show for my research was the knowledge where Shauna got the lead for her story about the socialite Hannah Scrimshaw, she of the clingy clothes and aversion to silent retreats with nuns. That and four bucks would buy me an Americano. Shauna hadn't blogged about the other two leads Noel sent her, and I'd already eliminated Hannah as a suspect, so I was once more batting zero. I might even be going backward.

I decided to try the second USB, simply so I could go to bed feeling that I was taking a step forward, a step toward helping myself out of a jam. I clicked on the desktop icon marked "silver" and when its menu appeared, double-clicked the lone folder, which bore the label "PPD67549 - 7/20."

It opened. I sat there looking at the contents in disbelief.

Chapter 41

THE SILVER USB contained a copy of the Prospect Police file about Shauna's murder. When I recovered from the shock of seeing the police records on my computer screen, I spent hours reviewing its contents.

I assumed whoever gave me the USBs believed they both contained information that might help me save my skin. Certainly, I would need to review the red USB's contents in more detail, but for the moment the silver USB, which I renamed "Case USB," had priority. In my mind, it presumably held all the information the professional investigators possessed. That meant the Case USB offered me the most help in finding Shauna's killer. The Case USB's information could only give my investigation a boost.

I concentrated on it.

First, I reviewed the Material Witnesses/Persons of Interest file, a.k.a. who the cops believed warranted a close look. Next to each name was a note about where the person was during the time frame for Shauna's death—between July 9 and July 12—as well as an indication whether that information had been verified. Shauna's brother Noel and all three of her former husbands, including Josh, were on the list. Of course, my name was there.

Noel and I were the two people who the police had not cleared.

The entry for Noel stated:

"on location in Los Angeles filming pilot for HBO series; in process of verification."

The entry next to my name stated:

"in Prospect at relevant time; at work during daytime and home alone in evenings; confirmed subject reported to work daytime; no supporting witness or other means of verification of subject's whereabouts during evenings."

I made a mental note: get myself a roommate before the next time I became a person of interest.

How had the police established a time frame for Shauna's murder? Surely Donner Lake's icy water interfered with forensic testing? The section titled Victim Video Surveillance, which documented evidence obtained from the security cameras at Shauna's ranch, answered my questions. It stated:

"victim exits property in red Land Rover 5:30 pm Thursday, July 9; no video of victim or Land Rover returning to property."

The report also noted my appearance at Shauna's ranch on the day her body was pulled from Donner Lake:

"No activity at victim's property until subject Olivia Mercier Bertucci, driving black Ford CMAX, attends victim's ranch Monday, July 13 afternoon."

The Witness Interviews section contained summaries of interviews conducted by Clapton. In addition to reporting interviews with me, Josh, and Noel, Clapton seemed to have talked with the entire town: Shauna's neighbors, her fellow board members on the Hospital Foundation and the Prospect Betterment League, her banker, her investment manager, and her lawyer Malkins.

I skimmed the interview summaries but put off reading the full text because there was one section in the file that screamed, "Pick me, give yourself palpitations, pick me." I knew it would be foolish to look at the section titled "Subject Mercier" in the dead of night, when all fears are amplified, and reason packs its bags and leaves town.

But I looked anyway.

The good thing about the section was that all the supposed evidence against me was conveniently in one place. The bad thing about the section? It was a one-stop-let's-fry-Olivia-Mercier shop. Clapton's affidavit to support the search warrant for my house and car was there. It spelled out the items he had noticed in my garage, and my appointment for a full detailing at Oasis Car Wash, as well as information from Shauna's lawyer that I was a significant heir to her estate. There was also a copy of my "eff off and die" response to the first email Shauna sent me begging forgiveness.

Clapton had also interviewed several of the diners at Chez Philippe who witnessed my screaming fit when I found Shauna's earrings in the bed in our cabin. The bow that tied it all together was a report of Clapton's telephone conversation with Noel, who confirmed the restaurant meltdown and then said Shauna had been receiving threats during the three weeks before her death and who else would do that but scorned and burned Olivia Mercier?

I stopped reading the file at that point and shut down my computer. Rather than giving my amateur investigation a boost, the file only ramped up my level of anxiety. Everything I'd read either cleared other suspects or pointed to my culpability. I turned off the lights at 3:00 a.m., disappointed and distraught.

Sleep came grudgingly much later.

Chapter 42

WEDNESDAY MORNING, I swatted the snooze button several times before the combination of the alarm's insistent buzzing and the glare of the morning sun through my bedroom window defeated me and I crawled out of bed. I'd stayed awake too long reviewing the contents of the USBs and was paying for it now.

I started the coffee brewing and stood in the shower, mentally composing my to-do list for the day. Reviewing the balance of the USBs' contents was on the list, but not the first thing I'd tackle today. I still had several things that required me to get out of the house and talk to people, so the USB files would have to wait.

A must-do on my list was to follow up with Shauna's blog targets and ask whether they'd been blackmailed as Quayle Jonasburg had been.

Collecting my car from the impound lot was high in priority as well. It was fun driving the T-bird and I reveled in the belief I was snubbing my nose at the local cops every time I got behind the wheel, but I liked to think that by driving a hybrid I was doing my small bit for the environment. Plus, I had to admit I wasn't really a member of the upmarket driver crowd—for one thing, the T-bird's trunk space would barely hold groceries, never mind wrought iron pieces I might buy at yard sales. I had entertained myself by pretending to be the owner of a T-bird for a few days, but in truth I fit firmly and comfortably into the look-good-but-be-practical crowd.

Third on the list was to find out who put the USBs into my mailbox and why. The Case USB gave me a huge clue. Even a person who was operating on three hours' sleep could make the connection when they looked at its contents—my mystery benefactor was someone with access to police files. As well, judging from the titles on the USBs, whoever had given them to me had accessed Shauna's file twice. The red USB, which I nicknamed "Shauna's USB," was identified as "7/15". I interpreted that as July 15, the date the body had been identified and probably the date the police seized Shauna's computer as evidence. Since the Case USB had "7/20" in its title, I concluded my benefactor had copied the police file on July 20. It was a safe bet the person was very comfortable dealing with the evidence room and computers and was someone whose presence the police would not question. That encompassed a large group of people, but I hoped I could narrow it down.

Last night I'd been disheartened when I read all the evidence against me. This morning, however, as I shampooed, rinsed, and repeated, I decided to take a positive view of the police file. When I finished reading it, I would know most of what the police knew. And that would enable me to spend my time investigating areas they had not covered. When the niggling and nasty thought "suppose they've covered it all" tried to destroy my positive outlook, I put my fingers in my ears and sang "nananananah, nananananah" at full volume.

No sooner had I blown my hair dry than I heard Duncan McAdams chastise the little schnauzer Charlie for some sin or another. That was followed by children giggling, small feet clattering onto the porch, and the doorbell chiming. Today was one of three official McAdams Family days at the Mercier household each week. I hollered, "Coming," yanked on a sweatshirt and jeans, and rushed to the door. I wrenched it open just as Claire's index finger stabbed at the doorbell again.

"Hi, Miss Mercier," she said. "We're here. Charlie wants to know if he can have a treat."

The pooch was investigating the lawn for places he hadn't yet peed, but when he heard his name, he turned toward us. His tail flashed back and forth, and he started his bark-whine-howl routine that I'd concluded was his way of making chitchat. He charged across the lawn, up the steps and past me through the open door. I looked over my shoulder in time to see his tail and rump disappearing around the corner into the kitchen. I stepped back and waved the children inside.

Ben handed me a brown paper bag on his way by. "Mom sent these." I peeked in the bag and smiled. Scones. Fattening, but I loved them.

Duncan tossed a tarp from the truck bed onto the lawn and then approached me. "I talked to Samantha last night about that restaurant. She wonders if you can stop by Sierra Bistro this morning? She'll be on her lunch break at 11:30."

I had done such a masterful job of pushing Abel's Table to the back of my mind that it took me a beat to realize what Duncan was talking about. I didn't have time to go down rabbit holes that had nothing to do with Shauna's murder. However, I remembered two things: Shauna's comment that there was something hinky about the restaurant, and Samantha McAdams' obvious anxiety about the place.

"Perfect," I said. "My day isn't too full, and I always enjoy a chance to have lunch at Sierra Bistro."

In the kitchen, Charlie and the kids stood by the walk-in pantry door, staring at me. "Go ahead. His bowls and the kibbles are in there," I said, which both children already knew. While Ben fetched water for Charlie, Claire retrieved the bag of kibbles and poured a small amount into his bowl. She returned the bag to the pantry and remained there, studying the contents of the shelves.

I put three plates and two glasses of milk on the island, and then left the room to exchange the grubby sweatshirt for a lighter, cleaner T-shirt. When I returned to the kitchen, Ben had joined Claire in the pantry. I poured my coffee, sat at the island, and extracted a scone from the bag.

The kids approached the island. Ben held a package of chocolate chip cookies. "Miss Mercier?"

I smiled at him.

"Are these for us?" Ben asked.

"Only if you sit at the island with me." The kids scrambled onto stools and when Ben opened the package, I said, "If your mother was here, how many would she let you eat?"

"Just one," Claire said. She sounded heartbroken.

"Why don't you have one cookie this morning, and put the rest back into the pantry for Friday?"

That was deemed an acceptable solution, and the kids immediately set about dunking their cookies into their milk.

"What do you do while your daddy works?" I said.

"We play with Charlie," Ben said. "He likes to dig in the dirt, so Daddy says we have to keep him occupied. And we make sure he doesn't jump all over people."

Claire giggled. "Charlie undid your mailman's tie."

"My mailman?"

She nodded. "I was scared he'd be mad, but the man said it looked better with Charlie's slobber on it."

"That's good," I said, thinking about lawsuits for dog-induced trauma.

Ben said, "He's nice. I hope he comes to your house again today. Charlie liked him."

Claire giggled again. "Charlie liked the tie." She turned to me. "Me too. It was a pretty bow."

Kids. They say the darndest things.

After they finished their milk and cookies, Ben and Claire

put their dishes in the sink, thanked me, and took Charlie outside. I reviewed my agenda for the day. Ever since I became a "person of interest" I'd been living in a state of acute anxiety. I didn't trust my memory to actually file anything of consequence in the correct drawers in my brain, so I opened the notes app on my phone and moved the three items from my mental to-do list onto the app: blog victims, USB benefactor, car. Then I added "Sierra Bistro."

It wasn't yet nine o'clock, too early to phone the blog victims I had interviewed earlier. I wanted to give them time to get their days under way, to ensure they were in a receptive mood when I called.

I didn't feel any such concern about calling Corporal Cassidy, however. Wonder Woman didn't need much sleep. No doubt she'd been awake since dawn. Before I could punch in her number on my phone, its chime announced an incoming text. I recognized the number—the same one from which I'd received the mystery text during Shauna's funeral. Even though he denied knowing what it was about, Dom had reacted to that text when I showed it to him.

Chapter 43

THIS MORNING'S provocative text message said:

> do u know real reason Cpt B is on marine unit.
> #thoseinblack.

My stomach felt like it held concrete. Two texts, one about hazing, and one inferring Dom's transfer wasn't for the reason he'd told me. Had he been harassing department staff or officers? It didn't sound like the man I knew, but the man I knew wouldn't have slept with Shauna, so maybe I didn't know the man.

I shook my head. No. This was too ridiculous to even consider. I'd seen Dom at department functions and his behavior was always respectful and above reproach, never arrogant or intimidating. "Yeah," my little anxiety-provoking voice said, "but that's when you were with him. Maybe he's different when you're not around."

I added a fifth item to my to-do list: check out harassment at PPD.

Then I tried to push the anxious doubts from my head by focusing on something else. Like retrieving my car.

Cassidy answered my call on the first ring with a "Hello Ms. Mercier, how are you?"

I ignored her attempt at niceties. "Dom mentioned I could collect my car from impound and told me to set it up with you."

"Sure thing. How's two o'clock. at the lot? Do you know where it is?" I didn't say more than "uhh" before she went on. "6743 North Pass Road. Huge chain-link fence. You can't miss it. Or would you prefer I pick you up?"

Oh sure. I really wanted to ride around in a cop car at the same time everyone in town was wondering whether I killed Shauna and holding their breath in anticipation of the perp walk. I said, "Thanks, but I'll grab a cab. I think I can manage on my own. You don't need to be there."

"Yes, I do," she said, and ended the call.

Around eleven o'clock, I packed up my laptop and drove to Sierra Bistro. I spotted Samantha McAdams in the open kitchen behind the bistro's counter and espresso machine. I waved at her and placed my order for a summer berry salad before choosing a table under one of the crisp crimson umbrellas on the outdoor patio. While I waited for my salad, I opened my laptop and closed my eyes, enjoying the feeling of warm air on my skin and the sounds of birds fluttering in the dense hedge behind my table. I hoped there was a nest there, maybe full of hungry fledglings.

"Gorgeous day, isn't it?" a woman said. I opened my eyes and smiled at Samantha McAdams as she placed my salad on the table.

"I could hang out here all day," I said. "Thanks for the delicious scones this morning."

Samantha placed a second salad on the table. "Can I join you for lunch? Duncan has encouraged me to talk to you. This is all off the record, correct?"

"Of course. How are you doing?"

"Okay." Then she shook her head. "No. I'm scared." She studied the only other two diners sitting on the patio, well away from us, then leaned forward and whispered. "Harlow says I can talk to you, and I know your husband is a cop, but I'm afraid. When I quit Abel's, the manager gave me my last pay check and said they usually held it back until they were sure employees respected the privacy of customers. Then he said in my case, he didn't have to do that, because he knew which kindergarten Claire would attend in the fall."

My heart sank at the thought of that little girl being in danger. "You're kidding."

"No. I didn't tell Duncan because he would have charged down there and bust up the place. I planned to stay quiet."

"Then I went there for lunch and became intrigued. And Duncan told me you used to work there."

"Yes."

"Okay, look. I won't print any of what you tell me. If I share it with anyone, it will be with Dom, and he would keep your name out of things. That is, if it ever came to anything."

She swirled her cup on the table and chewed on the inside of her cheek.

"Samantha, you can't stay quiet. He threatened Claire."

She nodded. "You're right. But really, I don't know much. We weren't allowed to go into that room. Ever. There's a coded lock and without the code, you don't get in. Now and then the code was changed, and some people didn't get the new one unless they had a special meeting with the manager. I think those people owed money for something and it was a way of cutting them off."

"I saw a slim guy come out of the room, dressed in a suit, carrying a briefcase," I said. "Is that the manager?"

"No. I don't know who he is, but he appeared once a week or so. He'd go into the room, stay a while, then leave, and we wouldn't see him for another week."

"I can think of two reasons for the traffic I saw in and out of that room. Gambling and drugs."

She thought about that for a bit. "Either would fit with holding back new codes until people met with the manager. But one time I overheard a woman pitching a fit in the manager's office. She said she needed her stuff and why wouldn't he cut her some slack."

"That sounds more like someone buying drugs than placing a bet."

"What are you going to do with all this?"

I shook my head. "Dunno. Who owns the restaurant?"

"No idea. The manager's Jimmy Paternik. He was always talking about the boss, so I don't think he owns the place."

"Okay, thanks. I promise this is off the record."

As Samantha prepared to leave the table, I said, "You should tell Duncan what the manager said to you, so he can be on alert. Tell him to ask Dom what to watch for."

She nodded. "I will. Thanks Olivia."

Once Samantha returned inside the café, I ran an online corporate search of AB Restaurants Inc. I'd learned the name of the corporate owner of Abel's Table when I visited the Town Clerk's office a few days ago. Because AB Restaurants was a private company, the search results wouldn't reveal shareholder information. However, the list of officers was available. It showed Malkins, Shauna's lawyer, as Secretary. The President was Jack Straw. His mailing address was a post office box in Miami, Florida. Google maps pinpointed Straw's residential address not far from Miami's South Beach.

I thought about Abel's Table and how strange it was that some guy in Florida would own a restaurant in Prospect, California. Then again, the company could own a string of outlets. It was conceivable the company didn't know what the manager was up to in the back room.

I phoned Dom, and told him about Abel's Table, Shauna's

belief there was something nefarious about it, and the threat made to Samantha. "Leave it with me," he said.

I relaxed against the seat back. Dom and his team would check out the restaurant and its manager. If there was something not right, they would find it.

Chapter 44

NOT LONG AFTER I spoke with Dom, Ingrid Schmuller, one of my contacts on the Police Advisory Committee, breezed out the door and hurried over to my table. "Oh, Olivia, how fortunate to see you. I intended to return your call today, but here you are, so we can chat now." She slid into a chair opposite me and put her coffee mug on the table. She flashed a wide smile at me. "I believe you wanted to speak about Shauna?"

"Yes. I'm doing a feature on her, and I know you were on the Police Advisory Committee with her."

Ingrid's face fell. "Yes?" The three-letter word came out in five syllables. Her voice had lost some of its breathy anticipation.

"Can you tell me a bit about Shauna's role on the committee and her interaction with the police?"

Ingrid studied her coffee as if it could foretell her fortune. "Well..." Silence.

"Of course, I wouldn't dream of quoting you without your permission. If you simply want to give me background color, that's totally fine."

She took a sip of coffee and studied the hedge behind me.

I played the someone-has-already-spilled-the-beans card. "When I spoke with Dr. Cigments, he mentioned Shauna often took the police brass to task. The performance audit, I think he said."

I could hear the relief in her chuckle. "If Norm thinks it's okay to speak with you, who am I to worry?" She looked over one shoulder, and then the other, as she checked out the patio for eavesdroppers. She lowered her voice. "Yes, she was disappointed with the last audit. More recently however, Shauna's concerns were about harassment."

"In the police department? Who was the culprit?"

"I don't know. Shauna spoke with Chief Gavric about conducting an internal investigation, but apparently, he shut her down. He told her to stop gossip mongering."

"Really? Sheesh."

Ingrid nodded. "Yeah. Shauna wanted the matter referred to the Conduct Review Board."

"Did the committee agree?"

"Oh, it didn't get to the committee. Shauna told me this privately. She intended to bring it up at last night's meeting. But of course she died."

"No one else knew about this?"

Ingrid shrugged. "I don't know."

"Did you bring it up at the meeting?"

She shook her head and studied her coffee once more. "The whole meeting was chaotic. We were in shock over Shauna's murder. I didn't mention the allegations because I didn't have any details."

I didn't say "or because you were gutless," but I thought it. Instead, I said, "This is helpful, Ingrid. Thanks for sharing your insights."

She sat there silently for a bit, smiling at me while I concentrated on my salad. Finally, Ingrid set her mug aside and said, "Olivia? One thing."

"Yes?"

"I'm wondering about the listing."

I stopped eating and looked at her. "Huh?"

"The ranch. Shauna's ranch. Do you know who her executor is? I'd like to talk to them, to see if the estate wants to list the property."

Well. That accounted for the chipper, breathy tone in Ingrid's voice when she first joined me. She had obviously thought that's why I'd phoned her in the first place.

"Her lawyer is Ronald Malkins. Try him."

"Oh, thanks. I don't need more work. My client list is jam-packed. But it would be my little effort to honor Shauna and do right by her estate. I *am* the top local agent."

I nodded at her. "I'm sure."

She slid her chair back and flashed another wide smile at me. "Must run, Olivia. So nice chatting with you. Ta-ta." With a wave, she was gone.

At what point in their training did some realtors lose their sense of basic decency? "My little effort." Baloney. "Honor Shauna." Right. "Don't need more work." Hah.

Shaking my head, I checked my to-do list. "Phone victims re blackmail."

I opened my list of *Cheat Sheet* victims and phoned them one by one, asking each whether they'd been blackmailed by the blogger. They all said no, except Hannah Scrimshaw, the Reno socialite who had an affair with her kid's soccer coach.

She said, "I received a text from a bogus number, offering to make the story go away. I know better than to let creeps like that get their fingers on my money. I declined the offer. They ran the story. What can I say? I rolled the dice and lost."

"Did you mention this to the police?"

"Heck no. That would mean admitting I'd been sleeping around, and at that point I was still hoping the *Cheat Sheet* would leave me alone."

"No, I mean recently, when they interviewed you about the blog and Shauna Wylie."

"The police haven't spoken to me. Why would they? The blog post came out months ago. It's old news. And what does Shauna whoever have to do with anything?"

Something didn't add up. I hemmed and hawed and then asked Hannah to send me the text from the blackmailer. She promised to look for it and send it on. "I have gobs of texts. Gobs and gobs, but I'll see what I can do."

Then she mentioned I'd caught her on the way to the airport. She was off to Italy for a month at a friend's villa near Lucca. I figured sending the text to me would be low on her list of priorities. Perhaps if she had a moment between appointments at the designer shops in Lucca, she'd remember to flick through her gargantuan number of text messages.

If I was a cop and I had a list of people whose misdeeds were exposed by a dead blogger, I'd definitely call a few of them. Especially those who stood to lose the most, like Hannah Scrimshaw. Yet, Hannah didn't know who Shauna was. Perhaps the cops hadn't made their way down the list to her.

I opened the Case USB on my computer again and did a quick search of the witnesses the cops had interviewed. Several names that should have been there were missing.

Chapter 45

AFTER MY TELEPHONE conversation with Hannah Scrimshaw, I returned to the *Gazette* offices and hunkered down in my cubicle, poking around in the information on the Case USB.

I skimmed the report on the recovery of the body from Donner Lake, most of which I knew since I'd been at the scene: a green and yellow oil drum found resting on an underwater shelf and filled with concrete encasing Shauna's body. Had the barrel been dumped a few yards further from shore, it would have missed the shelf and plummeted another hundred feet or more, making its discovery much more unlikely. Also retrieved from the surrounding area were a fish landing net, a few weathered pieces of wood washed up on the otherwise pristine shore, a partially empty bottle of Makers Mark bourbon, and a vintage fishing rod.

In the Witness Interview section of the police file, I learned police had traced Shauna's movements until around 7:30 on the evening of Thursday, July 9. Maggie had told them Shauna had visited her "sixish" and stayed until "seven-thirtyish."

One of Maggie's neighbors spotted Shauna's Land Rover

leaving Maggie's property about 7:30 p.m. Later, that same neighbor saw Chief Gavric arrive. A man around the curve from Maggie and a couple across the lake spotted her and Gavric on her deck from shortly after eight until sunset. I hoped Maggie and the Chief didn't think their relationship was a secret from her neighbors because the gist of the witness statements was "Oh yeah, the Chief shows up most evenings and stays over, but she never mentions him, so you know, why pop their bubble?"

Next was the autopsy report. I'd read a few since journalism school. Their clinical tone allowed me to stay removed from the subject and treat it as simply another part of my job. Today however, as I read the bare facts about the condition of Shauna's body and what likely happened to her, I fought waves of nausea. Still, I needed the information, so I gritted my teeth, prayed I wouldn't throw up, and read the report.

Thankfully, if one can be grateful for such things, Shauna died from a massive smack on the head. The M.E. found no foreign material in her lungs and no evidence of suffocation. She had been dead before her body found its way into the barrel of concrete, and to my way of thinking, that was a good thing.

Shauna's blood tests were negative for alcohol. Her stomach was empty. The M.E. estimated her last meal was between four and twelve hours before death. Her security camera had shown her leaving her ranch around 5:30 on Thursday evening, which presumably would have been when Shauna went to Maggie's cabin to discuss board matters. Since Shauna rarely ate dinner before eight, I concluded she'd had lunch that day, but not dinner.

Shauna was an extremely organized woman, meticulous about entering events and reminders on her calendar. Because Shauna's car had been found in the Aspen Heights country club parking lot, I'd hoped her calendar would reveal why it was there. Unfortunately, I found nothing on her calendar for that Thursday, not even a mention of her meeting with Maggie. Of course, Maggie had said Shauna had "popped by" unexpectedly. Shauna wouldn't put impromptu meetings into her calendar.

The only notation I spotted was a reference to "PI LOT - Scone" at two o'clock the following Friday, and an entry for the next Sunday mentioning "Spirit Rock Spa, Sedona." I had no idea what "PI LOT - Scone" meant. Presumably, the Sedona reference indicated Shauna had planned a getaway.

With no entries in her calendar to help me, it would be difficult to learn where Shauna had gone after she'd left Maggie's cabin Thursday evening. Then I remembered Corporal Cassidy had been one of the cops at the country club the day they found Shauna's Land Rover in the lot. I made a mental note to ask her if they found out whether Shauna had been in the bar and, if so, who she might have met.

The last thing I gleaned from the autopsy report was that Shauna's body was placed in the barrel long before the barrel was dropped into Donner Lake.

From the too-much-information department I learned that if Shauna's body had been placed in the lake close to the time of death, the iciness of the lake would have caused lividity, the pooling of her blood, to be bright red rather than a bluish or purple shade. Since Shauna's lividity was purplish, the M.E. concluded the killer left the body in the barrel for some time before dumping the barrel in the lake:

> "This would be consistent with allowing time for the concrete in the barrel to harden."

My guess was Shauna was killed some time after she left Maggie's on Thursday evening, and her body was immediately placed in the barrel of concrete. The barrel was then left undisturbed until the concrete hardened, which meant the killer needed to have a secure private place to store the barrel. The teens who'd been diving at Donner Lake saw nothing in the water on the weekend following that Thursday, which meant that between Sunday evening and Monday morning, the barrel was dumped in Donner Lake. The killer was strong enough to manipulate a barrel of concrete and had access to a boat. Perhaps also a boathouse.

While that might narrow the search somewhat, most of the cabins along the shores of Donner Lake had a boathouse. The lake also had a public launch ramp where anyone could put a boat into the water, so it was feasible the killer simply waited until dark and used the public launch. Not much help, I admitted to myself.

Even though it was closing in on 1:30 and I knew I should leave the office if I wanted to return the rental T-bird before meeting Cassidy at the impound lot, I took a moment to browse through a few more of Shauna's emails. I found a thread between Shauna and Noel, dealing with Clive Milliken's contact information. Grateful I wouldn't need to bother Noel about it, I jotted down the details.

More interesting was an exchange between Shauna and Noel dealing with money. Rather than read those emails now, I copied the entire thread and sent it to myself so I could access the information later on my phone.

I moved to shut down my computer, but a folder titled "Graceless" caught my eye. I'd noticed it several times previously and ignored it. Now I clicked on it. The folder contained a document called "*A Graceless Life.*" I read the first few lines:

> "Once upon a time, not too long ago and not very far from here, there lived two little girls, Victoria and Grace. They were best friends from the day they met, five years old and both knowing they could rule the universe."

It appeared Shauna had written a fairy tale. I recognized the names of the girls. Intrigued, I printed the story, stuffed the few pages in my bag, shut down my computer, and then hurried out of the office. I'd have to hurry to drop off the rental T-bird and still meet Cassidy on time at the impound lot.

Chapter 46

I BID farewell to my rental T-bird at Ritzy Car Rentals on Thunderhead Drive and climbed into the back of a spotless Checker Cab. "Impound lot on North Pass Road, please, and as long as I'm there by two, I'm happy."

The driver said, "You got it," put the cab in gear and crept away from the curb. He turned up the volume on the radio and sang along with Willie Nelson, while I opened my phone and accessed the email thread between Noel and Shauna that I'd copied earlier. It was all about money.

That is, Noel needed it and wanted Shauna to float him a loan. I knew from various conversations with Shauna that Noel often asked for advances from his trust. But the request in these emails was new to me.

The emails spanned a ten-day period starting mid-June. Noel had an opportunity to produce the movie of his dreams, one guaranteed to win accolades at Sundance. It was a small project, he said, requiring an investment of only five million dollars. It would mean he could finally make his mark in the industry. Shauna refused to advance funds to Noel, citing several other instances of funds loaned and not repaid. Noel's emails became more and more strident.

"Wait for your next trust payout," Shauna said. Noel complained the amount was only two hundred thousand and said, "Why won't you just give me the whole of the trust? It's my money, I'm a big boy."

Shauna responded: "Because our parents wanted me to manage it. When you're forty, it's all yours. Until then, the answer is no."

I relaxed against the comfy leather seat in the cab and mulled over the information. I wasn't sure whether the rules of the trust would permit Shauna to hand over the principal of the trust to Noel, but in any event, Shauna had refused. The battle over money changed the entire dynamic between them. Noel was only 31. Nine years is a long wait when you want to make the movie of your dreams. I wondered what happened to the trust now that Shauna was dead, and once more asked myself what Noel would do to lay his hands on the money he felt he deserved.

———

I JERKED upright when the cabbie said, "We're almost at the impound lot miss. Maybe five minutes." I realized I had nodded off in the cab's warmth. I straightened in the seat, yawned and rubbed my face. I needed to keep myself awake. I pulled Shauna's fairy tale from my bag and began to read.

A Graceless Life
By Shauna V. Wylie

Once upon a time, not too long ago and not very far from here, there lived two little girls, Victoria and Grace. They were best friends from the day they met, five years old and both knowing they could rule the universe. One of them was radiant and confident. The other was gawky and eager to belong. One of them was rich in material things. One was not.

Grace was my middle name. Victoria was Shauna's. It could have been a fluke she chose those names, but the next paragraph told me the story was definitely about the two of us.

Victoria, the rich one, shared her treasures with Grace freely. Grace learned to swim in Victoria's pool, learned to ride on Victoria's horses and learned to drive in Victoria's sports car.

My grip on the pages tightened.

Grace, in turn, shared her treasures with Victoria. She showed her the secrets behind magic tricks, taught her how to build igloos, and trash-talked anyone who treated Victoria badly.

I found myself nodding my head in agreement. If there was an Olympics of trash-talking, I'd take the gold. The more you practice, the closer you get to perfection, and being Shauna's friend gave me ample practice time. Between her teens and thirties, Shauna racked up at least thirty romances. Each time Shauna's heart was broken by an unfeeling cad, who either didn't understand her or only wanted her for the doors she could open, I did what all best friends do. I leaped into the fray and defended her with angry, righteous, cutting words. Josh was the only one of Shauna's exes not to be classified as a rat, the only one from whom Shauna parted amicably.

I picked up the tale again.

Then one day, a dashing dark-haired knight named Roberto came into Grace's life. At first Victoria celebrated their love and her friend's happiness, but soon a familiar imp, much like Poe's, settled himself on her shoulder. He began his whisper campaign, designed to put thoughts of failure in her head. It always worked.

At their annual celebration by the river, Victoria watched Roberto and Grace as they sat together near the fire. "Why are you doomed to loneliness?" Imp whispered. "Why can't you make a marriage work like Grace can? What is wrong with you?"

I remembered that party at the river. Shauna wasn't telling the whole truth in her little fairy tale. Of course, that was the point of fiction, wasn't it?

Victoria visited a local lounge more and more often, accompanied only by Imp. One evening Roberto happened upon Victoria as she stood by her vehicle, concentrating on her balance. "Are you able to find your way safely home?" he asked.

Victoria studied him, so gallant, so handsome, so concerned about her well-being. Imp whispered, "Grace has an exquisite treasure. You have nothing." She started to cry.

I began to wonder if the tale reflected reality. Even though I was astounded Shauna remembered any Poe at all from high school lit classes, I ignored her references to the imp and focused instead on trying to determine which night Dom, a.k.a. Roberto, might have come across Shauna outside a bar. Since he didn't work shift work anymore, it had to be an evening when he had been called out for a major crime. I hoped the tale would give me more clues.

Roberto escorted Victoria to her home, where she once more dissolved in tears. He listened as she sobbed and confessed how lonely she was, how she wanted nothing more than a perfect marriage like he and Grace had.

The cabbie's words ripped me away from the page. "Here we are. Twenty-seven bucks even."

I jammed the pages back in my bag and dug out my wallet. I thought about not tipping him because of his gross error in arriving at the impound lot before I could find out whether Dom/Roberto did the thing every man did in cheesy romance books, especially when the femme fatale cried. Did I not know him at all? Could he be so shallow?

I took a breath as I counted out some bills and admitted to myself the cabbie had done what I asked. He'd delivered me to the lot by two o'clock. Any bone I had to pick was with Dom and Shauna, and since she was dead, that left Dom. I tipped the cabbie, glanced out the window, and saw Cassidy leaning against a violently lime green SUV.

I had another bone to pick, and this one was with her.

Chapter 47

WHEN I WALKED across the gravel lot, Cassidy waved and smiled. I shaded my eyes. "That is a seriously bright green."

She patted the roof of the SUV. "This is Kermie, my pride and joy. Let's go. Jamworthy's waiting."

Cassidy led me through the gate into the impound lot and pointed at a tiny silver trailer in the center of at least twenty rows of vehicles. "We're heading to that Airstream," she said. "The office. Also, the staff break room."

"Spacious digs," I said.

"Staff of one," she said. "The PPD lives large."

We squeezed into the trailer where a cop well past retirement age slapped some papers on a foot-wide orange laminate counter. "Howdy. I'm Sergeant Melvin Jamworthy. Read this, sign here, lemme see your driver's license. So's I can compare it with the registration of the car. So's I don't give you the wrong vehicle and you sue me."

I dug out my license and placed it on the counter. I read the form. "It says I've checked the car and found it undamaged."

"Yeah," Jamworthy said.

"So, I want to check it before I sign. Where is it?"

He picked up my license and peered at it. Then he opened a drawer, pulled out a magnifying glass, and once more studied my license. "Olivia Grace Mercier." He pronounced it Mer-sigh-err.

"Mare-see-aye," I said.

Jamworthy squinted at me and then studied the license again. "I guess this could be you."

"It's me."

He pursed his lips. "Dunno. Says here you're five foot five. You sure? I dunno."

I turned to Cassidy, who was biting her lip. "Could you just tell him I'm me, and let's get on with it?"

"It's her. Let's get on with it," Cassidy said.

"Yeah, well have you even looked at her license? What's these two things on her head?" He handed Cassidy my license and then turned to me. "I don't think I ever saw that before. It's like post-surgery weirdness, like you had a couple extra appendages removed."

I ripped my license from Cassidy's hand. "For heaven's sake, what two things?"

Cassidy pointed at two whitish spots beaming at the camera, one on each side of my head in the photo, where overhead lights had bounced off my hair.

"Horns?" Jamworthy said.

Cassidy laughed out loud.

I placed my license back in my wallet. "I prefer to think of them as halos."

Jamworthy grinned. "You got a point there. Horns don't fit with your color eyes. Halos do." He waved toward the lot. "Your car's one row over, three spots down. Check it over, come on back and sign the form, and you're outta here."

Cassidy and I checked over my car. I had my head under the hood and was asking myself whether I'd even know if something in the engine compartment was out of whack when Cassidy said, "Jamworthy was playing with you."

"I wanted to jump down his throat but realized it wouldn't improve things."

"He pulls something with everyone just to see how they will react. It's why I wanted to meet you here, in case things went seriously south. But you handled it perfectly."

I closed the hood and did one more walk around the car. "Corporal, remember . . ."

"My name's Francine, but I prefer Frankie."

"Okay. Remember I told you Shauna was the *Cheat Sheet* blogger, and I thought maybe someone she slimed might bear a grudge?"

"Yeah, that was a good lead."

"If it was so good, why didn't you pass it on to the case investigators? I talked to some of Shauna's blog victims earlier today, and not one of them has heard from the police."

She frowned. "Hmm, that's strange. I told Clapton about it that same day. I'll check with him. But I wish you hadn't alerted them to a possible call from us. It could mess up the investigation."

"Mess it up? Are you kidding me? You bunch are doing a fine job of messing it up all by yourselves."

Cassidy's cheeks reddened. She folded her arms and glared at me.

I raged on. "In fact, I don't think there even is an investigation. I think whoever's in charge has decided I did it and is sitting there waiting for the right time to arrest me."

"And when would that be?"

The right time would be when the DNA test on the bloodstain in my car showed it was Shauna's blood. By my reckoning, that would happen Friday, maybe Saturday. But I sure wasn't going to tell Cassidy that. "How the heck do I know?" I said. "When they need one more arrest to meet their monthly quota. When they tire of sitting on their fat asses, watching me twist in the wind. Or when it will hurt . . . ahh, never mind."

I turned in a circle by my car, looking for I don't know what and blinking furiously to keep the tears at bay. "Just never mind. I apologize for my outburst."

"Off the record, Ms. Mercier, I don't think you killed Ms. Wylie."

We stood there staring at each other for a while until finally I broke eye contact. "That's ridiculously good to hear," I said. "But why not?"

"The horses." She handed me the key fob and my mobile. "We're hanging on to your computer for a while longer."

I was glad to have my old phone back. The burner had done its job well, but it didn't have my call history or contacts. I cradled the old phone in my hand. It felt like home.

"Thanks," I said. "Is this bugged?"

Cassidy laughed. "Nah. I'll talk to Clapton about those interviews and let you know what I find out. C'mon, let's go see Jamworthy."

We walked back to the Airstream and when Cassidy put her hand on the door, I said, "While you're at it, ask Clapton why no one's spoken with Shauna's colleagues on the Police Advisory Committee either."

"What would they have to say?"

I shrugged. "Something about harassment in the police department and a refusal to investigate. Have you heard anything about that?"

Cassidy pulled the door open, waved me inside and said, "Sergeant Jamworthy, get those forms ready. Ms. Mercier hasn't found a thing wrong with her car."

I signed in triplicate where Jamworthy's stubby finger marked the spot and then folded my copy and stuffed it in my bag. "Thanks Sergeant. Don't take this the wrong way, but I'm glad I'm saying so long."

He chuckled. "I definitely enjoyed meeting you. Not a lot happens out here that you could call a good time. But you were fun. You made my day, Ms. Mercier." This time, he pronounced my name with a flawless French accent.

When I left the Airstream, Cassidy stood beside her shimmering green pride and joy, studying her phone's screen. "Duty calls," she said. "I'll be in touch."

I turned on my old phone and checked the settings. Everything appeared to be the way I had left it, including the "Find My Phone" feature. Dom and I had activated family sharing on our phones, so if one of us misplaced our phone, the other could use Find My Phone to locate it. Did I want that feature now? Family sharing was brutally at odds with a couple living separate and apart. I debated turning off the feature, but decided to leave things alone for now. Dom and I might be separated, but I still misplaced my phone occasionally. Knowing he could locate it if necessary was reassuring.

Out of habit, I glanced at the home screen, looking for calls or text alerts, and found zero. Of course, the cops would have answered my phone and read text messages if any came in. I felt a little sick at the thought someone who mattered to me might have phoned me, only to find my answering service was the local police. I'd given all my friends and colleagues the number of the burner as soon as I'd purchased it, but on the chance I'd missed someone, I flicked through the call history. Three calls showed up, all robocalls—not in the category of someone who mattered.

When I checked my text messages, there were none I hadn't seen before the phone had been confiscated. Not even from my mystery texter. Now that I thought about it, how did the texter know the number of the burner? Was the person someone I knew?

As I stowed my phone, I remembered I'd intended to ask Cassidy if she knew whether Shauna had met anyone in the bar at the country club. In the kerfuffle with Jamworthy and my idiotic driver's license photo, not to mention my hissy fit in the lot over the cops' failure to investigate, I'd forgotten. I could phone Cassidy now, or I could take my hybrid for a quiet spin and do my own research. I opted for the latter.

Twenty minutes later, on the theory that the owner of a high-end vehicle would take care opening doors and not ding my car, I parked in the country club lot next to a silver Jaguar. I whistled at the sign on the building wall in front of the Jag that said "Manager." Who'd think managing a country club would pay that well?

As I climbed the three broad steps to the club's door, Maggie Shillingford came out of the building, her face grim. "Hello, Maggie."

She stared at me blankly for a brief moment before her face cleared and she said, "Oh Olivia, hello. Forgive me for almost walking past you, but that self-important Cupressis has put me in a state."

"Who?"

She scowled. "Our club manager, the officious codwallop." I bit back a smile. The British had marvelous denigrating expressions. Then Maggie brightened. "Are you meeting someone?"

"Not really. I want to speak with the bartender and staff about whether Shauna met anyone here the day she died."

"Ahhh, I see. I wish we had time to chat, but today's chock-a-block."

"No problem," I said, and moved toward the door.

She snapped her fingers. "Oh. I almost forgot. I spoke with Chief Gavric, and he'd be happy to give you an interview. Off the record, he's announcing his candidacy on Saturday. If I were you, I'd talk to him before then."

"That's fantastic, Maggie, thank you."

"My pleasure. Now, you'll excuse me, but I must move my car. A simple mistake, force of habit really, and the pipsqueak Napoleon is threatening to have the car towed. What nerve. I've half a mind to have him terminated."

I watched Maggie stomp over to the silver Jaguar. She got

behind the wheel, put the car in gear and laid rubber backing out of the manager's spot. There was no doubt in my mind whose head she envisioned beneath her rear wheels.

Inside the club, I chatted with the bartender, two servers and the club receptionist. They all told me they hadn't seen Shauna at the club since the annual Fourth of July picnic. I'd known discovering where Shauna went in the evening before she died wouldn't be easy, but still, I'd hoped.

On my way out of the club, my phone rang, but before I could wrestle it from my bag, the call went to voice mail. That was a good thing because the caller was Dom, and I didn't want to speak to him until I finished reading Shauna's fairy tale.

Chapter 48

Now that I'd reminded myself about it, I itched to read more of the tale. I couldn't decide if it was the masochist in me, or the wronged-woman-looking-for-ammunition, that made me want to know exactly what happened between her and Dom. But I needed to know, and since Dom wasn't talking, I was left with Shauna's fiction.

I drove to Donner Lake and parked near the Dockside Restaurant. I had a clear view of Maggie's uber-cabin on the knoll and a bare-chested fellow washing the deck of her powerboat as it bobbed in the gentle waves beside her dock. Maggie reclined on a sun lounger on the front deck of the cabin. She looked much more relaxed than she'd been an hour ago at the country club.

It was a scene that often played out along the shore of Donner Lake. The crowd who owned the lakefront mansions masquerading as cabins didn't need a regular job, or any job. They could lounge on their sundecks every day of the week if the weather co-operated. And if the weather was in a contrary mood, they could relax in any of their several indoor dens, solariums, sunrooms, or libraries.

It was still hard to believe that only a week and a bit ago

the serene surface of Donner Lake had hidden a body in a barrel of concrete. Yet, at the same time, it was easy to believe the lake could conceal gruesome secrets. From the first time settlers had come to the region, wanting only to pass through on their way to a better life, it had delivered desperation, horror, and grief. More than one hundred and fifty years had passed since the Donner Party arrived here, and danger still inhabited the land surrounding Donner Lake. Notorious for whiteout blizzards and impassable snowdrifts in winter, and fierce thunderstorms that whipped the lake into a frenzy in summer, the area continued to steal life from the unwary or ill prepared. Every year, a few poor souls lost their way and their lives around Donner Pass. This year, Shauna was one of them.

Shaking off my morose mood, I walked to the Dockside Restaurant, bought an Americano-to-go, and made my way down the bank to the lakeshore and a particularly sunny bench. I pulled Shauna's fairy tale from my bag and found the spot where the cabbie had interrupted me earlier. I noticed three asterisks at the bottom of the next page.

Shauna had evidently learned the universal sign for scene break, which made me hope I was only minutes away from learning what really happened with Dom, and when. Or should I say, learning Shauna's version of events.

When I'd left Victoria and Roberto on the page a couple hours ago, Victoria had told Roberto how lonely she was, how she wished for a perfect marriage like his.

Roberto sighed. "Every marriage has bumps."

"Not yours. That can't be," Victoria said, but her wretched jealous heart wanted it to be so. Imp danced on her shoulder and whispered, "Yes. Yes, it can. Offer him the elixir."

Victoria poured two glasses of cognac.

Roberto said, "A large bump tonight, one I don't know we can smooth out."

"Tell me," Victoria said.

Roberto resisted. "It's between Grace and me."

Victoria saw the hurt in Roberto's eyes.

"Drink your elixir," Imp whispered to her. "Fill his glass. Everything will be wonderful."

Victoria topped up Roberto's glass and drank deeply from hers. "Perhaps things will be better for you tomorrow," she told Roberto.

Imp whispered, "But not for you Victoria, no one wants you."

Victoria drank more of the cognac and said, "All my life I've wanted someone who wants me for me and instead . . ." Tears welled in her eyes and, as Imp promised would happen, Roberto's instincts to reassure and soothe took over.

If what was coming was treachery on Victoria's part and infidelity on Roberto's, it was an excellent trick. Blame it all on Poe's self-destructive imp so that Victoria/Shauna needn't take any responsibility for it. I wanted to stop reading. I didn't want to know that Dom could so easily fall for tears, even after a couple glasses of the so-called magic elixir. I wanted to stop reading, but I couldn't.

Victoria allowed reassurance and soothing to lead to other, more intimate things. Imp cheered her on, whispering, "Perhaps this time."

But if Victoria thought Roberto could love anyone but Grace, she was mistaken. He spoke in his sleep: "Gracie. Baby."

In the time before the dawn brings the promise of a new day, when fears are most pronounced, Imp took his leave of Victoria. She and Roberto spoke about the terrible thing they had done. It was a mistake, they agreed.

Roberto said he would confess to Grace. "You cannot,"

Victoria said. "Grace must never know. She may forgive you, but she will hate me."

Roberto shook his head, but Victoria begged him to stay silent. Eventually Roberto agreed that to confess to Grace, when this thing they'd done was never to be repeated, would hurt Grace for no reason. They would never speak of it, Grace would never know, and their lives would continue as before.

Within two days, Victoria received an ominous letter accusing her of being the ruination of good lives. Within a week, Grace discovered their treachery. Grace cast both Victoria and Roberto from her world, and Victoria's life was never the same again. ***

I crumpled the pages in my fist and squeezed them into a small ball that I threw toward the water. The breeze tossed the ball back at my feet. I stomped on it.

Your life was never the same, Shauna? What about mine? I lost my husband, probably the only man I'll ever love. I lost you, probably the best friend I'll ever have. Correct that, best friend right until you betrayed me big time. How could you do that? You were right, Shauna. I hated you. And I want to continue hating you, but you went and got yourself murdered, and now I don't know how I feel. Or how I'm supposed to feel.

I pounded my fists on my thighs and gritted my teeth, refusing to cry in public. I closed my eyes, turned my face to the sun and concentrated on a nearby chickadee's cheerful song. When the threatening tears passed, I relaxed against the back of the bench and thought about the reality behind the story.

I didn't know Shauna had been hanging out in bars, and I wasn't sure I bought the idea she'd been overtaken by envy and self-destructiveness. Apparently, the poor-little-lovelorn-rich-girl-baloney had struck a momentary chord with Dom.

And if Shauna based her self-worth on who desired her, then I bet that she'd simply played the sad and lonely card to get what she wanted.

I wasn't sure what to make of the reference in the tale to an ominous letter. It could be mere fiction, but then again, it might be worth looking into. If Shauna was into the bar scene and needed to feel wanted, she'd probably had a few flings. Perhaps a wronged wife or girlfriend sought revenge. I made a note to check the Case USB for notes about threats Shauna might have received.

Two things shook me after reading this last passage. First, I knew exactly which night Dom had slept with Shauna—it was the day Dom and I had had a massive fight. I also knew that, despite how he had felt about our argument earlier that day, he'd kept our private matters private. If Shauna's take on things was to be believed, Dom loved me despite what had happened between us that day. I definitely wanted to believe that.

The second thing that rocked me was what Roberto/Dom apparently said in his sleep.

Chapter 49

I WAS STILL MULLING over the fairy tale and the truths behind it when my phone rang. I dug it out of my bag quickly. Dom, calling again.

"Hey, bella," he said. "Thought I'd check in. What are you up to?"

I could have been forthright. I could have said I was wondering if Donner Lake didn't limit itself to stealing lives. If it slammed the unwary with brutal truths and made them admit they were actors in their own tragedies. Instead, I looked at the sun sparkling on Maggie's gorgeous boat and found a lighter topic.

"Sitting in the sun at the lake. Looking at Margaret Shillingford's capital B boat and watching her buff deck washer alternate between coiling his hoses and admiring his muscles in the boat's windows."

"Ahh. Enjoying local scenery then."

"This lake is known for it." I raised my gaze to Maggie's massive cabin, where she still occupied her lounge chair. But now a muscular silver-haired man stood behind her. "Oh, wow. You'll never guess who's giving Maggie a neck massage. Pretty sure it's Chief Gavric. I hear they're an item. And hey, while I think of it, did you know he's gonna run for mayor?"

"Interesting," Dom said, after a beat. "And speaking of the Chief, who we both know is the reason I've developed webbed feet, I want to tell you about my day on the marine unit."

"That reminds me. I received another strange text hinting your transfer is connected to something other than a conflict of interest in Shauna's murder. Is there something else behind your transfer?"

Silence.

"Dom? What's going on?"

"I don't want to talk about it on the phone."

"Okay, let's meet for coffee."

"I'm working till six. How about I treat you to dinner? Say six-thirty?"

A date with my husband. My estranged husband. Why not? We had agreed to be adult and civil about things. This time however, I'd make darn sure we had coffee at the restaurant, not back at my house.

"Sure," I said as I glanced over at the Dockside Restaurant and spotted Noel Wylie standing near the entrance looking my way.

"Great, see you then, bella."

"Dom, wait. Did you put a couple of USBs in the mailbox at the house?" Noel clattered down the steps from the restaurant and rushed along the path toward me.

"Huh?"

"USBs containing a copy of Shauna's computer, for starters. Was it you?"

"No. What's going on?"

"Don't know. I guess somebody thinks I can make use of the data. See you later."

By the time I stashed my phone, Noel was standing by the bench. "Hi Olivia, I noticed you here. Do you have a minute?"

Gone was the angry tone he seemed to have reserved for conversations with me. I smelled the liquor on his breath. His eyes were red rimmed and tired. He hadn't shaved since yesterday, his shirt was wrinkled, his hair compressed on one side of his head. Shauna would be worried to see him looking like this.

I nodded. "Sure."

He kicked at the path with the toe of his boot. "First, I'm sorry I mouthed off at you. I haven't been thinking too clearly. But since yesterday, I remembered how tight you and Shauna were, and how you were more like sisters than friends." His voice caught, and he swallowed twice and turned his face to the lake. After a moment, he sighed and turned back to me, a small smile on his face. "In the movies you would have killed her, but this isn't the movies, it's real life. I know you couldn't kill Shauna."

"You're right."

"I'm worried I'm to blame for it all," Noel said. "Some guys I know told me she had taken pictures of them and me. They aren't nice dudes, y'know? So maybe they killed her?"

I guess I'd been wrong when I assumed Noel had never found out about Shauna's video surveillance and her threats to expose his supplier.

"Did you mention this to the police?" I said.

Noel's jaw dropped. "Are you nuts? These guys are nasty. Anyway, what I really want to talk to you about is this: I live in Los Angeles. I don't need the ranch and sure can't afford to run it. So, I'm thinking of selling it."

"Uh-huh."

"Maybe you'd like to buy it?"

My mouth dropped. "What? Her ranch? I don't have that kind of money."

"But you will. She gave it to you."

My stomach tensed. All Noel ever wanted from Shauna, so far as I could see, was money. To finance his hapless acting career. I wanted to lash out at him, ask him how far he would go to get all of it. The ranch, the trust, Shauna's money.

From somewhere behind me, a robin trilled its song. Shauna had believed the male sang to his mate while she sat on the nest incubating the eggs. "He wants her to know he's there, and he loves her," she had said.

I studied Noel's dishevelment and saw pain in his eyes. Was the robin's song Shauna's way of letting me know she loved Noel, asking me to ease up? I took a deep breath. "I haven't really thought about the estate. But the lawyer seemed to think it would be several months before anything was settled. So can I think about it and let you know?"

Noel nodded his head rapidly and smiled. "That'd be great, Olivia. Call me or I'm at the ranch if you want to stop by. Any time."

Noel said goodbye and hiked the path back to the Dockside parking lot. I delayed a few minutes, drinking the last of the Americano. When I stood to leave, my foot slipped on the balled-up fairy tale. I thought about tossing it in the trash along with my coffee cup but instead put it in my bag. It was a bad fairy tale, but it was my fairy tale, and for now I didn't want anyone else to find it and read it.

Besides, the reference to an ominous letter niggled at me.

And then there was the word "baby." Shauna had it right that Dom talked in his sleep, but he'd never called me baby in all the time we'd known each other. Sweetheart. Bella. Livvielicious. All those, yes. Never baby.

Shauna thought it was an endearment.

Nope.

Chapter 50

MY LIFE HAD BEEN TURNED on its head over the last several days to the point where I didn't know what day of the week it was. Luckily, on my street I didn't need a calendar to orient myself in time. As I drove down Stoney Road, I noticed Baggie Bagnovicz tending to her garden gnomes. She stood with a gnome in one hand and a duster in the other. Ergo, today was Wednesday. I saluted her on my way by.

My mailbox held a letter from Malkins, Shauna's lawyer, advising me he had initiated the probate process and a notice to creditors would appear in next week's *Gazette*.

Dom had said he'd show up at 6:30 p.m. Even factoring in fifteen minutes to make myself presentable, I had two hours to work. I bashed out an article about the advances the food industry was making in providing gluten-free choices to consumers and submitted it to a new regional health magazine whose editor had commissioned a series of articles from me.

Then I got down to business on Shauna's case and searched the Case USB (the one with the police file) for references to threats Shauna had received before her death. Nothing. If the fairy tale was based on fact, Shauna must have tossed the threatening letter away.

I took a break from the screen and sorted through my closet for something suitable to wear to dinner with Dom. What would the *Sorority Fashion Handbook* have to say about appropriate attire for a date with one's estranged husband? Perhaps, "Dress in the style which you wish your alimony to fund. Designer clothes have a direct correlation with extravagant alimony awards." Or, "When dining with swine, no pearls please."

I owned only one designer outfit, and it was at the cleaners. And I wasn't particularly interested in schemes to enhance alimony payments. I opted for my next best outfit, the black slacks and white shirt that served as my food critic duds. I added a strand of fake pearls.

Back at the computer, I clicked on the Shauna USB, which held the contents of her computer. In the documents folder I selected a sub-folder titled "Blog Queue." It revealed a calendar of blog posts. I noticed two posts scheduled for the days before Shauna's body was discovered: *Mountain Man* and *Chopper*. Those posts, and others scheduled for the future, would now never be published.

Several entries, cryptically titled *Serene Siren, Mountain of Powder, Farmer Jones,* and *Dark Side*, were for posts that had already been published, but their titles gave no clue about their content. Even though I had read the *Cheat Sheet*, I didn't recognize those titles. However, the queue set out a specific date for the publication of each of those posts, so I made a note to reread the blog itself, particularly the posts on those dates, after Dom dropped me home from our dinner.

In a sub-folder named "Drafts" I found about thirty more files, each with a label. The first of these bore the label *Graceless*. It contained an earlier draft of Shauna's fairy tale. Evidently, Shauna had written more than one piece of fiction. These files must contain story notes and drafts. I rested my forehead on my desk. I couldn't do it. I just couldn't read thirty or more fairy tales. To be honest, hoping it would get me somewhere would be like believing in fairy tales.

I was relieved when the doorbell rang, and I could legitimately set my so-called research aside. I clicked on the button to shut down my computer and as the screen with its thirty files slowly grayed out, I caught sight of a label that rang a bell. *Farmer Jones.* I added it to my mental note of things to check later.

When I opened the door, Dom wasn't there. Two brown paper grocery bags sat on the porch. A bunch of asparagus spears and two wine bottles poked their heads from the top of one. The other bag's contents were hidden beneath a small bakery box. Dom's Jeep was in the driveway, the tailgate open. He maneuvered a large wooden crate from the trunk. "Guess what?" he said. "We're not going out. Guess what else? I'm cooking. You're gonna love it."

I muttered to myself as I schlepped the two bags into the kitchen and set them on the island. "Gonna love it? I dunno." Dom excelled at making cappuccinos. When it came to cooking food, however, he gave insurance agents everywhere nightmares. A quick-fire slide show of images from Dom's past efforts in the kitchen passed through my mind: tomato sauce boiling over on the range; innards of exploding baked potatoes decorating the ceiling; scorched skillets and broken dinnerware.

"A couple more trips should do it," Dom said, as he deposited the apple crate on the island. He disappeared back outside. I snooped in the crate: three cast iron skillets, a decanter, a food chopper, cutting boards, stainless steel mixing bowls, platters, an apron, a variety of tea towels and a potpourri of wooden spoons, and spatulas.

When I inspected the grocery bags, besides the wine and asparagus, I found spinach, pears, shallots, fresh thyme and tarragon, garlic, mushrooms, a pound of butter, and a butcher-paper-wrapped package weighing slightly more than the butter. There were other items in the bags, but I turned to the bakery box and was untying the string when Dom reappeared.

"Uh-uh-uh," he said. "Off limits until after the main course." He put the box in the fridge and then faced me, a huge grin on his face. "So. Madame, tonight I have for you spinach salad with *chèvre*, pears and candied pecans, followed by *châteaubriand pour deux*, *château* potatoes and seared asparagus. As well, if madame pleases and I believe she will, my *pièce de résistance* dessert, which for the moment will remain the chef's secret."

Had I eaten anything since breakfast? Judging from the way my mouth watered as Dom delivered his goofy imitation of a Food Network star's menu, no. Still, I looked at the bags and crate of cooking utensils and thought, "Smoke alarm. Scorched pans." Before I could open my mouth to object, Dom said, "And don't fret about the cleanup. I rented everything I need, and the deal is I return it dirty, and they do the heavy lifting. I should have thought of this a couple of years ago, hey?"

I relaxed and smiled. "Then all I need to worry about is the smoke alarm?"

"A little tension is never a bad thing. So, yeah. Maybe. Maybe not."

He grabbed the decanter from the apple crate and inspected the red wine. "The people at Wines to Dine For tell me this is an excellent Malbec, imported from a winery just over the Canadian border. 'Pair with beef,' they said. So we shall." After he decanted the red, Dom told me to stay put while he prepared the dining table.

I studied the wine's label and its picture of an owl. Burrowing Owl Estate Winery. I heard the snap of a tablecloth coming from the dining room and held my breath as I listened to the clatter of dishes and the clink of cutlery. I exhaled when nothing shattered. I heard Dom talking to himself: "Salad fork outside, dessert spoon above, salad plate on top."

He returned to the kitchen with his phone in one hand and two wine glasses in the other. He scrolled through items on his screen until he found what he wanted and then placed the phone on the island. "My crib sheet."

Dom opened the second bottle of wine, this one white, a Pinot Gris. He poured and handed me a glass. I asked what I could do to help.

"Nothing. Relax, enjoy the wine. I have it all under control," he said, and pulled the apron from the crate with a flourish. The chaos that erupted the last time Dom said he had things in the kitchen under control flashed before my eyes. I smiled bravely at him, took a sip of my wine, and quizzed myself on the exact whereabouts of the fire extinguisher. So long as he wasn't making bananas *flambé*, we might be okay.

I sipped the crisp and fruity wine, thinking the owl made a superb white, and watched Dom prepare the entrée for the oven and assemble our salad. He'd scan his crib sheet and then execute whatever step it outlined. The instructions must have been set out in excruciating detail because he never faltered. The only misstep was a few spinach leaves that hit the floor instead of the salad bowl.

While we waited for the *châteaubriand* to cook, Dom told me about his latest escapades on the marine unit. "We patrolled the Truckee River today. I'm almost comfortable on board the boat. I think I can dump the floater suit soon and just wear a life vest." He thought for a minute. "Right up until our next thunderstorm, that is."

"What's to patrol on the river? Isn't it just a few pleasure craft and inner tubes?"

"Mostly. Remember that's how I met McAdams? The homeless camps? We keep an eye on them."

"Do they stay there all winter?"

He shook his head. "We've got orders from the town to make sure everyone moves on by the end of September. If they don't find somewhere to live, a real home, the town will put them on buses to points west."

"The mayor probably wants to avoid a modern-day Donner excursion. I've been thinking about the fellow who said Shauna brought groceries to the camp. Is he a suspect? I mean, no one saw her after that."

Dom shook his head. "They can't find anyone in any of the grocery stores who remembers her coming in, but I don't think that matters because Frankie accessed video from a traffic camera. You know that high crash zone near the country club?" When I nodded, Dom said, "Video from that camera shows her Land Rover going past at 9:30 that same night."

Dom's phoned chimed. He pulled the cast iron skillets from the oven and covered them with foil tents. "Fifteen minutes to rest. Wait there," he said, and carried the salad bowl into the dining room.

I mentally drew a line through Stan-the-homeless-guy as a suspect, because apparently he had talked to Shauna an hour before the video camera caught her car on the road. I wondered how many people in the camp would be put on those buses. It was good Dom had found a way to help the McAdams family. Classic Dom, tending to strays. Last year, it had been the twins Connor and McKenna. This year it would be the McAdams family. Next year someone else.

Dom returned to the kitchen and picked up the decanter of wine. "Close your eyes," he said, "and take my hand." He led me into the dining room and guided me into a chair at the table.

"Can I look?" I said.

"Not yet." I heard him pour the wine. "Okay," he said.

The scene that greeted me evoked memories I thought I had stowed securely in the deepest vault of my mind. My bottom lip quivered, and I knew better than to look at Dom. I kept my eyes on my salad plate.

"I was sure you liked spinach salads," Dom said. "Did I screw up?"

I choked out a laugh. Then I cleared my throat, took a breath, and raised my eyes to meet his.

Chapter 51

DOM'S EXPRESSION WAS WORRIED. I focused on his comment about the spinach.

"No. I still like spinach salads," I said. "And this one looks fabulous. It took me by surprise, is all. Where did you learn to do this?"

"A guy can do anything if he's got the right tools. I'll show you." He whipped out his phone, found the picture he wanted, and passed me the phone. "See? All I had to do was duplicate this. Idiot proof."

On the phone's screen was a replica of the salad sitting in front of me: spinach topped with slices of pear, candied pecans and creamy droplets of chèvre, finished with drizzles of a balsamic vinaigrette.

"Amazing." I raised my wineglass. "A toast. To Chef Dom."

We tasted the salad, and I pronounced it worthy of a review in my column.

Partway through the salad, Dom said, "So, you got your hybrid out of impound okay?"

"Yep. Officer Cassidy was very helpful. If I overlook her

taste in automobile colors, I'm fairly impressed with her. Stanford. Crack shot. Olympic swimmer."

Dom raised his eyebrows. "You checked her out?"

I stretched the truth a bit. "I might do a feature on women cops. Is there anything she can't do?"

"Dunno. The department's real glad to have her on their swim team. This year we should win the first responders' challenge at the Truckee Open Water Swim." He chuckled. "Did you meet Jamworthy? Crusty old guy."

"It's a good thing Cassidy was there, or I might have smacked him up the side of his head. Isn't he seriously over retirement age?"

"Apparently, he needs the money to help his kid put her kid through college. He used to work major crimes, but the way I hear it, he did something and got himself transferred to impound."

There was my opening. I pounced. "Speaking of transfers, what about yours?"

"Finished with your salad?" he said. "*Châteaubriand* coming up." Salad plates disappeared, Dom with them. I fiddled with my cutlery while I waited. I stared at the three red calla lilies in their slender vase and felt heat flush my cheeks.

Dom returned with our entrées, the meat a perfect medium rare, the potatoes aromatic and crispy, and the asparagus a vibrant, luscious green. It was a plate worthy of a five-star restaurant. I cut into the meat and tasted. "Have you had a lesson from Chef Maurice at the Nevadan? Because this is as good as his food. Maybe better."

"I confess I've hidden this talent from you for years. I didn't want to intimidate you."

"Right, so all those fires in the kitchen, broken dishes, scorched pans were—"

"Subterfuge. I'm not proud of it."

"Thank heaven the secret's out." I savored another bite. "Now, we were talking about your transfer."

"What about it?"

"I told you about the strange text messages I received, hinting that harassment and your transfer are connected."

Dom frowned. "You think I harassed someone?"

"No, never. But someone's doing something. I discovered Shauna had a lead on harassment in the department. She asked Gavric to investigate, but he told her to get stuffed. Then someone hints you might know something and guess what? You're transferred. Did Shauna tell you anything?"

"No, and what she knew or didn't know has nothing to do with me. I'm on the marine unit because I mouthed off at Gavric. He's a vindictive prick." Dom shrugged. "He'll get over it in a year or two. But hey, if he becomes mayor, I can be reinstated."

I stared at Dom for a bit. He met my gaze without a hint of artifice in his expression. I believed him.

"What do you think of the Chief's chances if he runs?" I said. "There was that negative performance audit two years ago and another audit's due in September. Will it be better?"

"The upcoming audit explains why he's been so visible lately. Sitting in on briefings, taking a direct interest in several investigations, meeting with officers. Being his regular charming self." Dom's voice took on an edge. "Making everyone very aware of his status in the department."

"I hope to interview him again tomorrow. Maggie is one of his backers in the mayor's race, and she put in a good word for me."

"Maggie? Do I know her?"

"Margaret Shillingford? Has a place at Donner Lake. Shauna introduced us ages ago. I like her. She reminds me of Aunt Gaye. Except for the accent. I told you today, she was lolling about on her deck and the Chief was giving her a massage."

Dom cleared our plates. "Right, I remember," he said. "Ready for dessert? One of your favorites."

While Dom fussed in the kitchen, I poured more wine into our glasses. "That wine store was correct," I said. "This red is wonderful. Is there really such a thing as a burrowing owl?"

Dom laughed. "Oh yeah. Itty bitty. They live in holes in the ground. I saw another wine from Canada in the store. Quails' Gate. And I asked myself, what quail has ever needed a gate?"

I remembered Quayle Jonasberg then, but before I could mention the blackmail, I heard Dom say, "Ouch. Oops."

I slid away from the table and went to the kitchen doorway. "What's happened?"

"Nicked myself trying to cut the string on the box."

After I found him a bandage, we opened the bakery box. Inside were two *crème brûlées*. "I bought these at the bakery," Dom said. "I was leery about using a blowtorch in the house."

"Good thought," I said, as we carried our desserts back to the table.

The crust on the *crème brûlée* shattered with a satisfying crunch when I stabbed it. I dug in to the luscious custard hiding under the golden lid.

"How'd you find out about Shauna's run-in with Gavric?" Dom said. "That mystery USB you found?"

"No. I talked to Iris. She was on the Police Advisory Committee with Shauna. But it's not one USB, it's two."

Dom frowned. "What?"

Chapter 52

"THERE WERE two USBs in my mailbox," I said. "One contains the contents of Shauna's computer. And the other contains the police file."

"What file?" Dom asked.

"*The* file. The murder case. Shauna's murder file."

The incredulity on Dom's face told me he definitely was not the person who put the USBs in my mailbox. "Whoa."

"Yeah. Who d'you think made the USBs?"

Dom shook his head. "Whoever it is, they're playing a dangerous game." He thought for a few seconds and then said, "I'd like a copy. Can you make one?"

"The file? Sure."

"No, a copy of both USBs. Obviously, there's something on them, we just have to figure out what."

I loved the sound of "we" because now I wouldn't be alone in my search for Shauna's killer, and I hadn't had to beg Dom to help. I told him I'd make copies after dinner.

We were quiet then as we finished our desserts. I licked the last bit of creamy custard from the spoon and set it down. "Confession time. Tell me how you learned to cook *châteaubriand*."

"I told you. Natural talent."

"C'mon. The truth."

"Okay. What I did was visit Gourmet Gourmet. You know that new food-to-go place? I asked them for a menu that a novice couldn't screw up even if he tried. They told me what to buy and what to do. They said the meal would rival that of a pro chef."

"They were correct."

Dom cleared the table, and we moved into the kitchen, where he placed everything—dirty dishes, skillets, utensils, and linens—into the apple crate. "How about putting the coffee on, bella? I'll stash this in my Jeep, and we can have a coffee before I say good night."

While the coffee brewed, I copied the contents of the USBs for Dom. Well, almost all the contents. His copy of the data had everything except the fairy tale. After I placed the USB for Dom on the kitchen island, I rooted through the liquor cabinet until I found the port.

I handed the USB to Dom when he returned to the house. "Coffee or port?" I said. "I'm having port. A fitting end to a wonderful meal."

"If I have the port, I can't drive."

"There's always the guest room."

His shoulders slumped as he contemplated the port and the coffee. He sighed. "Guest room." He poured a glass of port and slid onto a stool at the island. He leaned against the seat back and gazed around the kitchen, drumming his tanned and solid fingers on the countertop. "This was fun. I sorta like cooking. I think because it was for you. You and me." He smiled at me, that quirky, crooked, sardonic smile that had been my undoing six years ago. My stomach did a small flip-flop. Maybe I'd had a bit too much wine.

I took another sip of port. In an effort to move the conversation onto safer ground, I said, "McAdams is making the yard look fabulous. You did a good thing helping them."

He shrugged and sipped his drink. "Kids, y'know? They need actual walls."

"And the motel has a pool."

Dom laughed. "Right. If I'd had one growing up, maybe I'd have learned how to swim." He ran his hand through his hair. Once more I was struck by the glints of silver in the black waves. More than I'd noticed a week ago, definitely more than a month ago.

"Livvie," he said. "Speaking of kids." My stomach clenched, and I fought the urge to leave the room.

Dom looked me square in the face. "I'm sorry I pushed you about a family. I want you to know: If we can patch things up, and I really want to do that, if you don't want a baby, I'm good with it."

Would I have had any insight into the role I played in the horrid mess that was now Dom's and my relationship if I hadn't read Shauna's fairy tale? I wanted to think so, but I could be like the little burrowing owl. Especially when it came to recognizing hateful things about myself.

"I'm so sorry." My bottom lip quivered. I squeezed my lips tight and jiggled my foot on the stool's footrest, determined not to give in to emotion.

"Don't apologize. It's okay. I can live without babies."

"I mean I'm sorry about the things I said that night."

Dom came around the island and hugged me. "It's my fault. I never should have sprung that bassinet on you."

I buried my face in his chest and bit my lip, willing myself not to cry.

Dom held me, stroked my hair, and kissed my forehead. "I only want us to be together again. I don't need kids. I need you."

His embrace was warm, reassuring. His arms were strong, sheltering me from everything that was rotten these days. "You need to stop saying that," I said, "or I'll cry and end up looking a wreck."

He brushed my hair away from my face and then ran his fingers lightly along my cheekbone. "You? Never. You are beautiful. I love you."

Dom kissed me then. A tentative kiss that matched the question in his eyes when he raised his head. I slid off the stool and stood facing him, then laced my fingers in his glorious thick, wavy hair and pulled his head toward me again. Leaving no doubt that my answer was hell yeah.

The second kiss was everything wonderful that I remembered about Dom and me. I didn't know how others might define swooning, but if it involved a jitterbugging stomach, tingly spine and mushy knees, then I swooned whenever Dom kissed me like he did the second time. Swooning was toe-curling good.

It wasn't only the wine that was my undoing. It was the whole evening. The apron with the bow at the small of his back and the ties resting provocatively against his firm butt; the muscles that rippled and flexed as he chopped and sliced and stirred; the tongue he ran over his full lips when he tasted the red wine-mushroom reduction for the *châteaubriand*; the single lock of dark hair that fell over his forehead when he shook the vinaigrette.

And when we moved to the bedroom, it was the huskiness of his voice, the curve of his lips, and the mischievous twinkle in his dark eyes when he said, "Livvie-licious." It was the way his hands shook as he unbuttoned my shirt, the way his eyes widened and the way he said "ohhhhh," when I touched him.

We sank onto the bed and as Dom leaned over me to kiss me, I caressed his naked chest. His skin was smooth and warm, his heart was pounding, and I was melting, and I closed my eyes. And I saw Shauna. Shauna dancing in front of the campfire that last cookout, her stilettos flashing like the flames of the fire. Dom saying, "Careful, you'll trip in those shoes." Shauna saying "Ahh, Dominico, if you weren't married to my very best friend, these shoes would be under your bed pronto."

I gasped and pushed on Dom's chest. "I can't."

Dom rolled away. His breath came in quick, short bursts. "What's wrong?"

Pins and needles raced along my arms, my palms were wet, my skin felt cold, and icepicks stabbed my lungs, forcing me to take small shallow breaths. My vision narrowed and although I was lying down, I had the sensation of falling. I sat up, struggled to get myself off the bed, upright. Then I tumbled to the floor, where things were dark and silent.

———

"LIVVIE, Livvie, Livvie. Breathe in. Deep breaths."

I became aware I was on the bed. I opened my eyes and saw Dom's face hovering above something brown that he held against my face. "The bag," he said, "breathe into the bag."

I did as he said. Slowly my heart stopped its panicked racing and my lungs once more allowed air inside.

"Panic attack?" Dom said.

I nodded. Then I pushed the brown bag away from my face. "Think so."

"What brought it on? Something I did?"

I could have said it was something you did, something Shauna did, something life did. But I said, "I'm not sure. I'm sorry."

He kissed my forehead. "You don't need to apologize. It's all good. Get some sleep. I'll be in the guest room. Call me if it happens again."

He tucked the quilt around my shoulders. He brushed at his eyes, exhaled a shaky breath, and switched off the bedside lamp.

Chapter 53

WHEN I WOKE the next morning, I took a quick look out the window facing the street. Baggie was in her front garden, repositioning the ceramic burro and its wagon of fake fruit. Today, the wagon sat three feet away from the miniature wooden fruit stand. So, today was Thursday. Tomorrow the burro would have that wagon snuggled next to the fruit stand just in time for what I knew Baggie envisioned as her very own farmers' market.

I heard water running and remembered Dom. "Oh geez, Olivia," I lectured myself, "what a catastrophically idiotic thing to do." I wasn't sure if I meant almost making love with Dom or dissolving in a panic attack.

I slipped into my Hello Kitty slippers and shrugged into my terrycloth robe, thankful I had washed it since last Friday when it bore splotches of dried oatmeal. You have to take your successes where you find them. I ran a brush through my hair and splashed cool water on my face. The result was fair to middling. Not the best I've looked, but definitely not the worst.

In the kitchen I turned on the espresso machine, ground some beans, and made myself an Americano. I heard the shower in the guest bathroom switch off and steeled myself.

Surely in a few days I'd see the humor in last night's debacle. In the meantime, I had to face Dom.

He came into the kitchen barefoot, but otherwise fully dressed. His hair was damp, and he had a day's growth of beard. "Coffee, my kingdom for coffee." He rubbed his face and smiled at me. "I couldn't find a razor. What kinda hotel is this, anyway?"

I was so grateful he was playing it light I almost cried. "The kind of hotel where guests make their own morning Americano."

I claimed a stool at the island, and as he scooted past me, he squeezed my shoulder. "Feeling better, bella?"

"Almost. I was mortified when I first woke up. Now it's eased off to extreme embarrassment."

Dom tasted his coffee. "Excellent." He joined me at the island. "The coffee, I mean. There's nothing to feel embarrassed about. However, it occurs to me you never reacted in bed like that before I messed things up. So, genius that I am when it comes to figuring out things of the heart, I think my huge never-to-be-repeated mistake, which I will regret for the rest of my life, is the reason you ended up breathing into a grocery bag. Amiright? Be honest 'cause you're talking to a homicide captain."

"A marine patrol captain."

"Amiright?"

I took a sip of coffee. "It could simply be the stress of everything—the last month, us, the murder—has me off balance."

He waited.

I sighed. "You're right. Last night in the bedroom, all I could see was you with Shauna."

Dom hung his head. "I knew it." He hunched over his coffee.

"Most of last night was very good," I said.

His shoulders relaxed. "Is there any chance I can make things right?"

Really, did I know what I wanted to happen between us? He'd done a rotten thing, and I'd been ripped to shreds, but there was so much about Dom that was so very good. I was still me, and a big part of me still loved him beyond all else. "Perhaps," I said.

He pushed his stool back, slapped his hands on the counter, and planted a quick kiss on my cheek. "Excellent. I'll take perhaps. I'm Italian. I'm going to turn that perhaps into a yes." He rinsed his mug and placed it in the dishwasher. "Gotta run, bella. Today we'll be sitting in the middle of Donner Lake, getting seasick, and keeping an eye out for litterbugs."

He charged out the door and down the walk. I found his socks and shoes on the guest room floor and went outside onto the porch at the same time as he exited his Jeep and ran back along the walk.

Pierre stood on his doorstep, grinning, newspaper in hand.

"Yeah, shoes," Dom said. "Handy when driving. Ciao, bella." He planted a loud smackeroo of a kiss on my cheek and hustled to his Jeep.

Pierre and I watched him drive down the street and toss a jaunty wave at Baggie, who stood mid-gnomes, arms akimbo and mouth agape. I waved at her and smiled at Pierre. "It's not what you think."

"But I hope it soon will be," Pierre said.

Later, as I stood in the shower, I thought about the things I needed to accomplish today. For starters, I owed the *Gazette* a column. Perhaps I could offer a review of last night's dinner. The headline could be something along the lines of *How to Light my Fire without Burning Down my House*. Or *Châteaubriand, Chèvre, and Shucking Clothes*.

Amanda would no doubt tell me she published news, not

romantic fiction. "Hard hitting news, Olivia," she'd say, emphasizing her words with fist pumps. "Not fluff."

An interview with the Police Chief would qualify, especially when Amanda learned he planned to run for mayor. I added more research into the Chief's background to my to-do list for the day. Shauna's murder went on the list too, because if I didn't solve it, I wouldn't have to worry about a job for a while. It was hard to hold down an outside job from prison.

After a quick breakfast, I dressed in what seemed to be my go-to outfit lately, a white shirt and black slacks. The ensemble should get me through my potential interview with the Chief. I packed my laptop along too, thinking I could squeeze a review of the USB data between tasks at the office.

Although it was a short trip to the *Gazette*'s office, I had ample time to replay part of last night's dinner in my head, particularly the scene that greeted me when I opened my eyes at the dining table—crisp linens and gleaming silverware, crystal goblets, white dinnerware rimmed with silver, and three stocky cream-colored candles surrounding a narrow vase holding three perfectly formed, deep red, calla lilies. Not coincidentally, on our wedding day I carried three deep red calla lilies and our reception tables held short creamy pillar candles. If Dom wanted to evoke memories of our vows, and I was pretty sure he intended to, he succeeded.

Maybe we could work things out.

First thing after I arrived at the *Gazette* I rapped on my editor's door. She stood by her desk, rummaging in her exercise bag.

I glanced down at her Louboutin pumps. If strappy red stilettos were Shauna's signature, Louboutin footwear was Amanda's. Along with her clothing straight from the runways of New York Fashion Week, and her Porsche Cayenne. Judging from Amanda's wardrobe alone, the *Gazette* had to be one of the few ultra-successful newspapers in the country.

"I get vertigo just looking at those heels," I said.

Amanda glanced down at her shining black Louboutin pumps and laughed. "They make me feel like a grown-up."

Then she took a look at me. "You are positively glowing this morning. A new exercise regimen? Tell me what it is, because I am *so* done with kickboxing. A person shouldn't have to work that hard to stay fit."

Amanda was nothing if not fit. Tall, lithe and sculpted, she gave new meaning to forty. I squinted and spotted a few lines by her eyes. Okay, maybe fifty.

"Not exercise. A story." I told her about the Chief and his upcoming announcement.

"Excellent. Forget the food column for now and focus on features of him and the race for mayor."

Chapter 54

ONE CALL to Chief Gavric's office was all it took to arrange an interview for five o'clock. His assistant said the Chief had been expecting my call and had told her to extend me every courtesy. Maggie obviously packed some serious weight with Gavric.

I turned to the *Gazette*'s archives, which furnished me with several articles and research pieces on Chief Gavric.

I hadn't read more than the first line of the first article before my phone rang. When I answered, I heard a familiar drawl.

"Quayle Jonasberg here. King George the Third and I are wondering if y'all are still looking into that exposé writer?"

"Yes, I am."

"Well . . ."

I swear I heard cattle lowing and the breeze ruffling wheat and pasture grasses in that one drawn-out syllable. I pictured Jonasberg astride his appaloosa at the edge of a paddock, squinting against the morning sun, and counting the dollars his prize bull King George was happily earning for him.

"Well," he said, "I remembered something about that

blackmailer. Something that mebbe could help y'all identify him."

"You mean her."

"Nah. Him."

That rocked me. Him? Shauna had a partner?

"So, it ain't much," Jonasberg said, "but the guy kept saying weird stuff to me, like 'this ain't the movies, bub.' I dunno if it'll help, but I figured I'd call."

My pulse raced. I could have kissed Jonasberg. His bull too. "Thanks. How's King George these days?"

"He's still real pissed about the suggestion he shoots blanks, but he's working hard to put the lie to rest. Take care now. See y'all on the range."

I punched Noel's number into my phone, was bumped to voicemail, and left a call back message, saying only "It's important." Noel was the only person I knew who'd use the line "it ain't the movies." How about that? Shauna and Noel, brother and sister, partners in crime.

I debated informing the police but decided to wait until I had more facts. Besides, it seemed the police weren't really interested in following up information unless it worked against their prime suspect, me. "Be honest," I scolded myself. "The entire department isn't against you. Someone gave you the file, someone copied Shauna's computer, and someone's tipping you about harassment. And at least Corporal Cassidy believes you're innocent."

———

"Ms. MERCIER, GOOD MORNING," Cassidy said, when she answered my call. "What can I do for you?"

"Can you talk privately?"

"Sure. What is it?"

"A couple things. I've been trying to nail down Shauna's

movements. Dom said you found a video of Shauna in an intersection by the country club?"

She hesitated. Finally, she said, "I shouldn't tell you any of this. But yeah. It shows her SUV at 9:35 p.m. on the Thursday, heading toward the country club."

"Only one way?"

"Yeah. My eyes are bleary from watching seventy-two plus hours of tape trying to spot her going the other way. I bet I saw every car in town at one point or another. Anyway, I didn't see her again. My guess is she parked the SUV in the club lot, and it sat there until we found it."

"Hmm. I talked to the staff at the club yesterday. They remember seeing her at the July fourth picnic, but not after that. So why would she park in the lot but not enter the building?"

"Beats me. Maybe she met someone."

"Yes, but there's nothing on her calendar."

"How do you know what's on her calendar?" Cassidy said.

"That brings me to the second thing I wanted to talk to you about. I've received two strange text messages recently that hint at trouble in the police department. Plus, someone sent me USBs with information about Shauna's case. I talked to Dom about it—"

"What did Captain B think?"

I punched the air with my fist. "Same thing I do—that the person has access to police records. Dom didn't make a guess, but I know the person is you."

"That's bullshit. I've got better things to do than tip you."

I blew by her protest. "What I really want to talk about is this. Yesterday at the impound lot, I mentioned the Police Advisory Committee had information about harassment among the officers. I asked if you knew anything about it. You ignored me. I think you hoped I'd let it slide. Nuh-uh. Here's what I know: Shauna had a lead on harassment, Gavric refused to investigate it, and Shauna planned to bump the harassment and failure to investigate to the Conduct Review Board."

"So?"

"I think you know all about Shauna's lead because you were it."

"Nope."

"I won't tell Dom, if that's what's worrying you. And I sure the heck won't tell Chief Gavric. I think you were her source. I think you've been sending texts to me, and I think you gave me the USBs with copies of Shauna's computer and the police file about the case."

"Giving you USBs? I don't think so."

"Okay, let's take one step at a time. You are the only person I've heard call Dom 'Captain B.' The texter called him that too. Shauna had a source about the harassment. Admit it, you were it. Unfortunately, she's dead, so I can't ask her for details about the harassment. What can you tell me?"

Cassidy sighed. "Okay, okay. Believe me, I didn't give you any USBs. But you're correct, I sent you a couple of texts, and I was Ms. Wylie's source. A female recruit was being bullied, so I told Ms. Wylie. I didn't know the Chief refused to pursue it, but I'm not surprised."

"I thought perhaps you'd been the victim."

She laughed. "No way. If he'd tried that with me, I would have broken his arm. For starters."

I didn't want to ask the next question because I was afraid of the answer, but I had to know. "Who was the bully?"

I lost ten pounds sweating during the time it took her to answer.

"Clapton."

"Will the victim talk with me?" I said.

"She quit. Moved home to Maine or New Hampshire or somewhere. I don't have contact information for her."

"Were there any other victims?"

Cassidy was quiet for a few seconds. "I don't know about any others, unless you count how the jerk treats civilian staff. Clapton believes everyone who doesn't outrank him is there to serve and entertain him. And he's plain mean."

"How so?"

She sighed. "I feel like the tattler in school. But what the hell, I hate Clapton, the infantile idiot. This is just an example, you know?"

"Okay."

"One day Clarence, our reception guy, brings Clapton a message and there's a spelling mistake on it. Clapton says to Clarence, 'In grade three, I knew how to spell better than this. Maybe your schoolteacher wife should focus on you? Or is she too busy helping teenage boys with their ABCs after class?' I figured Clarence was about to smack Clapton, so I jumped in and told Clapton he was being an idiot. And then he said he was merely joking."

"Geez."

"Is that it? I gotta be somewhere."

"One last thing. When you told Shauna about the harassment, did you know Shauna was the author of the *Cheat Sheet?*"

"I didn't find that out until recently," Cassidy said. "If I'd known she was spilling everyone's secrets, I probably wouldn't have approached her."

"Why *did* you go to her? Why not someone in the department?"

Cassidy was quiet for so long I thought my phone had dropped the call. "Hello? Hello?"

"I'm here. The episode happened soon after I joined the department and was still sorting out personalities. I knew she was on the Advisory Committee, and she had a reputation for being hard-nosed and dogged. So, I told her. After a while, after I started working with Captain B and I thought the advisory committee was doing squat about the harassment, I told him."

My stomach dropped. "Dom? When was this?"

"Must have been a month ago. He was furious."

Chapter 55

CASSIDY SHOULD HAVE PREFACED our entire conversation on Thursday with, "Do you want the good news or the bad news first?" That way I might not have let my guard down once I learned the good news (if ever there could be good news in a harassment case) that Dom was not the harasser. The bad news, had Cassidy known what I knew, was that Dom flat out denied any knowledge of harassment.

I'd raised the topic at least twice with him. The man I'd known for over six years and slept beside for most of that time had lied to me. Perhaps not a bald-faced lie. He might have been cagey enough to deflect the conversation, but when it came right down to it, he didn't tell me the truth. He knew about harassment in the department but lied to me. Plus, he insisted his transfer had nothing to do with harassment, preferring to blame it on mouthing off at a vindictive Chief. Doubts niggled at me. Had he lied then as well?

Dom didn't want me to know that he knew about impropriety in the department. Perhaps he believed I'd think less of him for not doing more about Clapton. Or he was still trying to figure out what to do. Or, and this thought made me pause, he had ignored it.

Maybe there was another way to discover whether harassment was rampant in the police department—via my interview with Chief Gavric.

To prepare for the interview, I scrolled through items on my computer and skimmed background information about Gavric. I had learned most of it when I prepared for my earlier interview with him about Clipper Milliken's kidnapping. This time, I focused on his policing career, which began in Chicago shortly after he finished college. He joined the Prospect Police Department when he was 28 years old and after three years on the force took part in a six-month long specialized training program in the elite First Responders Advanced Training center in Georgia. He rose through the ranks quickly and became chief eight years ago. The heroism Gavric displayed when he rescued six-year-old Clipper Milliken helped his police career, and I knew that in the race for mayor it would make him a favorite with voters.

When my stomach gave me the "you're hungry" signal, I opened Shauna's USB on my computer and sent the index of her "Drafts" folder to the printer. I also queued the Farmer Jones sub-folder that had caught my eye last night before Dom rang my doorbell. I would read all of it over lunch at the Dockside. My mouth watered as I envisioned their Ahi tuna salad.

Owen Starshult joined me at the printer as I pulled my copies from the tray. "Hey, Owen. How's your investigation into the Wylie story coming along?" I said. There had been a noticeable lack of coverage in the *Gazette* lately, either about Shauna or about the progress of the police investigation. Perhaps Owen needed some encouragement.

"It's stalled," he said. "Absolutely no updates."

Talking to Owen reminded me of the DNA results looming over my head. While I was working my way through an Ahi tuna salad today, the crime lab would be testing the bloodstain in my car. I envisioned a white-coated technician swabbing the stain and felt a familiar tightness in my chest. I forced myself to take a deep breath. Dom had said the lab was backed up. Surely the earliest results would be available would be tomorrow.

Anxiety bubbled up as I thought about the time I was taking away from my investigation by focusing on the upcoming interview with Gavric. I took another deep breath to calm myself. Yes, I needed to solve Shauna's murder to save my neck. But I also had a job that demanded a good portion of my time.

———

WHILE I ATE lunch at the Dockside, I mentally outlined the questions I'd ask Gavric. I wanted to learn what inspired him to run for mayor, what issues he planned to address, and what priorities he would establish for his tenure. I also wanted to ask whether he was aware of harassment in the police department. I knew better than to start with a controversial topic however, so I would start with background information and, since Gavric had asked to stay informed about the whereabouts of Clipper Milliken, I might mention I had a line on him.

Thinking about the young kidnap victim reminded me of Ben and Claire McAdams. Dom's soft spot for those children and their dog had roots in his own childhood because he grew up in a household full of children and pets. To him, babies and animals were what family was about. Not so for me.

I should have known it would only be a matter of time before babies became a critical issue between us. Long before we married, I knew Dom wanted children. Although I loved babies, I also knew they complicated things. When the topic came up, I had said "not now." At the time Dom was working his way up the ranks and agreed with me that the shifts he worked would interfere with his ability to be the hands-on father he felt children deserved. "Later, when I move up and stop working shifts, we can start our family, right?"

Later was a long time away, many things could happen, he could change his mind. I probably would not change my mind, but who knew what the situation would be when we got to later? Never say never. So, I said, "Sure."

Fast-forward five years, Dom became captain of homicide and said goodbye to shift work. I didn't realize "later" had arrived until he brought home what he called a vintage native bassinet—a woven basket that could be suspended from a frame or an overhead beam. "Isn't this fabulous, Livvie? I wonder how many babies have been rocked to sleep in this."

"Is this a new hobby? Are you going to refinish it and sell it?"

Dom ran his hand through his hair, my first clue he faced a situation where he felt unsure of himself. "No. It's my way of saying I'd like us to start a family."

"We are a family."

"You know what I mean. A little you or a little me." He hugged me and nuzzled my ear. "Maybe a little both of us, Livvie-licious?"

"You want a baby?"

"One for starters. More would be great. A couple of pets to go with them. You know, a family."

"What's wrong with what we have? We have jobs we mostly like, we have our house, we have friends, we can travel when and where we want, we have each other. A baby will complicate things."

"But what a great complication," Dom said. "I can't think of one that would be more fun, more special."

I didn't want to have this conversation. But it was even more. "I don't want a baby."

"Is it timing? We can wait a year if you'd like."

"No. I don't want a baby. Full stop."

Dom stared at me, the smile gone from his face. "What?"

"How many times do I have to say it? I don't want *any* baby."

"Not even mine?"

I crossed my arms and shook my head. Stared at the floor. "Not even yours."

"I don't get it, Livvie. We talked about this. You agreed we'd start a family when I didn't have to work crazy shifts."

I hated him for reminding me about my words. I wanted to end the discussion. "Yeah, well, I lied. Sue me."

Dom had stared at me, and then left the house.

Remembering the callousness of my words now made me almost choke on my salad. I pushed my lunch away, sat there, and beat myself up over the crass, unfeeling way I had treated Dom that night. Ironically, only a few hours ago I'd been upset that Dom might have lied to me.

I hated that he betrayed me with Shauna. But that did nothing to erase my angst at my betrayal of Dom. His betrayal was one night. Mine was a five-year lie. I didn't want to play the *One Thing Justifies Another* game. I only knew that I had done something hurtful. I needed to talk to Aunt Gaye. She would help me decide what to do.

I paid my bill and left the Dockside, hurrying across the parking lot. Maggie Shillingford hailed me from two spots over. "Yoo-hoo, Olivia! Time for a cocktail?"

"Oh Maggie, no. I need to prepare for my interview of the Chief. Thanks so much for putting in a good word for me! My editor will be ecstatic with our scoop, thanks to you."

"My pleasure. How is your husband doing? Is he still patrolling the lake?"

I grinned. "Yes, and scraping boat bottoms and swabbing decks. He's a landlubber at heart. He'll be glad to go back to his regular duties as soon as I'm cleared of suspicion."

"How's the investigation going?"

"Well, I don't know what the cops are doing, probably zilch. But I'm making progress. I found Shauna's notes for her

Cheat Sheet blog, which contain outlines for all her past and future posts. I think the killer could be someone mentioned in the notes. Unfortunately, she used some kind of code, so I have no idea who the notes refer to. Are you here for lunch?"

Maggie laughed. "Yes. My cupboards are bare, so I had a choice—go for groceries or come here for lunch."

I snapped my fingers and said, "That reminds me. I've been trying to trace Shauna's movements. When she visited you that Thursday, did she say where she was going later?"

Maggie concentrated, and then said, "Not specifically. She mentioned she had an errand to run."

"Apparently, she delivered groceries to the homeless camp by the river. But no one in any of the grocery stores remembers her shopping."

Maggie frowned. "Odd. Perhaps she shopped in Truckee or Reno? I remember seeing bags in her car when I said goodbye to her that evening. She could have shopped much earlier in the day."

"You're probably right," I said. I shook my head. "It doesn't really sound like something Shauna would do, though —taking groceries to the camp. She'd be the person to organize fund raising and make a huge donation to the food bank. I can't see her as the person to go out there with a few bags of food."

Maggie laughed and said, "True. Especially in those shoes she loved to wear. But perhaps Shauna had changed and was trying more of a one-person-at-a-time approach to helping." She squeezed my arm. "It was lovely to chat with you. My reservation awaits. Good luck deciphering that code."

"Thanks, I'll need it."

When I settled in my driver's seat, I remembered I hadn't even glanced at the documents I had printed out at the office. I opened my bag and retrieved the Farmer Jones document. It took fewer than three minutes for me to skim Shauna's notes and to recognize similarities to something I'd read days ago in another of Shauna's documents. My stomach went through its flip-floppy routine. My discovery could be a huge step forward in my hunt for Shauna's killer.

The answer would be in the contents of Shauna's USB. To look at that, I needed my computer. Some people might think that hybrids can't lay rubber, but mine did when I pulled onto the street from the lot. Five minutes later, slightly flushed and sweating, I rushed into the *Gazette's* office and logged on to my computer.

Chapter 56

FARMER JONES and his buddies took their own sweet time appearing on my computer screen. I drummed my fingers on the desktop as I watched the beach ball whirl, apprehensive that Shauna's USB contents had been erased. "C'mon, don't fail me now. Open." After an excruciating half-minute, the USB contents appeared. I clicked on the Drafts folder. Another fifteen seconds of drumming and there they were— all thirty of the folder's documents. Technology once more had answered my call.

Before looking at any of the files, I printed Shauna's Blog Queue document. I had recognized the title *Farmer Jones* from my earlier review of the queue. The copy of the Farmer Jones document I'd read in my car contained notes about a farmer with a sterile bull who was defrauding ranchers of stud fees. It was screamingly obvious Farmer Jones was a fictionalized Quayle Jonasberg. If Shauna had camouflaged her research about Jonasberg by changing names, I figured I'd find more of her blog victims in the "Drafts" folder.

Last night before Dom showed up with his groceries, I'd intended to reread Shauna's blog after dinner, but the disastrous way the evening ended had derailed those plans. Now I wasted no time accessing the *Cheat Sheet* on the internet so I could compare actual posts against items in her Drafts folder.

Four of the historical blog posts on the Blog Queue had titles that matched files in Shauna's Drafts folder: *Farmer Jones, Serene Siren, The Dark Side,* and *Mountain of Powder.* Using the dates on the blog queue for those posts, I accessed the actual posts on the *Cheat Sheet*: *A Bunch of Bull,* about Quayle Jonasberg; *Sex in the City,* about Hannah Scrimshaw's indiscretions with the soccer coach; *Salvation for Sale,* about Floyd Nash's church THE Way; and *Powder Baby,* about Councilman Hardy's recreational drug use.

Then I read the files themselves. In each case, the notes mirrored the actual blog post, with the exception that names were changed. To a casual observer, the notes in Shauna's Drafts folder would likely appear to be story outlines. When I compared the published blog post to the fictionalized version, the details matched. Shauna wrote her exposés using fictional names and titles. When she published a post, she changed the title of the piece and used her targets' real names. Farmer Jones became *A Bunch of Bull.* Serene Siren became *Sex in the City;* Mountain of Powder became *Powder Baby;* and The Dark Side became *Salvation for Sale.*

I sat in my cubicle, still and quiet, but mentally celebrating. Somewhere in those thirty files might lurk Shauna's killer. I compared the queue with the files and found several more historical posts with matching files. Two were scheduled for publication in the week Shauna had died. A few were scheduled for the future. Many did not appear on the queue at all, and I could only guess that Shauna had not yet scheduled their publication.

I'd already combed her published posts for people who might have a reason to kill Shauna and come up dry. Now, however, the Drafts folder gave me more possible suspects, especially if they had been blackmailed like Hannah Scrimshaw and Quayle Jonasberg had.

Why would Shauna first write a fictional post using fake names and then publish it with a new title and real names? Was it fear that someone would hack her computer? Was she in danger? Was Noel right about the threats?

Whatever Shauna's motive for the subterfuge, I knew I'd be able to match some of the draft files to published exposés. Those I could eliminate as sources for new suspects. The remaining files, ones that related to yet-to-be published posts, would be a problem however, because of the fictionalized names. If I wanted to identify possible suspects from those stories, I'd need to figure out Shauna's code, if there was one, or hope that the notes in those files would point me to the obvious target.

I was on my way out the door, heading to the *Gazette* parking lot, when Dom phoned. "We checked out the company that owns Abel's Table. Can you talk, or are you at your office?"

"I'm walking to my car. Got an interview with Chief Gavric."

"Okay. So, AB Restaurants. The president is Jack Straw, which you know. Frankie couldn't find out who owns the shares. But the interesting thing about this Straw man, pun intended, is his address in Miami."

"What about it?"

"We tracked down the owner of the condo who said the lessee isn't Jack Straw. It's Amanda Brammell."

I stopped dead. "My editor? No way."

"Yep. We'll dig around a bit more, check out Paternik, the restaurant's manager, and see what's what."

"You'll keep Samantha out of it?" I said.

"Completely. And it would be good if you didn't say anything to Amanda."

"You think?"

On my way to the Gavric interview, I thought about Dom's bombshell. Amanda, the owner and editor of the

Gazette was involved with AB Restaurants, which owned Abel's Table, the restaurant with the mystery back room. Did Jack Straw even exist? Did Amanda know what was happening at the restaurant she probably owned? What else might Shauna have known about the goings on at Abel's Table?

My phone rang at 4:30 p.m., when I was about fifteen minutes away from my rendezvous with the Chief. The dashboard display told me it was Noel calling. Since my appointment with Gavric was at five o'clock, I had time to talk to Noel and find out who else he had blackmailed. I pulled over and answered the phone.

"Olivia, hi, how're ya doing?" Noel said. "I got your message. So, I'm guessing it's about the ranch? You thought about what I said?"

His suggestion that I buy Shauna's ranch from him once Shauna's estate was settled had been pushed into the furthest recesses of my memory over the last two days. Still, it gave me an opening into the topic of money and his need for it.

"I'm not sure I want a ranch. Why don't you want it?"

"It's like I said at the lake. I live in L.A. and can't really afford to run the ranch. I've got better uses for my money."

"You mean buying scripts, producing a movie?"

"Sure. But I'd need capital for that."

"Like the advance you wanted from Shauna."

He stammered. "Ummm. How'd you find that out?"

"I saw your emails about it. She turned you down."

"Yeah." He was silent for a moment. Then words rushed out. "But listen, if you think I would kill her just because she didn't advance money to me, you're nuts. She's my sister. Was my sister. I loved her. So, she said no, so what? There're other ways to get capital."

"Like blackmail?"

Noel was silent.

"What I don't get," I said, "is how you convinced Shauna

to give you the information you needed to blackmail her blog targets."

As soon as I said it, I remembered Noel bragging at the lawyer's office that he'd helped Shauna set up the blog's security system. "Or let me guess, you just hacked her computer and fished around for juicy bits. I bet the cops can analyze her computer and easily find out whether you accessed it. I'm going to give one of the officers on the case a call."

"Wait, Olivia, don't do that. Okay, you're right. I looked at her computer."

"How'd you identify her targets? Her research uses fictitious names."

"She liked to talk about the blog. Who else could she share it with? I got her talking and soon enough I'd have the name I needed."

"And then you blackmailed them."

"Geez, that sounds so criminal. It wasn't like that. I contacted some of the people she was looking into and offered to help them out, but they didn't pay me anything. No harm, no foul, right?"

"Somebody killed Shauna. If the killer was a person you contacted, and they connected the blog to Shauna, I'd say there was huge harm. Shauna died."

"Nonononono. The security on the blog was tight; she had voice-altering software; no one knew Shauna was the blogger. I'd stake my life on it."

"Well, you sure staked her life on it, Noel. I want names."

"What for?"

"To give them to the cops so they can find the killer, what do you think? And you'd better prepare yourself for a visit from the police."

"Oh, geez, Olivia, don't do that. A person could go to jail. I can't do jail."

"You should have thought of that before you tried to get money from her targets."

"Okay, look, I'll give you the names. But only if you promise not to tell the cops where you got them, or that I was involved."

I said nothing and let the silence drag on for a minute.

"Olivia? Olivia. What do you think of that idea? Hey? You'll have the names. Isn't that the important part?"

"Okay. You better not pull anything, Noel. Send me the list of names, and I won't connect you to the blackmail."

"Great, thanks. And listen, I still want to sell the ranch to you. I'm really not a ranch type. I'm moping around while the lawyer's doing his thing. Me and the horses. It's too quiet. You like horses, right? I can give you a good price. What d'ya say?"

"Noel, don't push your luck with me today. Send the names."

It was too bad Noel didn't have the code to Shauna's naming protocol for her blog, but on the upside, he'd agreed to send me a list of his blackmail victims. A small step forward perhaps, but I'd take it.

Chapter 57

CHIEF GAVRIC and I had agreed to meet at the Donner Lake pier since he wanted his candidacy for mayor to remain private until Saturday. He said if I showed up at the Police building to interview him again, it would prompt questions from officers and staff. I had my own reasons for wanting to avoid the police building, not the least of which was that it housed the jail cells. The thought of occupying one made me hyperventilate.

When I parked in the lot at the lake, I spotted Gavric leaning against the railing on the pier. He still had the physical bulk of a wrestler, and, unlike many former athletes, his upper body muscles hadn't slid toward his middle. The Chief's stance projected a don't-mess-with-me message that would be reassuring to the average law-abiding citizen and intimidating to ne'er-do-wells. Also, to lowly reporters.

I shrugged into my sweater to ward off the lake breezes and made my way toward him on the pier. When he spotted me, he walked to meet me. He clasped my hand in a firm, two-handed grip. He smiled the way a politician does: teeth showing and eyes crinkling. "Let's walk, shall we? Police chiefs don't get enough exercise."

When we set off along the lakefront, I said, "I assume it's acceptable if I record our conversation?"

"Have at it. Let me say I hope you understand why I shifted Dom away from Ms. Wylie's case? Not that I think you had anything to do with the murder, but your name has come up in the investigation, and we must avoid any appearance of conflicts."

"Of course."

"Admirable. Now, where shall we begin?"

I pressed the record button on my phone and said, "I'm aware you plan to announce your candidacy for mayor on Saturday and would like your views on issues facing the town. A bit of background however, before we get into that. I have plenty of information about your schooling and your heroism in the Clipper Milliken kidnapping for the article. Can you tell me about the First Responders' Advanced Training? I wasn't able to access the government information."

"Yes, FRAT doesn't enjoy sharing information. I was lucky enough to be accepted into the training program in 1990. It's an elite program for first responders. Training in handling many crisis situations, forensics, leadership, and so on. We spent six months, January through June of that year, studying and training in Georgia. A valuable experience that has opened many doors for me and enabled me to do the job I do today."

"That's great information. Now, what are your policies should you become mayor?"

He treated me to a monologue about Prospect's issues, such as homelessness, a faltering economic base, the need for more schools, and concerns over the quality of our drinking water system. All issues I agreed needed addressing and ones that the current mayor had not fixed during his tenure.

"You make a convincing case that you are a worthy candidate for the job," I said.

"Thank you. I think voters will agree the only thing in

town that doesn't need fixing is the police department. As a chief, I am quick to recognize and remedy problems."

"Can you give me an example?"

"Dom would be one. He isn't a problem per se, but a perception of a conflict of interest would be. Another example is an officer who exceeded his mandate and was generally disruptive. In both cases my remedy was the transfer of the officer. In your husband's case, the transfer is merely temporary."

"The other transfer was permanent?"

"Yes. I perhaps should have terminated the officer in question, but he has a family and needs the job. My record as chief will give voters confidence I can run the town in the same pragmatic, yet compassionate, way."

"So, you're expecting this year's audit of the police department to be better than the one two years ago?"

Gavric bristled. "That is old news, Olivia. I'm surprised you would bring it up. But yes, I expect an excellent review of the department. Morale is up. Our officers are well-qualified, and their closure rate is superb. The department is an excellent place to work, as evidenced by our increased numbers of recruits."

"But are those recruits working out? I heard recently about one recruit who quit as a direct result of on-the-job harassment. Are you aware of that?"

He stopped in his tracks and turned to face me. The look of fury in his eyes was so quickly quashed that I wondered if I had imagined it. "I'm surprised you would put credence in an unsubstantiated rumor, Olivia. I thought you were a better reporter than that. The whole suggestion of harassment was fabricated by an unhappy employee."

He gazed at me like a disappointed father. "I was good enough to give you an interview at the request of a friend. Am I wrong in thinking you did not want to conduct an interview so much as talk about false stories of harassment?"

"No, I mean yes. I did want the interview, but I wanted your thoughts on the harassment," I said, backing a step away.

"Again, that is a fabrication. Any publication of that false claim would be cause for a lawsuit, as I'm sure you know." He shook his head. "This interview is over, Ms. Mercier."

Gavric stomped away.

It was a short walk back to my car, but I spent every second remembering the fleeting fury in his eyes. I jumped at the slightest sound, and swiveled my head from side to side, trying to spot ogres behind trees who might leap out and gut me.

The minute I was inside my car, I locked all the doors and started the engine. I told myself it was July, and no one uses either the heater or heated seats in summer. Then I turned both on high and hugged myself until I stopped shivering. I placed a call to Dom. When I was bumped to voice mail, I left a message. "Hey, it's me. My interview with Gavric deteriorated because he objected to a couple of questions and I'm sure he's aggravated with me. Just a warning in case he takes it out on you."

Then I placed a call to Aunt Gaye. Gavric's eyes had scared the pee out of me. I needed my aunt's reassuring words and voice to calm me down.

"Olivia!" Aunt Gaye said when she answered. "Have you been traveling? Is that why I haven't heard your voice for weeks?"

"There's been a lot going on here, and most of it is shitty. I didn't really know how to tell you about it."

"Like I always told you, start at the beginning. Or the end and work back. Even the middle. But start."

I breathed in. And let it out. "Okay. First, Shauna's dead. Someone killed her."

"Oh my god! How terrible! I loved that girl. You must be devastated."

"Second," I said, "they think I killed her."

Aunt Gaye laughed. "Well, that's about the most ridiculous thing I've ever heard. What would make anyone think you could have killed your very best friend?"

I told her: inheritance, bloodstain in my car.

"But they'll test that blood and see it's not hers, right?" Aunt Gaye said.

"It's hers," I said. "My trunk lid smacked her, and she bled on the carpet."

"Okay, but you told Dom that, right? Isn't he head of homicide?"

"Yeah, he is. But I didn't tell him. He has assumed it was my blood and I didn't bother to correct him."

"Oh, Olivia, whatever possessed you to do that?"

I sighed. "Because Shauna was stuffed in a barrel of concrete, and I have the makings of concrete in my garage. There's more, but basically, everyone in town thinks I have the world's best motive."

"The inheritance? Surely, they jest."

"That's part of it. But the nail in my coffin is Shauna slept with Dom. I found out and screamed at her in front of a bunch of diners."

"Shauna? Dom? Oh dear Olivia, that's awful. I'm so sorry. Whatever possessed either of them?"

"Even though she was gorgeous, Shauna had low self-worth. And I think she wanted what I had—the love of a good man."

"Hmm. And Dom?"

I told her about the argument Dom and I had when he bought the bassinet. I winced inside as I told my aunt the ugly truth that I'd let Dom believe we'd start a family, even though I didn't want children.

"Olivia! Why did you lie to him?"

"Because I was selfish. I loved him and wanted to marry him. He wanted kids. He wouldn't marry me if I told him I didn't."

"Did he say that?"

"No." I stared out the windshield at Donner Lake. "It's ironic. If I'd told him the truth, he wouldn't have married me, and a marriage with children wouldn't have worked, and now we aren't together anymore anyway, so damned if I did, damned if I didn't."

"Why do you think having children wouldn't have worked?"

"Because my father left Mom when she got pregnant. You told me that, Aunt Gaye. He said babies complicated things and he wanted her, not babies."

"For a smart woman, you can be so unaware of what's right in front of your face. Dom loves you beyond everything. He has told you he *wants* children. He's not like your father, who never wanted children. Your mother knew that about him before she got pregnant, but she hoped he would change his mind."

I wished I'd had this conversation with Aunt Gaye five years ago. Or at least before my argument with Dom about the bassinet.

Aunt Gaye said, "How much of this does Dom know?"

"I told him babies complicate things. He doesn't know why my father left Mom."

"Well, I'm not saying that I excuse Dom for betraying your love. But I think you need to come clean with him."

"I know."

"And not just about the baby. About the bloodstain in the car as well."

"Yeah, I know. But I'm worried he won't forgive me for lying about wanting children."

Aunt Gaye was quiet for a beat. Then she said, "Knowing Dom, I think he will understand why you lied and kept it a secret for so long. And given sufficient time, forgiveness is always a possibility, isn't it?"

"I suppose so. Although I'm still a long, long way from

forgiving Dom for sleeping with Shauna and for keeping it from me."

"Most people tell lies and have secrets. Some tell bigger lies than others. Some secrets are more dire, life threatening even. Be thankful yours are ones that don't rise to that level. Talk to Dom. Get the angst off your chest."

I resolved then that I would do it tonight. I would drive over to Dom's and come clean. I breathed a sigh of relief. Talking with my aunt always helped me see the way forward. I put the phone away, drove to Sierra Bistro, and ordered an Americano-to-go. When I dug in my purse for change to pay for the coffee, I noticed a ball of paper tucked in the corner of my bag. It took me a moment to remember Shauna's fairy tale.

I hadn't yet read all of it. Did I really need to know the entire story? What's left to discover after finding out your best friend caught your husband at a vulnerable moment and seduced him? Suppose the story went on to talk about how they spent many more evenings together?

Did I want to find out? Or did I want to stick my head in a burrow? Again.

My phone chimed, announcing a text message. My mystery texter, who I now knew was Corporal Cassidy, saying:

> Clapton says Chief vetoed interviews of advisory committee and Cheat Sheet targets.

Well. That explained why it appeared no one was investigating Shauna's death. Why would the Chief direct Clapton not to do those interviews, particularly the members of the police advisory committee? To suppress the fact Shauna pressured him about the harassment? Or was he intent on pinning the murder on me? Well, if he could mess with me, I could mess with him. I texted Cassidy back:

> Check out Chief's padded resumé re Poland and Olympics.

The barista called my drink. As I collected it, another text arrived, this one from Dom:

> What could Chief do that's worse than marine duty. Ciao, bella.

The "bella" made me relax. Dom seemed unconcerned about repercussions, and the tone of his text was affectionate.

I was reassured that surprising Dom at home and coming clean with him was a good idea. I smoothed out the pages of Shauna's fairy tale and took a seat at a table by the window.

Chapter 58

AT THE DOCKSIDE pier the other day, when I had squeezed *A Graceless Life* into a tight ball and tromped it underfoot, I had reached the point in the story where Grace had discovered that her husband Roberto had slept with her best friend Victoria. Grace had cast both of them from her life. I flicked through the wrinkled pages, found the three asterisks at the bottom of the page where I'd stopped reading, and turned to the next page. What followed was not more of the fairy tale. Rather, it read like a journal and had an apt title.

After Disgrace

June 27

Fairy tales always end happily, don't they? I don't see how this one can, so I'm putting it aside. Besides, I'm not a writer, as Olivia reminded me a few months ago when we talked about the Cheat Sheet. I was on the verge of admitting it was my blog, but when she said the writing was too horrid for words, I zipped my lips and took my gawky, needy self to the bar where a few G&Ts made the world rosy again.

Shauna's characterization of herself as gawky surprised me. When I'd read the first lines of the fairy tale, I'd assumed Grace, my alter ego, had been cast as the gawky one. I remembered that conversation about the blog. I had called the writing trashy, saying the blogger would never make it in the world of real writing. How cruel of me.

June 28

I'm still trying to make things right with Olivia, but am losing hope. I've sent emails, left messages on her phone. I even wrote a couple of letters. She responded to my first email with "FOAD." I don't know what else to do. I convinced Dom to meet me at the Dockside for lunch and asked him for suggestions. He had no answer other than if Olivia had to choose between their marriage and me, he hoped she'd choose their marriage. I'm sure our server wondered what was going on. I was crying a river and Dom was all stone faced.

I recalled my lunch at the Dockside Restaurant when the violet-haired server told me Shauna had an intense lunch with a man who was "good-looking for an old guy." I filed that knowledge away. Dom didn't need to know that in some quarters, the age of 36 was old.

July 2

Another anonymous letter. This makes three, all telling me to stop ruining lives. When the first one arrived, I thought Olivia had sent it, but then realized the letter arrived days before Olivia threw my earrings at me at Chez Patrice. There's a mystery: who nabbed my earrings from the gym and planted them at Olivia and Dom's cabin? Who wants to mess with our lives that much? Back to the letter, however. I know how Olivia operates. The day she threw my earrings at me was the day she found out about things.

She's fiercely swift in responding to wrongs. Plus, anonymous letters aren't her style. Throwing jewelry is. God, I miss her. Life without Olivia's friendship sucks.

Dom had insisted her jewelry ended up in our cabin, in our bed no less, because someone stole them to play a mean prank. I hadn't believed him, but it appeared to have been the truth.

This part of Shauna's notes confirmed the fairy tale's reference to an ominous message wasn't mere fiction. Shauna had, in fact, received threatening letters. But why hadn't the police found them when they searched her house? I could easily believe the cops wouldn't dig deep into the documents on Shauna's computer, especially when the documents appeared to be draft short stories. But surely if there were letters at Shauna's house, they would have found them. Had they found the letters and ignored them?

July 5

Another letter. This one said I'd pay an extreme price if I didn't stop. The more I think about it, the more I think the letters are connected to my blog. Which is scary as shit because no one except Noel knows I write it. Could someone have hacked the blog? I'd love to talk to Olivia. She'd know what to do. But she's cut me out of her life. And I'd tell Dom, but at our Dockside lunch he told me not to contact him again. Noel insists the blog is hack proof but said I should do what they always do in movies. Send him a list of who could want to hurt me and then put a post on my blog telling everyone that if anything happened to me, I had made sure evidence could be produced. He thinks that will make whoever it is leave me alone. I rarely listen to Noel's "it's just like the movies" mantra, but he might be right.

I took a picture with my phone of this entry. I typed a text to Officer Cassidy:

> Found this on Shauna's computer. Someone threatening her. Was not me.

I could share that much of the journal with Cassidy without humiliating myself or Dom too deeply. Before I hit the send button, I read the next part of Shauna's journal.

July 7

I did it. Wrote out a list of people who could be sending those letters. I'm so worried about my computer being hacked I wrote it longhand. I mailed it today. In a few days, I'll put a note on my blog like Noel said to do. Maybe I should have kept the anonymous letters, just in case. But too late. I burned them all a couple days ago, trying to get them out of my mind, I guess.

Damn, damn, damn. Why did she burn those letters? I took a picture of this entry too, attached it to the text to Cassidy and expanded my message:

> I will tell Noel to send you Shauna's letter.

Then I sent the text, drank the last of my Americano, and read Shauna's last entry.

July 9

No more letters. I think it's over. Probably putting something on my blog is silly. I'm going to book a few days at a resort in Sedona, work on inner peace, pray (there's a switch!) for forgiveness. Maybe by the time I get back Olivia will have read my letter with the list. Maybe she might open the door a bit?

Shauna had still hoped that I would relent, that I would open her letters, read them and forgive her. I looked again at the last entry. Shauna referred to "my letter." Singular. She'd also said, "with the list." I thought of the final letter from Shauna—now in shreds in the shredding bin. Could she have sent her handwritten list to me instead of Noel?

It would take ages to piece the letter's contents together, and I didn't have the time to do that now. Dom would be off shift and at his apartment. I needed to do what Aunt Gaye said: make things right. I would confess that the blood in my car was Shauna's and explain why I hid the truth from him. I would tell him why I'd lied about wanting a family—that I'd been frightened I would lose him. I hoped Dom would forgive me, but I might have to settle for a mere understanding of motivation. Whatever the outcome, I needed to talk to him, and I needed to do it tonight.

The more I thought about it, the more ridiculous it seemed Shauna would have sent me a list. Her journal entry said Noel had told her to send it to him, which is what she probably did. Besides, sending me anything would be useless. Ever since she received my email telling her to eff off and die, Shauna would have known I would ignore further communications from her. The person she trusted with her life might have been me at one time, but not after her betrayal. Like she'd said, she knew how I operated.

I drove to Dom's apartment building, going over what to say to him. Wondering if perhaps we could ever get past Shauna, put our marriage back together.

I turned onto Dom's street and hit the brakes. Up ahead, under the streetlight in front of his building, was a violently bright green SUV. Kermie, she called it. I pulled over and turned off the ignition.

A few minutes later, I watched Dom and Cassidy exit his building and walk to the SUV. I watched Dom toss a small overnight bag into the back seat. I watched him say something to her over the roof of the SUV. I watched her throw her head back and laugh. Her ponytail swung and shimmered under the streetlight.

I watched Cassidy and Dom drive away.

I started my car, made a U-turn, and headed home.

Chapter 59

BACK AT HOME, I sat in my dark living room, numb. What a dupe I was. Last night, this morning, even an hour ago, I'd been ready to believe Dom had been the victim of a conniving seductress. That he'd merely slipped.

Taking an overnight bag along when you join a woman in her SUV did not meet any definition of slip that I knew. No, that was more like forward thinking and planning. Call it like it is, I told myself: serial cheating.

Blind. Idiot. Naïve. Brainless. Fool. I could sit here all night and not run out of things to call myself.

Cheater. Lothario. Pond scum. Pants-on-fire-lying Casanova. I could sit here all night and not run out of names for Dom.

Part of me wanted to believe there was an innocent explanation for Dom getting into Cassidy's SUV with an overnight bag. The other part of me said he had cheated with Shauna, and now here he was, reverting to type. Francine Cassidy had moved to Prospect from the Bay Area. Dom had lived and worked there too before he moved to Prospect. I had a sick feeling they could be rekindling an earlier relationship.

But in the fairy tale, if Shauna was in fact writing the

truth, Dom was the seduced one, not the seducer. Why was I so quick to believe the worst about him? Why not? What had he done to make me believe anything but the worst?

I considered my options. I could hold my head high and carry on as if nothing untoward had happened. That didn't promise much in the way of revenge, which at the moment was what I wanted above all. I could kill Cassidy, but the loss of a partner never stopped a serial cheater from cheating. I could kill Dom, but that hardly seemed fair. He'd be dead and unfeeling. I'd be alive and still feeling like a bag of crud.

I could put up a billboard at the entrance to the public parking lot by the police station. It would have Dom's picture on it above the caption "Local Lothario Services. References Available." That had potential. How much did billboards cost?

When my left leg went to sleep, I knew I'd been pouting on the sofa too long. I shuffled into the kitchen, shaking the pins and needles out of my left leg with every other step, and studied the contents of my fridge. Marmalade. Teriyaki sauce. Wilted lettuce. My mouth watered when I thought of deep-dish pizza loaded with sausage, mushrooms, peppers, and bubbling cheese. "When times get tough," I told myself, "the tough order in."

I ordered a pizza from a place nearby. "Fifteen minutes," they said.

Maggie phoned me shortly after I'd changed into jeans and a sweatshirt. "Olivia," she said. "I was just now speaking with the Chief. He was upset, disappointed in you, he said. Whatever happened?"

"I asked him about harassment at the department and he denied it was happening. But I have a reliable source who says differently."

"Who told you about this harassment?"

"I'd prefer not to say, but they have no reason to lie." I gave a weak laugh. "I also found out the Chief told Corporal

Clapton not to interview Shauna Wylie's blog victims or her colleagues on the Police Advisory Committee. I'm wondering if he simply wants to convict me."

"Oh, that doesn't sound like the man I know. He always says one must look at everything because one never knows where the truth is hidden. I will talk to him. If you believe your source, then I believe you and so should he."

"I doubt it will make any difference, but thanks. If you'll excuse me, I have a lengthy list of things to do tonight." What they were, I didn't know. I merely wanted to end the call and wallow in self-pity over my lonely dinner-for-one.

As soon as the pizza arrived, I ripped open the box and groaned as I smelled the wonderful aroma of sausage and cheese. I sat at my island, dug into the pizza, and thought about next steps. Usually I would ask myself, "What would Wonder Woman do?" Tonight I was afraid to ask that question because I knew the answer would be, "At this very moment, Wonder Woman is in the sack with your cheater of a husband."

Instead, I asked, "What would Aunt Gaye do?" Her voice immediately filled my head: "How the heck do I know, Olivia? What needs fixing most?"

Sheesh. What didn't need fixing? Without a doubt, the most urgent was the whole Shauna thing. It was Thursday evening. Odds were the DNA results on the bloodstain would arrive tomorrow. If I were lucky, they'd be delayed over the weekend. Did I want to rely on luck? No, better to keep digging.

I remembered Shauna's fairy tale-journal combo and her reference to a list of people who might want to harm her. Noel had told her to write one out and send it to him. Although I'd texted Cassidy and said I would ask Noel to send it on, I hadn't yet contacted Noel. When I realized that I also needed the list, I texted Noel:

Shauna sent u ltr July 7. Did u get it. Pls send
2 me.

I ate another slice of pizza and thought again of the final
envelope from Shauna. What if? What if it wasn't another
forgive-me-please letter?

I went to the shredder and retrieved what I hoped were all
the strips of paper from her last letter. I grabbed tape, spread
the strips out on my table and started putting them in order.
Shauna's spikey, assertive handwriting made the job somewhat
easier.

One hour and three slices of pizza later I had a single,
handwritten page that contained two columns of names under
a short paragraph that said, "Olivia, please please please read
this. The Cheat Sheet is my blog. Someone is threatening me.
If anything happens to me have a look at my computer and a
folder called Drafts. This list will help you find out who might
have done me wrong. P.S. I'm sorry. Always will be."

Shauna's journal entry at the end of her Graceless fairy
tale said she'd sent a letter with the list to me. Despite the
knowledge I was irredeemably angry with her, despite my
telling her to stay out of my life, Shauna had trusted me with
her life. She had believed that no matter what, I would come
through for her.

I sat there, holding Shauna's taped-together note, feeling
like I might vomit. She had trusted me with her life, and I
hadn't opened the envelope. I had shredded it, and now she
was dead. All through this terrible last month, I'd felt righteously angry with Shauna, even after she died. Because, after
all, I was the wronged one. I had been comfortable in the
knowledge I had nothing to do with her death. Now, however,
I wondered if that was so. If I'd opened her envelope, could I
have saved her life?

What would I have done if I'd opened the envelope? At a
minimum, I would have given the note and the list to Dom.

He would have started an investigation. He could have given Shauna some form of protection.

I sat at my desk with the list in my hand. Then I remembered Pierre. The mail carrier had mistakenly delivered all my mail to his house for the week he'd been in London. Pierre had handed me Shauna's last envelope the Sunday after they found her body. I started to breathe again. Perhaps it didn't matter whether I had opened the letter.

The little doubt that picked at me was which day the envelope had been delivered to Pierre's house. Suppose it was Thursday or earlier? Suppose I had received it on a day when Shauna was still alive? I checked the cancellation stamp on the envelope. Shauna had mailed it Tuesday, two days before she was last seen leaving her house. The guilt gods were not going to let me off the hook. If the carrier had not messed up, the envelope could have made its way to my house by Thursday.

And try as I might, I knew that had the envelope come to my house instead of Pierre's, the self-righteous me would have taken that envelope and shredded it as I did with all but the first of Shauna's envelopes. I wouldn't have opened it.

For the first time since all this mess started over a month ago, I wanted to apologize to Shauna. But she was dead. She couldn't hear me or accept the apology. I realized then I couldn't stay angry with her. You can't stay angry with the dead. They no longer know how you feel, and they can't apologize or beg forgiveness. Had Shauna lived, she would have lived with her remorse over seducing Dom. I would have to live with the knowledge that, even if I'd received that letter, I would have ignored it and could have played a role in her death.

All I could do now, I told myself, was keep trying to find out who killed her. At least do that for her.

I skimmed the handwritten columns on Shauna's note. When I found *Farmer Jones* in the first column, which was aptly titled Fake, I looked at the name in the opposite column, which was titled Real: Quayle Jonasberg. In the Real column I found Hannah Scrimshaw's name not far below Jonasberg's. The corresponding name in the Fake column was Delilah, which matched the name Shauna had given her seductress in the Drafts file titled *Sex in the City*. I did a little jig around the kitchen island. These columns of names were the code to Shauna's blog.

When I scanned the names in the Real column, I recognized several. Besides Jonasberg and Scrimshaw, I found Councilor Hardy, Andrew Gavric, Clive Milliken, Brian Clapton, and Melvin Jamworthy. Absent from the list was Amanda Brammell, which told me Shauna had not discovered anything about Abel's Table. I assumed Gavric and Clapton were on the list because of Shauna's crusade against harassment at the police department. Why Clive Milliken was on the list was a mystery.

The code to the names got me only so far. I still missed two vital pieces to the puzzle.

First missing piece: the names of Noel's blackmail victims, who I believed were the best suspects. Until I had those names, I would need to look at all the names on Shauna's list, tie each to a blog post, and decide whether the relevant exposé was enough to kill for. I sent Noel a text:

> Forget ltr. Send names of blackmail targets.

Second missing piece: the key to the titles of the files in the Drafts folder that had not yet been turned into published blog posts. Shauna had given her drafts coded titles that she changed when she published the blog posts. Without that key, I had only one way to match people in the Real column with files in the "Drafts" folder: I'd have to read every one of its files in order to discover what dirt or alleged dirt Shauna had dug up on each person listed in the Real column. Even if I eliminated the published posts, I was left with ten files to read.

Logic demanded I read the stories Shauna had queued for publication first. Then I could move on to files she had not yet added to her calendar. I opened my computer and accessed Shauna's USB contents, noting the two posts queued for publication on the week after Shauna's body was pulled from Donner Lake: *Chopper* on the Wednesday, and *Mountain Man* on the following Friday.

The *Chopper* file contained notes about a man named Neil Swiper who owned a local auto detailing shop that, in reality, was a chop shop, specializing in funneling stolen high-end vehicles to auto traders in San Francisco. Except for his penchant for flipping stolen vehicles, Swiper seemed to live a blemish-free life. According to Shauna's unnamed source, police were aware of Swiper's activities, but he stayed one step ahead of them.

I checked Shauna's Fake column and located Neil Swiper. The name in the opposite Real column was Zack Lockhart, someone I'd never heard of.

Next, I opened the *Mountain Man* file. Instead of notes, this file contained Shauna's draft blog post. It began, *"Let me tell you a story about a man named Big Pinocchio."*

I checked Shauna's code—Big Pinocchio was in reality Andrew Gavric. I expected to find details about the harassment Cassidy had mentioned. It struck me as odd that Shauna had used the name Pinocchio as her code for Gavric. Perhaps she branded him a liar because he'd denied knowing about harassment.

When I read the balance of the story, I realized I wasn't even close.

Chapter 60

THE *MOUNTAIN MAN* story was short.

"Let me tell you a story about a man named Big Pinocchio. A man sworn to protect and serve the people in this town. A hero they say. But is Big Pinocchio the man he wants us to believe he is? Let me pose two troubling questions.

"First, Big Pinocchio was an accomplished wrestler in college, even winning awards for his skills. We are told that Poland, his country of birth, invited him to join its team for the 1984 Olympics. Big Pinocchio tells us he turned down the offer, as he was months away from becoming a U.S. citizen. Question one: why is there no record anywhere of Poland's offer?

"Second, and more troubling. Many years ago, when Big Pinocchio was new to town, he rescued a kidnapped child. Most of us know the story. Big Pinocchio disabled the kidnapper and then, when his snowmobile broke down, he hauled both the child and the kidnapper over five miles through a terrible blizzard to safety. Question two: what would you say if the child, Skippy Jones, remembered the rescue differently?

"If he lied about these two things, I wonder what else he lied to us about. **"

I didn't need to look at the codes to know that Skippy Jones would be Clipper Milliken. Luckily, when I had read Shauna's emails earlier, I had noted down Milliken's contact information. I punched his number into my phone.

When Milliken answered my call, I heard bells and chimes and cheering in the background. I introduced myself and asked if he had a moment to talk about Shauna Wylie.

"Noel's sister?" he said. "Yeah, hang tight a minute." He hummed into the phone and the background noise gradually lessened until it had almost disappeared. I heard him order a large coffee, no room, and then he was back talking to me. "Okay, sorry about that. Things are rockin' in the casino. Is this better?"

"It's great. Where are you?"

"Bellagio in Vegas. Sitting outside the Palio coffee shop. What can I do for you?"

"I'm following up on Shauna's death and wondered if you could—"

He interrupted me. "Shauna's dead? What?"

"Sorry, I assumed everyone knew. Shauna was murdered about ten days ago. I've been looking into it and wanted to ask you about the recent conversation you had with her about your kidnapping."

"I haven't talked to Shauna since elementary school. And back then, I didn't feel like talking about the kidnapping."

It took me a second before I realized Shauna hadn't told him who she really was. "Do you remember talking to anyone, say in the last year, about what really happened the day the cop rescued you?"

"Sure. I talked to a reporter from some newspaper I've never heard of. They said they were doing a feature on the cop. Gavric?"

"That was Shauna you talked to."

"Nah. It was a guy. He had a weird nasal voice, and his name was Joe something. Some horsey thing. Joe Palomino."

I grinned. Shauna's horse. I supposed even Shauna figured calling herself Rocketman wouldn't fly. "Trust me, Clive, that was Shauna. She published an anonymous newsletter and Noel set her up with lots of security tricks, among them voice-altering software. She could have made herself sound like Barry White if she wanted to."

Milliken laughed. "If she'd made her voice sound like Lauren Bacall I woulda told her my story and then asked her out for dinner."

"What did you tell her?"

"Pretty much all about that lowlife grabbing me and how I was scared pee-less, and how the cop found us in the cabin and got us outta there on a snowmobile and toboggan. The dude, I mean Shauna, was real interested in the gunfight by the sand shed."

"Sand shed?"

"The shed they keep all the sand in for the roads in winter?"

"There was a fight there?"

"Yeah. The cop needed to take a leak, so he stopped by the shed and went into the trees. The lowlife was laying in the toboggan like he was unconscious, but pretty quick after the cop left the guy told me to zip it and stay put. Or else. He followed the cop and soon I heard shouting. I found a rock that fit my hand nicely and went looking for them. The rifle was leaning against a tree. The cop was on his knees, and the lowlife was standing there with his back to me. I couldn't see his hands, but the cop kept saying 'don't shoot, don't shoot,' so I figured he had the cop's gun. I wound up and threw the rock and hit the lowlife in the head. Stunned him pretty good. Then the cop took over."

"Impressive pitching," I said.

"Yeah. Little League. First string pitcher."

"But I thought the kidnapper was shot at the cabin."

"Hah, nope. At the cabin Gavric, the cop, caught him by surprise and took him down like one of those guys on W.W.F. The guy was out cold before he knew who smacked him. The cop put handcuffs on him and flung him into the toboggan. He didn't shoot the guy until the sand shed, after I hit him with the rock. The cop snatched his gun back and shot the guy in the leg. Then he got the rifle and put the guy's hand on it and fired a shot into the trees."

Clive paused, and I heard him slurp his coffee. "That's about it. The cop stashed the snowmobile behind the shed and said we'd walk from there. He dragged the guy on the toboggan, and when we were near the town's lights, he insisted on carrying me the rest of the way."

"Five miles, I heard."

"Way less. Go check out the sand shed if it's still there. About half a mile west of town. Big red roof and a sign saying Shed No. 1. We kids used to ride our bikes out there all the time in the summer. I don't think Prospect had more than one sand shed in those days. Anyway, the cop and I walked half a mile or so and the cop dragged the toboggan. Then the cop carried me maybe a hundred yards."

"Why didn't you tell people this when it all happened?"

"No one really asked me for too many details. And Gavric said if we told the story his way, the guy couldn't sue my parents because I'd hit him with the rock. He said the guy coulda had brain damage, and my parents would have to pay. Now that I'm all grown up, I think he was conning me, right?"

"You mean rather than admit a Little League pitcher saved his life?"

Milliken laughed. "Yeah, that's what I thought. Anything else? I have a poker table waiting for me."

I thanked Milliken for his time and promised to buy him a

coffee next time I went to Las Vegas. I wondered why Shauna had not included all of Clive Milliken's story in her *Mountain Man* post. Was this a teaser with the real exposé to follow?

It was then I focused on the two asterisks at the end of the last line of the story.

Chapter 61

I SCROLLED down the page and saw two more asterisks with a note that said, "Talk to Scone about transfer."

When I checked the codes, Scone was Shauna's nickname for Sergeant Jamworthy. I laughed out loud. Pure Shauna. Scones were a favorite food for both of us. Every time I passed one up in an attempt to diet, she would bite into hers and say, "Yummers, you're really missing something, Olivia. This is totally jam-worthy."

First thing Friday morning, I would take a drive. I'd go find Milliken's sand shed, and then stop by the Police Impound lot for a chat with my favorite crusty oughta-be-playing-shuffleboard-at-the-old-folks-home cop.

I phoned Dr. Cigments, one of my contacts on the Police Advisory Committee, and asked him what they would do if they discovered a padded resumé or mismanagement at a high level.

He said, "The committee has no power to fire someone. We would refer it to the Conduct Review Board, who can discipline members of the department. And the Mayor can fire the guys at the top. Something egregious, we would refer to both the Review Board and the Mayor."

At nine o'clock, Dom phoned me. I let the call go to voice mail. I was done with him. Over the next hour I read through all of Shauna's files, looking for suspects. Two files contained material significant enough to make the target angry.

The first, titled "*35 mm*" had notes about Nelson Leadbetter, a prominent local doctor, who filmed porn in his examining rooms and marketed the videos as part of his libido enhancement and rejuvenation program. According to Shauna's notes, not all the stars of his videos were aware they were being filmed.

Another file, named "*Play On Boys*," suggested Ivan Klingover supplied steroids to the junior hockey players he coached.

I jotted down a to-do list for Friday morning: sand shed; Jamworthy; Dr. Leadbetter; and Klingover's players. My phone rang again—another call from Dom. That was followed by a text from him:

> where r u. calling about my day on the high seas.

If I didn't answer him, Dom would continue psycho dialing and texting. I texted him, using complete words so he could not misunderstand:

> Fool me once, shame on you. Fool me twice, shame on me. We are done.

It was after eleven when I cleared my dishes, tidied up the kitchen and moved through the house, turning off the lights. I heard the garage door slide open at Pierre's house and peeked out the sidelight by my front door. It was Thursday. He'd be on his way to the late showing of *Rocky Horror Picture Show* to visit Darlene, his favorite popcorn lady. I watched him back out and then hit the brakes as a sleek, light-colored car advanced up the street, slowed as it passed Pierre's driveway, and then sped away.

I turned off my front porch light, double-checked my locks, and headed to the bedroom to watch the late news. A few minutes later, Noel's email arrived with the list of people he had "offered to help."

I recognized four of the six names: Quayle Jonasberg, Hannah Scrimshaw, Nelson Leadbetter the porn videographer, and my editor Amanda Brammell. Amanda's name surprised me because she didn't appear anywhere on Shauna's list of blog targets.

Of the last two names, Patrick O'Hagen was a complete cipher. Annabelle Bonaventure rang a distant bell, but I couldn't place her. I grabbed Shauna's list of codes. Neither of those names appeared on Shauna's list.

I punched Noel's number in and waited for him to answer.

Noel's voice was peevish. "It's late Olivia. I'm tired. I sent you the list. No need to keep bugging me."

"It's not my fault you delayed so long. I'm tired too, and cranky. I have questions. Answer them and you can go to bed."

"Fine."

"Three of your names don't show up in Shauna's blog files. O'Hagen, Bonaventure, and Brammell. Was Shauna investigating them?"

"Not Shauna. Me. But I told them the *Cheat Sheet* was on to them and would expose their naughtiness."

"Who's Bonaventure?"

"Annabelle Bonaventure, wife of a Miami banker who made a fortune laundering money. A buddy and I saw her skiing at Heavenly last winter."

I remembered. "Right. I saw an email exchange between you and Shauna about the woman." Noel had also attached a copy of a newspaper article about the case.

"Then you know she testified against her husband and he's sitting in jail."

"Shauna turned down the story."

"Yeah, she thought the woman was a hero. Giles, my bud, poked around a bit more when he went back to Florida. Turns out the cops never found all the money they think the guy made. They traced it to Panama, where it disappeared. Annabelle disappeared too. I bet it's not a coincidence. I offered her the chance to keep her whereabouts out of the *Cheat Sheet* and private from her husband."

"And O'Hagen?"

"Mr. soccer-coaching-sex-machine Patrick O'Hagen. Clive Milliken introduced him to me at a party in Las Vegas. O'Hagen was real pleased about the number of soccer moms who wanted to share the sheets with him. Hannah Scrimshaw was one of many. I offered him the chance to avoid having his gigoloing ass exposed in the *Cheat Sheet*."

"What about Amanda Brammell?"

"That upstanding member of Citizens Against Drugs owns a restaurant that sells much more than pork and beans. Smack, grass, meth, whatever you want, her manager Jimmy Paternik is the man to see."

"How'd you find this out?"

"Duh. When I'm not in L.A. I need a source, don't I? I promised Jimmy a part in my next movie, and he was my newest best friend. Told me all about his boss lady, Amanda Brammell. So I thought she'd like to keep her dabbles in the drug trade secret."

"Did Shauna know about this?"

"I dunno. I mean, I know she followed me around, trying to keep me straight. So maybe."

He laughed. "Anyway, it was all for nothing. No one responded to my offers. Except the guy with the stud bull who told me to screw off. I heard nothing from the rest even though I kept the pressure up until Shauna died."

"Yeah, kind of hard to blackmail people when the person you were hiding behind is murdered. Or were you afraid if they could find Shauna, they could find you?"

"No, I told you. That blog was safer than a vault in Switzerland. Shauna used voice-altering software when she interviewed people, never met them face to face, never used email or texts, and the security on the website made it impossible to hack."

My body ached with fatigue. "Maybe."

"I never talked to them either, except for the bull guy and that was a big mistake because he threatened to sic every cop in the county on me. After that, I only sent anonymous letters, and used a service to do that." Noel took a breath. "We're good, right Olivia? I gave you the names. You won't squeal on me?"

"If you're playing straight with me, yeah. One thing before I let you go. Why not Gavric? Shauna had damaging stuff on him. Why not offer to help him out?"

"Are you nuts? Gavric? I want to, one, stay out of jail and, two, keep on living."

Chapter 62

FRIDAY MORNING, I didn't need to spy on Baggie to know what day of the week it was. Giggles, sharp barks, and a clattering of small feet on the porch told me this was another McAdams Family Day. When I opened the door, Charlie paused long enough to give my palm a quick swipe with his tongue before scampering toward the kitchen. Ben and Claire stood still and smiled at me until I waved them inside. Then they broke into a run down the hall.

I took a moment to wave hello to Duncan McAdams, who had watched his children and pooch scramble past me and raised his shoulders in a "what can I say" motion. By the time I returned to the kitchen, Charlie's bowls were full, the cookies were on the island countertop, and Ben and Claire sat on stools at the island.

I poured two glasses of milk and set them on the island. "Only one cookie, remember."

The kids dunked and munched their cookies while I turned my computer on and searched for Patrick O'Hagen and Annabelle Bonaventure. I found O'Hagen easily because he ran soccer camps and advertised online. Bonaventure was more of a challenge, and I had to search neighboring towns before I finally found an A. Bonaventure in a small one-traffic-light town about thirty miles west of Prospect. I jotted both O'Hagen's and Bonaventure's phone numbers on a slip of paper, next to their initials.

Once Ben and Claire finished their snack, they headed outside to join their father in the garden. Charlie snatched the last kibble from his bowl and raced after them. I made a mental note to buy more treats for Ben and Claire to discover in the pantry when they showed up for the next McAdams family day.

Patrick O'Hagen sounded hurried when he answered my call. I introduced myself. "Have I caught you at a bad time?"

"I have five minutes," he said. "Are you calling about soccer camp?"

"No, about the *Cheat Sheet*."

His voice cooled. "What did you say your name was?"

"Olivia Mercier."

"I've written it down. If you're looking to get money outta me, think again."

I trotted out my ruse about doing a story on bottom-feeder journalism, and said I merely wanted to talk to him about the story the *Cheat Sheet* had run about Hannah Scrimshaw. "What do you mean about money?" I asked.

"I got lots to say about that newsletter, blog, whatever they call themselves. But I'm not talking except face to face. I'm busy until late this afternoon. So where do you want me to meet you?"

I suggested four o'clock at the Sierra Bistro.

"Suits me," O'Hagen said. "You better be on the up and up or it won't be good for you."

He disconnected. Did I really want to meet this guy? When I asked myself whether he could be trying to lure a blackmailer into a trap, a shiver of concern ran down my spine. I hoped Sierra Bistro would have a crowd at four o'clock. Preferably a crowd of large, aggressive cops.

When I phoned the number I'd found for A. Bonaventure, I was greeted with, "This is Alvin." I asked to speak with Annabelle.

"No such here," the guy said. "Just me and the pigs. And ain't none of them called Annabelle. Although that would be a real good name."

"Do you know Annabelle Bonaventure?" I said, idly drawing a circle around the initials "AB" on the slip of paper.

"Nuh-uh."

I sent a text to Noel asking for contact information for Bonaventure, frustrated that I hadn't asked last night. I could chalk it up to exhaustion, or I could blame it on being in a tizzy over Dom and his cheating ways. "No," I lectured myself, "you erased Dom from your life before the chat with Noel. You were not in a tizzy."

Dom chose that moment to phone me. I let the call go to voice mail.

Noel's admission he'd blackmailed my editor, Amanda, made me wonder whether she might have killed Shauna. I stared at the slip of paper with the phone numbers and focused again on Bonaventure's initials. AB.

According to Dom, Amanda leased a condo in Florida. According to Noel, Annabelle Bonaventure was originally from Florida. Annabelle seemed to have disappeared. Could Amanda Brammell be Annabelle Bonaventure? I shook my head. No, surely Noel would have said something. Unless he had never met or seen Amanda.

I tried to recall what, if anything, Amanda had told me about herself. Not much. She had worked at the Miami Herald before moving to Prospect. She lived alone, was a fitness addict, and President of the local chapter of Citizens Against Drugs.

I suppose it didn't matter if Amanda Brammell was the mysterious Annabelle Bonaventure, wife of the money-laundering banker. The fact remained that Noel had tried to extort her for at least one misdeed, perhaps two. Would blackmail drive Amanda to murder, assuming she could identify the blackmailer? Did that explain why she had been so eager to identify the author of the *Cheat* Sheet, not because of scoops, but because she believed the blogger was blackmailing her?

If I were on speaking terms with Dom, I could mention the AB coincidence. I thought briefly about calling him and then decided against it. There was no need to share my suppositions with him. Dom and his crew were already looking into Amanda's involvement in Abel's Table. If there was anything else fishy about her, I was confident they'd find it.

Before I left on my trip to the sand shed, I scrolled through the pictures on my phone, found one of Shauna, and showed it to Duncan McAdams. "Did you see her at the camp by the river a couple weeks ago, maybe around Thursday, July 9?"

He studied the picture and shook his head. "Nope. I'd remember her."

"You sure? A fellow named Stan says she delivered groceries out there that Thursday. In the evening, around 8:30?"

"Stan Drozeny said that?"

"I don't know the guy's last name, but yeah."

McAdams scratched his head. "There's only one Stan out there, so it has to be Drozeny. Maybe he's got his days confused. Thursdays at the camp, everyone broke out board games after dinner. Stan and I always played snakes and ladders with the kids until bedtime, and then he and I would play crib. He whipped me every time, loves the game, never misses a Thursday. If he got groceries from someone, it wasn't on a Thursday night."

"How do I find the camp?"

McAdams gave me directions and said, "Want me to come with you?"

"No, I'll be fine. I have some things to do but should be back in a couple of hours."

"Right. If I don't see you by noon, I'll drive to the camp. It's rough country, you could twist an ankle easily. Or worse."

Just talking to McAdams calmed me. It was good to have someone else around the property. I felt less vulnerable.

I accessed the GPS on my phone and typed, "Prospect sand shed." Instantly I had a choice of three sand sheds, proof the town had grown since Clive Milliken was called Clipper. When I tapped on sand shed one, a map popped up. The shed was a short distance along an offshoot of Donner Pass Road.

When I arrived at the sand shed, I took a picture of the red roof and the sign Milliken had remembered. Then I turned the car around, zeroed the trip meter, and drove back to the outskirts of town. I hit town limits within a quarter mile, which I figured accounted for a bit of urban sprawl. After half a mile, I was definitely back in the land of streetlights. Gavric's estimate of a five-mile hike was grossly exaggerated.

Chapter 63

CLARENCE WAS at the reception desk when I entered the police building. His eyes lit up when he saw me. "Hey Olivia, how's by you?"

"I'm glad to find you here," I said. "I need someone to come with me to the homeless camp by the river. Why not take a long coffee break, Clarence?"

He fiddled with his bowtie and chuckled. "I don't think I can swing that. Want me to call an officer for you?"

"No. I need someone riding shotgun for appearances only. No danger involved. And I'd like it to be you. On the way, we can discuss the USBs someone left in my mailbox."

His face paled. "Huh?"

"USB drives. I haven't had them tested yet for prints. Maybe I'll get Dom on it later."

Clarence cast his gaze around the room and waved at a young woman across the lobby. As she approached, he said, "You know, I think I could use a break." He asked the woman to spell him at the desk and then glanced at me. "About how long?"

"Thirty or forty minutes, max," I said.

According to McAdams' directions, the camp was a

hundred yards down a trail off the south end of the public park by the Truckee River. As we drove to the park, I told Clarence that Claire McAdams had outed him. "She likes your bowtie."

Clarence sighed. "Yeah, those kids, that dog. In my plan, they weren't supposed to be there. Are you going to turn me in?"

I laughed. "Would I ask you to tag along if I wanted to burn you? I appreciate what you did, and the data on those USBs is helpful. But it was a dangerous thing to do."

"No one saw me. I'm kinda invisible around there. I wanted to help."

"Why?"

"You and the captain are good people. I don't think you killed your friend. That day you got the T-bird delivered? When the captain sent me to see Cassidy about your computer information, I heard her telling Clapton there was no way you'd done it. She's okay, Cassidy. I like her a lot. Anyway, Clapton told her to leave detecting to the big boys. He's what the missus would call a difficult personality."

"You're not the only one to say that."

"So that evening I copied everything on Ms. Wylie's computer. Then, several days later, when I heard the captain had been shipped to the marine unit, I copied the police file. I held on to both the drives for a bit, not really sure what I was going to do with them. And then I overheard Clapton bitching on the phone about how the captain had accused him of harassing someone. 'A stupid broad,' Clapton called her. He said if the captain could mess with his life, he could mess with the captain's. 'I've already thrown a couple wrenches into his world,' Clapton said."

Clarence glanced at me. "That's when I decided to put the drives in your mailbox. End of story."

After we parked in the lot by the river, I explained why I wanted to speak with Stan Drozeny. "I don't expect trouble, but I feel better having someone along. So even though I sorta coerced you into this, thanks."

We hiked along the trail McAdams had told me about and even though it wasn't as rough as he'd led me to believe, I couldn't imagine Shauna negotiating the ruts and tree roots in her stilettos, especially with her arms full of grocery bags.

Five minutes later, we spotted the first of the tents. I asked a woman hanging wash on a makeshift line between trees where I could find Stan Drozeny. She pointed me to a balding man supervising a teenager who was studying the engine compartment of an ATV. Stan looked up as Clarence and I approached. "Help you?" When the man spoke, the teen wiped his hands on a rag and turned his attention toward us. His eyes were the exact shade of blue as Stan's.

I told them who I was, showed them my picture of Shauna, and said I was trying to trace the movements of a friend of mine who'd been killed. "Shauna Wylie. The police said you might have seen her. She brought some groceries out here?"

"Yah, yah. That's right. Thursday, July 9. 8:30 or so. Nice lady."

"Are you sure about the day? Could it have been earlier in the week? Because I talked to someone else who's pretty sure no one came out to the camp with groceries that night."

Stan snorted. "I'm positive it was that night. She didn't actually come out here. I mean not to the campsites. Hank and I were in the parking lot when she pulled in. Snazzy SUV wasn't it, Hank?"

The teen jerked his head toward his father. "Yeah."

"Okay, thanks. Did she mention where she might have been going later?"

Stan shook his head. "Not a word."

I pulled out my card and a twenty and handed them to him. "I'm sorry it's not more, but hopefully it helps. Please call me if you think of anything else."

On the road back to town, Clarence said, "I recognize that young man, Hank. I think he was in bail court a while ago. He seemed surprised when his dad asked him about the SUV."

"That's what I thought, too."

I dropped Clarence back at the station and thanked him again for giving me the USBs. Then I plugged the Police Impound Lot into my GPS. I followed the map's route to North Pass Road and soon arrived at the high chain-link fence that surrounded the small Airstream trailer and its collection of abandoned and seized vehicles.

Even if Sergeant Jamworthy hadn't seen me enter the yard, which I doubted, my tires crunched over the gravel in the lot and announced my presence. I turned my phone off to avoid interruptions and walked to the Airstream. When I entered the trailer, Jamworthy stood at the orange laminate counter, head down, right hand extended, palm up. "Driver's license," he said.

I dug out my driver's license and slapped it into his palm. He put it on the counter and studied it. "Geez, it's just as bad as the last time you were here, Ms. Mercier. Still got those halo things."

"You thought I'd go running to the DMV and get a new license?"

"I woulda. Course, it's only been a few days. They're noto-riously slow." He handed the license back and grinned at me. "I already gave you your car. What else do I have that you want?"

"I hope you have information that can help me. Did you know Shauna Wylie?"

Jamworthy turned away and fussed with the coffeemaker, busying himself with the water, adding grounds to the filter. "I know who she was," he said with his back to me. "Never met her." He pushed the brew button and turned to face me. "We were supposed to meet a while back, but she never showed up. Then I heard she died."

That explained Shauna's calendar entry of "PI LOT-Scone." Police Impound Lot-Jamworthy.

"She was my best friend," I said. "Some people think I killed her, but please believe me, I didn't. I found something on her computer, amongst notes about Chief Gavric. It said, 'Talk to Jamworthy about transfer.' So here I am, hoping to talk to you."

The coffee machine beeped. Jamworthy poured two mugs. "Milk, sugar?"

"Black," I said.

"Have a seat, Ms. Mercier. Let's talk."

Chapter 64

I sipped my coffee and watched the sky darken as thunderclouds rolled up their sleeves and formed fists. Jamworthy told me about his transfer to the impound lot.

"I was with the NYPD for twenty years," he said, "working major crimes. My wife wanted to get outta the city, be closer to our kids, who by then were having their own kids. We kept our eyes open and when Prospect advertised an opening, I applied. Our son lives in Reno and our daughter is in Sacramento, so it's sorta halfway. The Prospect police chief back then was old man Hardson, and he hired me right then, over the phone. I showed up two weeks later, and he put me on the homicide team."

He added sugar to his coffee and stirred. "When I joined up, Gavric was a sergeant, rising quickly in the ranks. You know he rescued that kid?"

I nodded, and Jamworthy slurped his coffee. "Chief Hardson told me I was joining a force that could claim a bona fide hero who'd done special training with FRAT. Meaning Gavric. What Hardson didn't know was I'd trained at FRAT too. I just never mentioned it when I phoned about the job."

"When were you there?"

Jamworthy went on as if he hadn't heard me. "I asked Hardson if he knew when Gavric had done his training. He said of course he knew, because he'd recommended Gavric for the program and got the Town to cough up money to send him. 'January through June 1990,' he told me. Cost the Town $18,000."

"Expensive."

Jamworthy nodded. "Yep, and worth every penny. The thing is there are only thirty-six trainees in each of those special sessions. I was one of the thirty-six at FRAT from January through June 1990. I knew every one of my fellow trainees. Gavric wasn't there."

"Could Hardson be mistaken about the dates?"

Jamworthy refreshed his coffee, then waggled the pot, and raised his eyebrows at me. I shook my head.

"No mistake," Jamworthy said. "I peeked at the files, copied all Gavric's paper—application, references, acceptance. It was all neat and tidy and looked legit, but you can fake almost anything with a good computer. I kept my head down and nosed around a bit and found out Gavric had actually spent those six months in the Florida Keys, fishing, lazing on the beach, taking private martial arts courses, hanging out with some rich guy and his wife."

"Can you prove it?"

He smiled and shook his head. "If I could, would I be sitting in this silver bullet? In the NYPD I trained a kid, Lawrence. Great young fellow. He moved to Florida in the late eighties, to the Keys. In 2000 when I left the NYPD to come here, I sent my new contact information to Lawrence, and invited him to visit if he ever got tired of oranges. About six months later he emailed me, saying he remembered meeting a cop from Prospect and did I know him. I guess Lawrence met Gavric in the martial arts course and they hit it off, hung around together a fair bit. Gavric had slipped up one day and mentioned Prospect to Lawrence. When I received Lawrence's email, I called and asked him to tell me everything he knew about Gavric, which is how I knew about Gavric's frolics in the Keys."

Jamworthy stared out the Airstream's window. "Gonna storm," he said. "Lawrence died not long after that. Aneurism or something."

"I'm sorry."

He sighed and cleared his throat. "Yeah. Good kid. Gavric was our golden boy. Chief Hardson loved having a hero to brag about. But no one wanted to work with Gavric. He bullied other officers and took credit for their collars. Gavric and I had a run-in over a case, and when he tried to push me around, I told him not to mess with me, because I knew who'd been at FRAT in 1990 and it sure the hell wasn't him. Then Hardson says he's retiring, and he recommends Gavric as the new chief. And not long after that, Gavric just happens to be in the locker room when I open my locker and find a stash of cocaine. Gavric accuses me of lifting it from the evidence room. He says I can go to jail, or I can go to the impound lot and keep my mouth shut."

"He planted cocaine?"

"Someone did. So here we are. It's my word against his. He promised to ruin my life, and my kids' lives, by smearing me. In the big scheme of things, proving he was lying about FRAT didn't seem so important."

I rinsed my coffee mug in the small sink. Dom needed to know this, but I wasn't talking to Dom. Not even for something like this. Cassidy either. I said, "Shauna Wylie had proof Gavric embellished that kidnap rescue story. The young victim actually saved Gavric's life."

Jamworthy laughed. "Gavric probably hates that."

"I've asked Corporal Cassidy to check out Gavric's resumé. Please tell her what you told me. Maybe she can talk to someone at FRAT."

"I thought of doing that, but he still has the cocaine."

"He lied about parts of the rescue. If you can prove he lied about FRAT as well, people may not be quick to buy his story about the drugs. Isn't it worth a shot?"

When I left the trailer, Jamworthy was standing at the orange counter, staring at his phone. I offered up a prayer he would make the call.

Despite the short jog from the trailer to my car, I felt cold when I slid onto the driver's seat and closed the door. The outside air was as chilly as the sky was dark. Definitely a storm coming. I cranked the interior temperature to 75 degrees.

When I turned on my phone, I noticed calls from Dom and Maggie. I ignored Dom's call and returned Maggie's.

"I have good news," Maggie said. "The Chief will look into the harassment allegations. I told him there must be something to it if you brought it up, that you didn't go around making up stories."

"Well, thank you—"

"That's not all. I asked him about telling Corporal Clapton not to pursue those interviews. I was quite upset with him, to be honest. And the Chief had no idea what I was talking about. Corporal Clapton has not talked to the Chief at all about who to interview. The Chief is going to have words with him and will probably call you later to apologize for being rather abrupt with you yesterday. He feels properly rotten about it."

I thanked Maggie for her concern, disconnected and then sat in my car, letting the warmth of the heater waft over me. What did I really know? Gavric made his rescue story a bit more heroic. A past-retirement cop who carries some baggage involving Gavric says he's a fraud. I had no proof Gavric didn't go to FRAT. At least not yet.

"But—Maggie," my conscience said. Yes. Then there was Maggie, who I knew to be romantically involved with Gavric. A woman I liked. And it wasn't just romance. Maggie was putting her money behind Gavric's political aspirations. If

Aunt Gaye had become involved with someone who was not what he appeared to be, was risking her heart and her money, wouldn't I have wanted someone to warn her?

"Maggie," I said, when I called her the second time. "This is difficult to ease into, so I will just say it. I don't think the Chief is who we think he is. Some things in his background don't check out, at least not yet."

"What are you talking about?" she said, defensiveness rising in her voice.

"It could be nothing but for starters, his resumé is padded."

"Pshaw."

"I've also heard he lied about his special training, that he spent the time vacationing in Florida. He could have defrauded the town."

"That's ridiculous. Honestly, I must have misjudged you, Olivia. I'm surprised you would listen to nasty rumors."

"It could be nothing. But I know you care for him and are putting money into his campaign. I simply wanted to alert you to my concerns."

"I'll thank you to allow me to manage my life. I don't believe a word you've said. He's a good man and an honorable one. Such stories could ruin his life. And mine. I'm very disappointed in you."

Maggie disconnected the call.

"That went well," I said out loud as I drove home. A clap of thunder made me jump. The heavens obviously agreed with my assessment.

Chapter 65

THE MCADAMS CHILDREN waved at me from the cab of their father's old truck when I parked in my driveway. I waved back and saw Charlie put his front paws on the dash, his tail doing its metronome imitation. Duncan McAdams came around the corner of the house with an armful of tools. "Glad to see you," he said. "I was becoming concerned."

He stashed the tools in the back of the truck and when he joined me on my porch said, "How'd it go at the camp?"

"According to Stan Drozeny, Shauna was definitely at the camp that evening. He said he and his son Hank met her in the parking lot."

McAdams shook his head. "He's lying. One, Stan never misses crib night. Two, Hank rarely rolled in to the camp until the wee hours. Usually drunk or stoned. I wonder what gives."

What was going on with the whole bit about Shauna and the groceries? I believed McAdams when he said she was never at the camp. Why would someone insist she was?

I shrugged. "I don't know that it matters because they have video of Shauna at 9:30 that night from a traffic camera near the country club. So, you're done for the day?"

He nodded. "Sorry to stop earlier than usual, but it looks like we're in for a storm, and I'd like to get the clan indoors for the duration."

I caught sight of Baggie Bagnovicz standing on her front lawn cradling a bunch of cut flowers. I tossed a distracted wave her way and turned my gaze back to McAdams. He was a calm, reassuring presence.

"I'm wondering if you know of anyone looking for a place to live," I said. "There's a suite in my basement, two bedrooms, furnished. We used to have tenants, but they've moved on, and with Dom being, um, elsewhere, I'm rattling around the house all by my lonesome. I thought I'd rent it out again."

McAdams looked over his shoulder at his truck and then back to me.

"I don't know what to charge," I said. "The last tenants were students and looked after the garden in exchange for the suite. Something like that would work. If you know anyone, let me know. Children, pets would be fine. But no smokers."

"I might know someone," McAdams said. "I just might. Let me ask her." He jogged to his truck, climbed in, tossed me a wave, and they were gone.

A quick tour of the back garden convinced me McAdams had coaxed the ugly duckling to reveal much of its hidden personality. Where dandelions and stinkweed once formed the border along the back fence, now delicate columbines poked their heads over mounds of fountain-like grasses. A California lilac anchored one edge of the garden, and a sensational glory tree brightened the other. The formerly patchy lawn was gradually becoming a series of small oasis-like areas linked by pathways that invited visitors to wander and explore. A few more weeks, I estimated, and the transformation would be complete.

When the first drop of rain splatted on my arm and my

phone rang, I decided now was not the time to wander and explore. I hurried inside, answering the call as I closed the door.

"It's Noel. I don't have Bonaventure's contact info."

"For crying out loud, you must. How did you write to her without it?"

"I told you I stayed out of things. I didn't want a starring role, if you know what I mean. This ain't the movies. I hired a guy to deliver letters."

"But where did he deliver them?"

"How the hell do I know? Look, here's what I did. One weekend, I came to visit Shauna. I was out and about, minding my own business, when I saw the woman, the one Giles and I had seen at Heavenly, come out of a store. I snapped a picture. Then I went to see good old Zack and he did the rest."

"Zack?" My phone beeped then, indicating a waiting call. I let it go to voice mail.

"Yeah, Zack Lockhart. Runs an auto detail shop. Among other things. I told him to find her, follow her, and put my letters in her mailbox. That's how I did it with all the people I offered to help. I'd send Zack stuff from L.A., and he'd get it delivered. I don't know if he did it himself or if he got kids to do it."

"I need you to get me that address. Send it to me, and the picture, okay? And one more thing, could Amanda Brammell be this Bonaventure woman?"

"Dunno never met Brammell. Just sent letters."

"Okay. Last thing. I need you to be at the Sierra Bistro today by 3:45."

"What for?"

I heard a second beep on the line. Dom, I thought. I ignored it. "Have a coffee," I said to Noel. "I'm meeting Patrick O'Hagen there and frankly, he scares me. I need you to be there. If he makes me leave with him, follow us and call

Dom."

"I dunno. Can't you put it off? I got stuff that needs doing today."

"No, I can't put it off. You must do this. Do it for Shauna, if not for me."

"Sheesh. You're not giving me much time. But okay, I'll be there."

"Send me that picture and address."

As soon as I ended the call, I texted Noel with Dom's telephone number. Just in case. I shook my head at Noel's attitude. Not giving him much time, he said. It was 2:30. Shauna's ranch was maybe half an hour from downtown Prospect. He'd already complained to me that he was bored at the ranch, so I would have thought he'd jump at the chance to hang around a place with more people than animals.

When I checked my voice mail, the first message was from Clarence. He spoke in a whisper. "Hey Olivia. Officer Cassidy and I looked up Hank, or Henry, Drozeny. He was brought in for possession with intent in May. I knew I'd seen him in bail court. Anyway, funny thing, the evidence in his case went missing not too long ago. Gotta go. Good luck."

The second message was from Dom. "Frankie checked out the USB you gave me. She pulled Shauna's computer from evidence to compare things. Your USB has a file called Mountain Man. That's not on Shauna's computer. She's checking further, but are you sure your USB is an accurate copy? BTW, what gives? What have I done?"

No matter how angry a person was with someone, no matter how vehemently she vowed never to talk to him again, there were times when pragmatism trumped petulance. This was one of those times. I texted him:

> Mtn Man = Gavric. Shauna was on to him.
> BTW you know what you did.

My to-do list this morning directed me to follow up on the other blog targets I'd found in Shauna's files, but after my discussion with Jamworthy I suspected Gavric had killed Shauna. Granted, I didn't know Jamworthy well, but I instinctively believed him. Gavric had been quick to transfer Dom when Dom mouthed off at him, so Jamworthy's transfer fit the pattern of Gavric moving obstacles out of his way.

Gavric seemed to be a better suspect than my editor Amanda, because he definitely knew Shauna was on his case. Shauna had been right on the money about Gavric's lies about the kidnapping. She'd made a note reminding herself to talk to Jamworthy, which made me think she felt Jamworthy had information about Gavric. If she believed that, how could I not? I'd known her for thirty years, give or take, and knew she had an excellent bullshit detector.

Initially, I had dismissed Shauna's blog posts as based on rumor and innuendo, but that was before I spoke with some of the targets and before I'd discovered she had done her homework. Her blog posts were accurate. Well, all except for the bull semen magnate, and I could only chalk that up to the fact she hadn't talked to Jonasberg. If she had, I knew Shauna would have killed the story and invited the man to bring himself and his appaloosa over to her ranch for a spell. His voice alone would have been enough to make her want to meet him.

Since I had convinced myself Gavric was the best suspect, there was no need to talk to any of the other blog targets. That would allow me to cancel my meeting with O'Hagen and to relieve Noel of babysitting duties. Instead of venturing out into what looked like it was going to be a rotten afternoon, I could stay at home and concentrate on proving what I believed to be true.

When my phone chimed to announce a text message, I assumed it would be Dom, psycho-texting, trying to get me to talk to him. But it was a text from the number Cassidy always used when she contacted me about the case.

My stomach plummeted to the bottom of my gut, and I immediately broke out in a cold sweat as I read her message.

Chapter 66

I STARED at Cassidy's text:

> DNA results arrived. Clapton seeing judge re warrant.

Knives stabbed at my back, my lungs spasmed, and I found it impossible to take a breath deeper than a weak puff. My skin felt icy and damp. My hands shook, and my phone tumbled to the floor. When I reached for it, my fingers seemed disconnected from my brain, and all I managed to do was scrabble at the phone, sending it skittering across the floor. My legs went to jelly. I sank down to my knees, and then lay on the floor in a ball, whispering, "oh god oh god oh god oh god."

After a minute or two, the stabbing sensations in my back eased enough for me to take slower and deeper breaths. Feeling came back into my hands, and my legs felt like they once more contained bones and muscle. I lay there, trying to think rationally, trying not to provoke another bout of panic.

If Clapton obtained an arrest warrant, he would come for me. I would be handcuffed and taken away. The cold sweats began again. I took in a slow breath, held it for a count of three, and then exhaled. I forced myself to take more deep breaths until I felt calmer. As calm as a person can feel when arrest is imminent.

Self-preservation finally motivated me to get off the floor, to pick up my phone, to find a warm sweater, to check for cash, to find my car key. I would go somewhere, pay cash for a room. Where? Anywhere, somewhere far from here. And once there, I would call someone. Dom? He would try to convince me to give myself up. Ditto Francine Cassidy. Maggie? No, she had made it clear I was on her outs list. Aunt Gaye? Yes, once I was somewhere safe, I would call her.

I now knew the fallacy of the statement, "If you aren't guilty, you have no reason to run." Whoever coined that line had never faced arrest for something they hadn't done. They had never been branded a person of interest or a prime suspect. They never had police looking solely at evidence pointing to their guilt, never had police refusing to follow other leads. And they definitely had never hidden the truth from police, failed to admit a bloodstain came from the victim, failed to explain the innocent reason for the stain's existence.

I left lights on in my bedroom and the main floor den so anyone driving by would believe I was home. Then I grabbed my bag and left the house, locking the door behind me. The wind had picked up since I'd come home less than an hour ago. I was glad I'd thought to put on a sweater. Hugging myself, I hurried to my car. Before I could open the driver's door, a silver Jaguar pulled into my driveway and stopped.

Maggie's window lowered. "Olivia, I'm so glad I caught you. I owe you an apology."

I rushed over. "I'm on my way out, Maggie. Can we talk another time?"

I shivered and hugged the sweater tighter. Maggie squinted at me. "You're very pale. Is anything wrong?"

I couldn't help myself. I covered my face with my hands and began to cry. Wracking sobs, shaky gulps of air in between. "I can't be here," I said. It came out as more of a high-pitched wail. "I have to go. Can we talk later?"

"Good heavens, Olivia. What is it?"

I took in a breath. She was the person I had thought I could call once I found somewhere safe to be, but I'd believed she was angry with me. Now she seemed not angry, but concerned. In fact, she'd said she came over to apologize. She would help me.

"I think they're going to arrest me," I said. "I don't know what to do, but I can't be here when they come. So, I'm going somewhere."

She sat quietly for a few seconds, appraising my face. Then she patted the passenger seat. "Get in. We'll go to my cabin, get out of the weather, put on a fire and have tea or something stronger, and work this out. Your car will be here. They will think you are at home. You'll be safe at my place. No one will find you."

"Are you sure? You could get into trouble for helping me."

She laughed. "Trouble? For what? I stopped by a friend's place, and we decided to share tea by the lake. How could we know anyone was looking for either of us? Trouble? I don't think so."

She was right, of course. Leaving my car in the driveway was a good idea. I hurried to the Jaguar's passenger side and opened the door. I glimpsed Baggie Bagnovicz just then, chasing after her small outdoor rug that the wind must have blown onto her lawn. When Maggie and I drove past, I hoped Baggie was too busy struggling with the wayward rug to notice us.

The Jag's interior was warm, and I leaned back against the luxurious leather seat, feeling some of my tension melt away. When we reached the relative safety of the next block and stopped at a light, I said, "Thank you Maggie, for doing this."

She adjusted her rear-view mirror, her chunky silver and turquoise bracelet hanging from her delicate wrist. "It's no problem. Now, why do you think they are going to arrest you?"

"The DNA."

She glanced at me briefly and frowned. "Pardon?"

I let out an enormous sigh. "A while ago, Shauna and I were unloading wine from my car, preparing for our annual camping trip. She was removing a case from the trunk and my hatch lid, which is a bit wonky, smacked down on her head. She got some blood on the carpet in my trunk. The police eventually seized my car, found the bloodstain, and tested it. And discovered it was Shauna's blood."

"But surely they understand how it got there?"

I shook my head. "I never told them."

"Oh."

She was quiet. I knew she was thinking what a stupid thing I'd done. Or maybe she was thinking only a person with something to hide would mislead the cops about the origin of the blood.

I said, "If I had it to do over again, I might do it differently. But Corporal Clapton had already noticed a bag of cement in my garage, and I know how cops' minds work, and I'd had a public blow up with Shauna, and honestly, I was feeling vulnerable. And I thought, why complicate things? I couldn't prove how Shauna's blood got there. It's not like she went to emergency or even her doctor. We simply put ice on the cut and had a glass of wine."

I looked at Maggie. Her face was thoughtful. "I never dreamed they'd think I killed Shauna," I said. "Never dreamed they'd search my house or start testing bloodstains."

Lightning slashed through the sky ahead of us. I counted one thousand one, one thousand two, before thunder clapped overhead. Fat drops of rain splashed down. Maggie slowed at the intersection with Donner Pass Road, signaled a left turn, and waited for a break in the traffic. "I think you should tell them the truth. Maybe they can verify your story."

"How? No one except me saw it happen."

"Where on her head did the lid hit her?"

I touched my head, just above my forehead. "About here."

"Do you think it left a scar? Didn't I hear that what killed Shauna was a blow to the back of her head?"

"Yes."

Maggie accelerated onto Donner Pass Road, leaning forward slightly and squinting through the rain. "Perhaps they found blood on your trunk lid to support your story? Maybe since they have no explanation for how it got there, they assumed the worst. If they could match a mark on her head with your hatch, wouldn't that help? I imagine a trunk lid makes a different mark than something like a poker, don't you?"

Relief washed over me like warm Maui waves. "You are making me feel so much better. Things may not be as awful as I thought."

"Why not tell Dom? Won't he be able to straighten things out?"

"We're not on speaking terms at the moment. And before you offer to intervene and talk to Chief Gavric, I have my doubts he'd want to help me."

Maggie glanced over and smiled. A small, sad smile. "Earlier, I said I owed you an apology. I did some thinking about what you told me. I must admit there are some things Andrew has said that make me think your suspicions have merit."

"Oh?"

"For example, once he mentioned attending a friend's wedding in the spring of 1990 and I said, 'Wasn't that when you were at your special training?' Then he backtracked and said he'd got the dates confused and the wedding was 1991."

She shrugged. "You know, we all make mistakes. Who remembers dates exactly anyway? But last year he mentioned sitting on the beach in Florida. He'd once told me he'd never been to Florida and had no desire to go. I said, 'You told me you'd never been to Florida,' and he said I was mistaken, that I must have been talking to someone else or I dreamed it. Pshaw. I did no such thing."

She slowed as we turned onto South Shore Drive, the road that would take us to her cabin on the knoll. "I've contributed to his campaign and am committed to give more. It's not an enormous amount so far, but the costs will rise, maybe by several hundred thousand dollars." She shook her head. "I don't want to be one of those silly women who men scam. Can you tell me exactly what you've learned?"

Chapter 67

"SOME THINGS I learned aren't that horrid by themselves," I said to Maggie. "But they may make voters turn their backs. And some have yet to be proven."

"I understand," she said.

"First," I said, "there is doubt he received an offer to wrestle for Poland, to which I say big deal, a bit of resumé enhancement. Next, and more worrisome, is that the kidnap victim, Clive Milliken, tells a different story about his rescue. Clive says if not for him, the kidnapper would have shot Chief Gavric."

"Oh dear."

"I'm sorry if it hurts you to hear this about someone you care for."

"I'm tougher than I look. Is there more?"

I nodded. "I haven't verified this, but it appears he didn't attend the First Responders Advanced Training program, at least not when he says he did. The Town spent thousands to send him there. It looks like he used that money to vacation in the Florida Keys, where he studied martial arts and partied with a wealthy couple."

Maggie turned off South Shore Drive and passed between

two stone pillars. Both bore plaques: one with the number 4655 and the other with the word "Aerie." The driveway climbed two hundred yards and near the top Maggie pressed the garage door opener. The massive wood and iron door slid upward silently. She drove into the garage, which could have easily held three Jaguars, and said, "That would account for his knowledge of Florida beaches, I suppose."

"I'm so sorry you're hearing this from me."

As we climbed from the car, Maggie said, "No, it's better to be armed with information. That way, I can protect myself. Come. Let's go inside. Somehow, tea doesn't seem appropriate. I'll start a fire and then we'll have wine, shall we?"

When we entered the gleaming mudroom, Maggie stopped me from removing my sneakers, saying her floors were indestructible. She waved me through to the kitchen. "Excuse me while I start the fire. Perhaps you can root around in the fridge for some wine, or if you prefer red, I have a bottle of Merlot on the counter."

I took in Maggie's kitchen, with its soaring vaulted ceiling, natural timbers and granite counters, and compared it to my looks-good-but-no-Ferrari model. I knew better than to play the *Measure Up* game. The rich lived an entirely different life than the rest of us, and for most of it they were not even aware that what they spent on a prime rib roast at an upscale grocery store could feed a family of six for three days. Maggie didn't flaunt her wealth, but it was there for anyone to see if they paid attention. Case in point, today was a crummy, wet, and stormy day, and I wore jeans, T-shirt and a four-year-old cardigan. Maggie, who I assumed had been kicking around her lakeside mansion most of the day, chose linen slacks, a cashmere sweater and a heavy knit jacket. I wore no jewelry while she wore matching silver earrings and bracelet.

I snooped in her Sub-Zero fridge and extracted a bottle of white wine. Something French. With a real cork. I found crystal wine glasses on the sideboard and poured a small amount into one. I held the wineglass up to the light and admired the prisms reflected by the glass. Crystal was to the rich what dollar store plastic was to the poor and homeless. Dollar store plastic and food bank handouts. Or as Stan Drozeny would have everyone believe, groceries from Shauna.

I believed Duncan McAdams when he said neither Stan nor his son Hank met Shauna that night. Why would Stan lie? What was in it for him to say he'd seen her?

I thought I knew. His son. Stan tells a story about Shauna, and the evidence in his kid's drug case goes away.

It wouldn't be hard for a police chief to mess with evidence. Cassidy couldn't find the Mountain Man file on Shauna's computer. A witness whose kid was in mega trouble says he met with Shauna the night she was last seen. But why would Gavric want people to believe Shauna was alive and doing good deeds at 8:30 on Thursday evening?

Some people at Donner Lake had seen Shauna leaving Maggie's cabin around 7:30 that evening. Others saw Gavric arriving at eight o'clock that night. Could Gavric have killed Shauna in that window of time? Was Stan Drozeny the witness Gavric needed to establish he couldn't have killed Shauna?

Then I remembered the video Cassidy had found of Shauna's SUV at the high crash zone near the country club, at 9:35 p.m. Did Gavric know about that video camera? Most people in town did. But then again, the camera had been there for a long time. We were all used to it and never gave it another thought as we drove that road. Had he arranged for someone to dispose of Shauna's vehicle? Someone who didn't know about the camera or, like many, never gave it a thought?

I was pulled away from my mental wrangling with those few hours in Shauna's life when my phone pinged, announcing incoming messages. A text from Dom, saying:

Emails re Bonaventure missing where r u.

It took me a moment to shift gears and decipher Dom's text. Cassidy had been comparing the USB data to Shauna's computer contents. If I was correct and Gavric had cleansed Shauna's computer of references to himself, had he also done this? Why? Or did Amanda, who I figured could be the mysterious Annabelle Bonaventure, have a guardian angel in the department? My head began to ache.

The email icon blinked then, displaying the number "1," and when I tapped on the icon, I saw an email from Noel. I took in the first few words: "It's after four," when I heard something clatter to the floor in the great room. Maggie let out a curse. I put my phone on the counter and hurried to the other room where Maggie stood by the fireplace with a pair of log tongs in her hand. "Are you alright?" I said.

She replaced the tongs in the rack of tools. "Yes, my hands are chilled, and I lost my grip on the tongs."

I looked at the cheerful fire and the set of fireplace tools next to the screen. "Oh."

"Yes?" Maggie said.

"You mentioned Shauna was hit by a fireplace poker. I didn't know that."

"Well, I'm not surprised. The Chief told me only this morning. He said he'd just then got word about it." She pushed an errant lock of hair away from her forehead and then gestured at a chair near the fire. "Why don't you relax by the fire? I'll wash my hands and be back in a flash."

I sat and carefully set my crystal glass of wine on a coaster on the side table. I stared at the hearth where Maggie had stood, and pictured her raised hand pushing hair away, the bracelet dangling and obscuring part of her face. I'd seen that picture before, hadn't I? A woman shielding her face, her wrist adorned with distinctive jewelry, in a newspaper clipping about the trial of a money launderer? No, that was ridiculous.

I went back to the kitchen and picked up my phone. I told

myself I was being silly, jumping at shadows. Maggie is British, I told myself. And a widow.

Still, I couldn't quite get that newspaper clipping out of my head.

My hands shook as I punched in my password. The screen opened to Noel's email: "It's after four. You are late. Here's the info." The name Annabelle Bonaventure and a picture appeared below his message, along with an address.

Chapter 68

I WAS WRONG. Amanda Brammell was not Annabelle Bonaventure.

Maggie might have been British and a widow, but that was definitely her face in the picture Noel attached to his email. And the address Noel listed, 4465 South Shore Dr., was definitely the address of the house in which I stood.

The *Mountain Man* file was missing from Shauna's computer. The Bonaventure emails were also missing. Gavric and Maggie were romantically involved.

Little bubbles of anxiety popped up in my stomach. I gritted my teeth and pushed them back. I couldn't afford a panic attack right now. My lungs felt tight, like my breath could fill them only half full.

If I left now, just walked out, and then ran like mad down the street, I could make it to the neighbors. I could call 911. I could phone Dom as I ran. I could outrun Maggie, I had maybe twenty years on her.

"*There* you are," Maggie said. I jumped, whirled to face her. My phone clattered to the island counter. I snatched it back up, clutched it to my chest, and stared at Maggie.

"I have to leave Maggie." My throat was tight. My voice

quavered. "Something's come up and anyway, it's not right for me to be here. The police wouldn't understand. I'm going to leave. The rain's letting up, I think. I'll be fine. I can flag a cab, I'm sure."

Maggie frowned and, in an instant, stood next to me. She grabbed the phone from my hand. When I reached to take it back, she said, "I wouldn't," raising her right hand and the gun it held.

She studied my phone's screen, which still displayed Noel's message. "Not the best picture of me, is it?" she said. Her British accent was gone.

Maggie tapped on the phone's screen. "Let's see. Ahh yes, I thought you'd have the Find my Phone feature. It's so handy, isn't it?" She tapped again. "Family sharing, too. Even though you and Dom are splitsville. That's touching. Well, let's turn that function off, shall we?" She tapped the screen and said, "Hmm, it appears I need your fingerprint for verification."

Before I could move, she grabbed my right hand and pressed my thumb to the home button. Maggie smiled at me. "Ahh, wonderful, the phone recognizes you, dear. And presto, no more Find my Phone." She turned the phone off and tossed it back into my bag.

Maggie waved the gun toward the wine bottle on the counter. "Do me a favor, Olivia, and pour me a glass of that Merlot? This situation positively demands something to soothe the nerves."

I poured some wine into a glass for her. She picked it up and waved the gun toward the great room. "Let's sit by the fire."

I trudged ahead of her and sat in the chair I'd vacated earlier. I had an unimpeded view of the lake, its slate-colored surface marked with white-tipped waves. I smiled at her or tried to. "Maggie, I don't know what the big deal is. So you used to have a different name, so what? And frankly, I admire what you did, testifying against him. Your civic duty, really. If you want to keep it all secret, I'm good with that."

Maggie sipped her wine and placed the gun on her side table, its muzzle pointing toward me. "I never liked the name Annabelle. I prefer Annie." She sighed. "You're quite right, Olivia. I do want to keep my real name a secret. More important, however, is Annie's whereabouts."

She gestured at the room and the lake. "All of this is compliments of Peter. If he finds out where his Annie is, he will surely come looking for his money. He's not thrilled with her as it is, so I imagine he will be apoplectic when he finally gets out of jail and discovers she absconded with his money. I'm sure he will be furious enough to kill."

"Okay, no one needs to know where you are. I won't tell anyone."

"No? Well, that makes two differences between you and your friend Shauna. One, she was rich, you are not. Two, you say you'd keep Annie's secret. Shauna was going to put it into her little tabloid blog. She wanted to blab it to the world."

"No, no, you have it wrong. I saw Shauna's files. She thought you were right to testify, she wasn't going to write about you."

"She sent me letters saying the *Cheat Sheet* would expose me, asking for money. Shauna Wylie, one of the richest people around here, a common blackmailer. I sent her letter after letter, telling her to stop what she was doing, but she kept up the threats. Until I had to make her stop."

"No, Maggie, you're wrong."

She shook her head and sipped her wine. "You're not drinking your wine. Don't you like it? It's not like you'll be driving anywhere later." She shook her head again. "I know it was Shauna who blackmailed me. When the first letter arrived, I told Andrew. He hired someone to hack that silly blog. Imagine my surprise when I find out it's my fellow board and club member."

"Chief Gavric? He knew about you, I mean Annie?"

Thunder rumbled overhead and rain pelted against the windowpanes. Maggie threw back her head and laughed. "Of course. Who do you think he was partying with all those months in the Keys? Peter and Annie. Andrew and I became quite close during the long stretches when Peter was slaving away laundering money, taking his cut."

She glanced at the window. "Andrew should have been here by now. I wonder if the storm is slowing traffic. Where was I? Right, Florida. When Andrew and I decided we absolutely needed to spend our lives together, Andrew sent information to the authorities and Peter's lucrative banking career was over."

"Oh."

"Yes, oh. He helped me move the money Peter had socked away. Then Andrew came back here, and I stayed in Miami to testify. After the trial I left Florida, traveled some and then about a year after Peter was sent to prison, I moved here to be with Andrew. As Margaret Shillingford. It's amazingly easy to get new identification if you know the right sources, and Andrew does. British birth certificate, fictional husband's death certificate. I told Andrew to make me British as I wanted to have a bit of fun and make use of my years of amateur theater."

Maggie finished her wine and picked up the gun. "Now, you tell me something, Olivia. Why are you so sure I was wrong about Shauna?"

I didn't want to expose Noel to the dangerous side of Maggie/Annabelle. I shook my head. "I'm not."

"Yes, you are. You told me she wasn't going to write about Annie." She cocked her head. "Why would Noel Wylie have Annie's picture and my address? Was he working with Shauna?"

I opened my mouth and then closed it.

"Of course he was," she said. "Two rich kids in it together.

I've never had the pleasure of meeting Noel. I must take care of that oversight soon." She looked at her watch and then stood and waved the gun at me. "Shall we go?"

"Where?" I stood and calculated the odds of lunging at her and disarming her. My legs were jittery, and I doubted they would hold me upright, never mind enable me to rush Maggie.

"We're going out on the boat for a brief tour of the lake. Andrew was in Reno when I called him. Traffic must be terrible. Time's passing, so you and I will go ahead without him. He'll catch up."

"The lake looks rough."

"I've had the boat out in worse. I love being on the water during thunderstorms when the sky is almost like night and the lake's frothy and excited."

In the mud room, Maggie donned a slicker and rain hat before motioning me to a door opposite to the door we'd entered earlier. This one opened onto the outdoor staircase that led down the high bank to Maggie's boathouse and dock. Wind blew my hair behind me as soon as I stepped onto the landing. I shivered and hugged my sweater to me.

"Down we go," Maggie said.

By the time I'd gone down ten steps, the rain had plastered my hair to my head and face. I picked it away from my face and wiped it from my eyes. My hair clung to my shoulders, my sweater and jeans soaked up the rain, and by the midpoint of the staircase my feet sloshed inside my sneakers. If she didn't kill me, I figured I'd die of hypothermia in half an hour.

Maggie's boat, named *Bye Gone*, rocked in the waves, but instead of going straight to it, Maggie pushed me into the boathouse. She flicked on a light and grabbed a set of keys from among several hanging on pegs by the door. In addition to her sleek red Sea-Doo, the boathouse held a canoe and two kayaks. I sucked in a breath when I noticed a small concrete mixer next to a dented green and yellow oil drum full of floats and swim noodles.

"For a short time, I had two of those barrels," Maggie said. "If fact, it was Shauna who told me about them. Andrew and I bought that one recently. I phoned her that Thursday and asked her to be a dear and pick up another one for me. Her Land Rover was much better than my Jaguar for hauling such things. She was always so helpful, a real generous person, wasn't she?"

"She brought it over?"

Maggie chuckled. "I had it all worked out, you know. I brought the poker down here earlier, leaned it right there." She pointed to a spot near the door. "Shauna helped me bring the barrel down the staircase. She did most of the work. Once she'd moved the barrel inside, I picked up the poker and hit her. She was standing just about where you are now."

Involuntarily, I looked behind me.

Chapter 69

WHEN I LOOKED BEHIND ME, Maggie smiled. "No poker today." She motioned again with the gun. "Okay, let's get on the boat."

"How did you get Shauna and the barrel on your boat?" I asked.

"I didn't. I told you I had worked this out. The former owners left an old wooden dinghy in the boathouse." She pointed to a partially submerged shell of a rowboat. "What's left of it is over there. I put the empty barrel in the dinghy, retrieved Shauna's car key from her pocket, and then dumped Shauna into the barrel. That took a bit of doing, but she wasn't very heavy, and I was motivated. She almost fit, only her lower legs stuck out."

Maggie smiled. "Those shoes! I debated about removing them. But you know, the way her legs stuck out of the barrel, with the bright strappy stilettos on her feet—it looked like a couple of stir sticks, like you'd see in a martini. Quite festive, really. So, I left them alone.

"I mixed concrete and put it into the barrel, one bucketful at a time, until the barrel was full. I encased her legs and feet in bags of ice to slow decay. Couldn't risk a stink, could I?

"Then I locked up and left the concrete to set. I popped back here now and then to refresh the ice and to toss some water on the concrete, to help the hardening process along."

The expression on Maggie's face as she talked made a shudder run down my spine. How could I have thought this woman was a kind, caring person? How could I have compared her with my aunt?

We climbed onto *Bye Gone*, and Maggie directed me to sit on the banquette at the stern. "The only miscalculation I made," she said, as she zipped a life jacket over her slicker, "was not evaluating the dinghy's condition. The night I put Shauna in the lake, I used the inflatable to tow the dinghy, planning to shove the barrel over the dinghy's side in the middle of the lake. But the weight of all that concrete in the barrel must have been too much because the bottom of the dinghy gave way when I was only about a hundred feet from shore. If I'd been another fifty feet toward the middle of the lake, no one ever would have found Shauna."

I sat on the bench, shivering, staring at the blank windows of the neighboring cabins, hoping someone might be standing there watching us. Someone who might wonder why a woman in a slicker was taking her boat out in the storm and why she had a gun in her hand.

"But that won't happen in your case, Olivia," Maggie said. "You will be three hundred and sixty feet down; I'll make sure of that."

She lifted a metal bucket from beside the driver's seat and lugged it over to the bench. The bucket was filled with hardened concrete. "I mentioned I thought things out, didn't I?" My stomach turned over, and I gagged when she pulled a pair of handcuffs from her pocket. "I hate to lose these. Andrew and I love playing with them, but he can always get more." She grabbed my wrist and snapped a cuff on it. The other cuff went on the bucket's handle.

Maggie put the gun on the driver's seat. "Whew, that's a load off my mind." She climbed off the boat, untied the tethers, and nimbly jumped back aboard.

"It's too bad really," she said. "If you hadn't looked into her death, we wouldn't be here today. But when you mentioned you had a copy of Shauna's computer files, I knew I couldn't risk you putting things together."

I sat in the rain and shivered, staring at the concrete-filled bucket with its faded label proclaiming, "A-One is All You Need." My heart skipped. I grabbed hold of the handle and began moving the tab connecting it to the bucket back and forth, hoping that all A-One buckets were the same piece of junk as mine had been.

Maggie started the engine and pulled away from the dock, heading toward the middle of the lake. *Bye Gone* plowed through the two-foot waves. I worked away at the handle and metal tab and tried to keep her talking. "Does Chief Gavric know any of this?" I said.

"Of course he does. In fact, Andrew helped me work out how to cover my tracks. All I needed was an auburn wig. I drove Shauna's SUV to the sand shed outside town and left it there. My neighbors swear they saw Shauna leave here that evening. Andrew met me at the shed, and we drove back here in his car. I hid out of view when he neared my cabin, so my nosy neighbors would think he was alone. He simply pulled into my garage like he always does. Then we lounged on my deck as usual. Once it was dark, we went back to the sand shed where I picked up Shauna's SUV."

"And you drove it to the country club," I said, as I continued to worry the metal tab on the bucket back and forth.

She let out a heavy sigh and nodded. "I said one miscalculation, didn't I? Actually, there were two. The first was the rotten wood of the dinghy. The second was where I parked

Shauna's vehicle in the club lot. It was simply force of habit, but I left it in the manager's spot. Which had been my spot until the officious pipsqueak decided he was more valuable to the club than I was. With an attitude like that, he's not long for the job."

She turned and smiled at me brightly. "But with you, I don't have that problem. We left your car right where people expect to see it, didn't we? And if anyone saw you with me, I'll simply say I dropped you at the grocery store not an hour ago. Andrew will easily find someone to verify that. Perhaps the same fellow who Shauna supposedly delivered groceries to."

She cut the engine and picked up the gun. "I think it's time, Olivia. Come join me by the rail. The pail's heavy, but if I can lift it, I'm sure you can."

I stood and clutched the bucket with both hands. I'd bent the metal tab on one side of the bucket and thought it would separate if I could pleat it back and forth a few more times. I looked over Maggie's shoulder and saw a small red shape in the water coming toward us.

Seconds later, I heard a high-pitched whine and recognized the shape as a Sea-Doo.

Maggie must have heard its engine too because she turned to look, saying "That must be—"

Using both arms, I flung the pail as forcefully as I could at Maggie, catching her in the shoulder. The gun flew from her hand, slid across the deck, and came to rest under the passenger seat in the cockpit. I lunged for *Bye Gone*'s controls and smacked the anchor button. When I turned around again, Maggie screamed and came at me. She swung her arm at my head. I grabbed hold of her wrist with my free hand while I hugged her with my right arm and, of course, the bucket, which was still attached to the handcuff on my wrist. We did a drunken dance around the deck, pitching and lurching as *Bye Gone* rocked in the waves, until a sickening moment when I felt the railing behind my legs, and Maggie pushed, and I toppled backward, reaching out, grabbing at anything I could find to stop myself. And then the dark, frigid waters of Donner Lake enveloped me.

Chapter 70

PEOPLE SAY life flashes before you when you face death. Not so.

When I recovered from the icy shock of hitting the water and realized I was immersed in rough, deep water, with a bucket of concrete attached to my wrist, I did not see pictures of my life. Instead, one thought jarred me: *I'll never know how the stories end.*

I wouldn't know whether Pierre would ever do more than sweet talk his popcorn lady; whether next spring Baggie would once more replant her wooden tulips; whether the McAdams family wanted to rent my suite; whether Dom would regain his spot on the homicide squad or would become a father; or what it was about horses that made Cassidy so sure I was innocent.

A person should not face death with so many unanswered questions. Perhaps my questions ought to have been grander and more spiritual, but they weren't. The lives that flashed before my eyes were the lives of people *in* my life. More than anything, I wanted to know how their stories played out.

I kicked my feet, and my head broke the surface so quickly I could not have been more than a foot beneath the waves. The bucket dragged on my right wrist; my left hand felt pinched and cramped. I took in a gulp of air and opened my eyes to find myself staring at a blue pillow on a shiny bunched up piece of yellow oilcloth. I thought of the bright tablecloth my aunt put on our patio table every summer. Why was it out here in Donner Lake?

I shook my head to flick water away from my eyes and focused. The fingers of my left hand clenched Maggie's bracelet and were jammed between the bracelet and her wrist. The bottom of her yellow slicker floated and swirled around us, and her blue life jacket held us both aloft. *Bye Gone* was about ten feet away from us, rocking in the waves, its stern turning away from us as the anchor held the bow firm. Maggie struggled with her free hand to pry my fingers away from her bracelet. "Let go, dammit."

Oh sure, I'll do that post haste. I raised the bucket and pinned it between my legs, relying on Maggie's life jacket and my death grip on her bracelet to keep me afloat. I concentrated on working the handle's tab back and forth rapidly, praying once more to the build-a-crappy-bucket gods. I felt the metal give slightly. Hope blossomed, and I pleated the tab faster.

Maggie pushed my face under the water. I took in a mouthful of water, wrenched my head sideways, breached the surface, and spewed the water at her. We had drifted even further from *Bye Gone*. Even if I freed myself, I doubted I would have enough strength left to swim to the boat.

With my fingers still firmly clamped around her bracelet, I lifted my left hand up and over Maggie's head, dragging her right arm across her body. Now I was behind her, relatively safe from any further attempts to drown me. She turned in the water, trying to face me again, but each time she did so, I moved with her, keeping my body behind her. Once more, I began wrenching the bucket's handle with my right hand. I grasped the handle as close to the tab on the bucket as possible and worried it back and forth.

The high-pitched whine of the Sea-Doo's engine was louder. I realized it had almost reached us. Any minute now, Gavric would be beside us, able to help Maggie, and send me to the bottom of Donner Lake. I was freezing and exhausted. Part of me wanted to let go, let it end. I looked at the man on the Sea-Doo. Hypothermia must have set in because I saw not Gavric, but Dom.

The man shouted. "Livvie."

Dom. It *was* Dom.

He stripped off his life jacket and, when the Sea-Doo was within five feet of me, threw it to me. "Grab it." The vest sailed over my head and landed just over an arm's reach away. The waves batted it, pushed it to me, then away. Lifted it up. Dropped it into the valley between their crests.

I watched it rise and fall and when it looked like the vest was on a path toward me I released my grip on Maggie's bracelet and lunged. My fingers grazed the canvas of the vest. I felt the zipper slide through them and then I closed my fingers around the clasp. A wave slapped into my face and the bucket shifted in my right hand, pulling me down. The life jacket's clasp slipped from my fingers.

I kicked my feet, pushing upward against the pull of the bucket's weight, all the while wrenching the handle in its tab. When I broke the surface, I gasped in air and spun around, searching for the life vest. It was nowhere. The bucket's weight pulled me down, almost underwater.

I heard the Sea-Doo again and saw Dom approaching. He held the life vest in his left hand, slowed beside me and tossed the vest again. This time, it hit me on the head. I grabbed it by an armhole, slid my free arm through the hole, and clutched the vest to my body. I gulped in air, treading water like mad.

Dom shouted at me. "Going to get her." He turned the

Sea-Doo and headed toward Maggie, who was perhaps fifteen feet from *Bye Gone*, trying to reach the swim board at the stern.

The noise of another engine broke through the wind and thunder. A small motorboat headed directly for Dom and the Sea-Doo. I screamed at him, but my voice was overwhelmed by the motorboat and the storm. At the last possible moment, Dom glanced to his side, saw the motorboat approaching, and leaped from the Sea-Doo into the lake. The motorboat veered, but its bow clipped the Sea-Doo. The machine spun again and again, each time raking the side of the motorboat, until it spun free. Then the Sea-Doo listed to one side and slowly sank beneath the waves.

I hollered for Dom, scanning the waves for his head. He was in the water without a life vest. He couldn't swim. I had to find him. I wrenched on the bucket in desperation and felt the metal tab give. I wrenched again and this time the tab broke away from the bucket's side. The handcuff slid off the handle, and I felt light. Free. Hurray for piece-of-crap A-one buckets.

I turned circles in the water, searching the waves for Dom. Rain pelted down and blurred my vision. After an excruciating half-minute, I spotted Dom between *Bye Gone* and me, swimming toward me. Not flailing around. Swimming strongly. I swam toward him. When we reached each other, I said, "You don't swim," gasping between the words.

"Frankie," he said. "Good coach."

We reached the swim board of *Bye Gone* in time to see Gavric pull Maggie from the water into his motorboat. When Dom and I scrambled onto *Bye Gone*'s deck, I pointed at the passenger seat. "Gun, over there."

"Go below," Dom said. "Blankets, towels, anything dry and warm." He made his way to the driver's seat and started the engine.

When I came back to the deck with an armload of blankets, Dom had the gun trained on Gavric and Maggie in the motorboat. Gavric, in turn, pointed a gun at Dom.

"Give up, Chief," Dom said. "You can't win this."

The waves tossed the smaller motorboat like a tennis ball. *Bye Gone* towered above Maggie and Gavric, but still Gavric pointed his gun at us.

"You're sinking," Dom said. "Look at your hull."

Maggie leaned over the side of the motorboat and screamed. The Sea-Doo had ripped a gash along the entire side of the boat. It was taking on water with every wave that smashed against it.

Dom yelled in the wind. "Give it up. Toss your gun down, and we'll drop the inflatable for you."

Maggie and Gavric stared at each other. She said something to him. He laughed and said something back. She slapped him, turned to us, and shouted. "Drop the Zodiac." Then she removed her life vest and slicker. She donned her life vest again before jumping into the lake.

I released the inflatable from its cradle at the stern and played out about twenty feet of line. When I rejoined Dom, the motorboat had taken on so much water that Gavric was wet to his knees. "Chief," Dom said. "Enough. We're all cold and wet. It's time to come in."

Gavric slumped and let the gun fall from his hand. He sloshed to the edge of the boat and smiled at Dom. Then, in one quick motion, he removed his life vest and jumped into the water. And went under.

"Dammit," Dom said. He handed me the gun and snatched up the life ring. When Gavric resurfaced and called to us for help, Dom tossed the life ring. When Gavric clutched the ring, Dom pulled the attached rope until Gavric could crawl onto *Bye Gone*'s swim board.

Then Dom hauled Maggie from the inflatable onto the boat. I handed the gun back to Dom, raised the anchor, and pointed the vessel toward Maggie's dock.

When I parked Maggie's boat alongside her dock, Dom

said, "Help should be here soon. I told Frankie where I was heading and to send backup."

"How'd you know where I was?" I said.

"A trio of superheroes."

Sirens drowned out my "Huh?"

Cassidy and a crowd of uniformed officers clattered down the staircase toward us. Dom grinned at me and said, "I hate to admit it, but I'm going to enjoy making this arrest."

Chapter 71

Eleven Months Later

It TAKES two and a half minutes to roll a recycled oil drum from Pierre Roche's garage to mine. It takes another thirty minutes to pry off its lid, remove the contents. and carry them inside the house. From that point on, the time it takes to rebuild a life can vary. In my case, it's been eleven months and reconstruction remains a work in progress.

———

Let me back up to that Friday, the day Dom arrested Maggie Shillingford and Andrew Gavric.

Cassidy and her team hurried the four of us to the hospital to be assessed and treated for hypothermia. Gavric and Maggie were detained in a secure area overnight and then transferred to the County Jail. Dom and I also spent the night in hospital but were free to move about so long as we stayed warm. Mostly we stuck to our two-bed room and its hefty layers of quilts.

It didn't take long for Dom to proclaim his bed too cold.

"Don't panic," he said. "All I want to do is hold you and exchange body heat." He slid in beside me, pulled the quilts over our heads, and wrapped his arms around me. I lay my head on his chest and listened to his heart's steady thump. I had to admit his way was warmer.

Soon, I poked my nose out from under the quilts and said, "Who are the trio of superheroes?"

"Mmmm?"

"How you knew where I was."

"Oh. Mrs. Bagnovicz and Claire. Plus Noel, after a bit of prodding," Dom said. "You weren't answering my calls. I was going nuts trying to reach you. Then Noel phoned and said he was supposed to meet you and you hadn't shown up and you'd told him to call me if anything weird happened. He said you planned to talk to a guy called O'Hagen, and he definitely knew you weren't with O'Hagen, because Noel was sitting in Sierra Bistro looking right at him."

"Reno's resident soccer coach slash gigolo."

"Really? I roared over to the house and was relieved to see lights on and your car in the drive. When you didn't answer the doorbell, I started pounding on the door, hollering for you. Then Mrs. Bagnovicz came over and told me she'd seen you get into a car earlier. She'd apparently seen that same car come along the street last night and a few times this morning, driving slowly."

I gasped. "I saw a car go by the house last night, but dismissed it as someone looking for an address. Maggie must have been stalking me. She bragged she had it all thought out."

"About then, the McAdams clan arrived. Duncan wanted to rent the suite and couldn't reach you on the phone. When I asked Baggie about the car, she said she didn't know what type of car it was, and she didn't catch the plate. All she could tell me was it was silver and had an animal on the hood."

"A Jag," I said.

"Yeah, we figured that. Then little Claire pipes up and says, 'I saw a car with an animal. And a sign on the front. Mommy Daddy Ben.' No one knew what she was talking about, except Ben. He asked her, 'Do you mean the license plate?' Claire said yes, and Ben said, 'I think she means MDB.' Claire said, 'Yes, I know my ABCs.' Do you believe it, Livvie?"

I laughed. "Yes, I do."

"Right. Then I called Frankie and got her to search DMV. I called Noel back and asked him if you'd told him anything else that might help me find you. After much bafflegab and angst, he finally admitted sending you an address of a woman you wanted to investigate. He flipped me the email, and I had the address."

"Hurray for Claire and Baggie and neighborhood nosiness. I'll even say hurray for Noel."

"Want to tell me why he had that picture?"

"Nope."

He sighed. "That's what I thought. Anyway, I called Frankie and told her I might have a lead. She said DMV had a silver Jaguar with the plate MDB 733 owned by Margaret Shillingford. I told her to send backup. And you know the rest."

"Except why Noel would phone you when I didn't show up at Sierra Bistro. I'd only told him to call if O'Hagen got weird, and Noel isn't my biggest fan."

"Who else could buy the ranch from him? He wants cash and you have it. And if anything happened to you . . ."

"That makes me feel better. For a moment there, I thought Noel had turned into a regular person."

Dom and I were discharged from hospital the next morning in time to watch Frankie Cassidy lead the Prospect Police Department's swim team to a record-breaking finish in the Truckee Open Water Swim at Donner Lake. The day was warm, sunny, and calm. Except for downed branches, you'd never know a storm had ripped through the area the previous day.

I pushed my way through the crowd celebrating the win and congratulated Cassidy.

"Thanks," she said. "It felt good to compete again. Maybe next year Captain B can join the team."

"He told me you taught him how to swim."

She towel-dried her hair and nodded. "Yeah. He wanted to do it in private because, you know, being over thirty and skittish about water." She shrugged. "No biggie, but whatever works. I would pick him up and we'd go to a pool in Reno. Then I took him here to the lake a couple nights so he could practice in open water, which is a completely different thing. He's a natural."

"Thanks for teaching him. It saved his life. Now, I have to know. What was it about horses that convinced you I was innocent?"

She grinned. "Shoot, you were so worried about who was going to take care of Ms. Wylie's horses. No one who cares about animals the way you do would kill their owner and leave the horses untended. Just wouldn't happen."

I smiled at her and turned to go, when she stopped me. "About the harassment? Captain B reported it to Gavric, who then made his life hell. Refused to approve expenses, told Clapton Captain B was after him, messed with evidence to make him look incompetent. When the murder happened, Gavric made sure Clapton was on the case, and eventually Gavric found a reason to ship Captain B out."

She cursed softly. "Piece of work, hey? And for what it's worth, I heard it was Clapton who found a way to steal Ms. Wylie's earrings and hide them in your cabin. He thought he was being hilariously funny."

"Yeah, a laugh a minute, that guy."

A few days after the Open Water Swim, police raided Abel's Table and arrested the manager. Then they paid

Amanda a visit and arrested her on suspicion of drug trafficking. Their case was strong because they had a solid witness in Noel Wylie, who agreed to testify against the druggies in exchange for the authorities turning a blind eye to his attempts at blackmail.

It took a few weeks for Maggie and Gavric to cave in. Maggie insisted I was deranged because of my husband's cheating, and that I had actually tried to kill her. She had a difficult time explaining why I would encumber myself with a bucket of concrete while trying to kill her. When tests on the fireplace poker in her house revealed Shauna's blood, Maggie's story broke down.

Gavric claimed Maggie had told him what she was going to do, and he had come to the lake to stop Maggie from killing me. Ramming Dom's Sea-Doo was an unfortunate accident in the stormy conditions on the lake. Maggie was unstable, and he'd suspected her of Shauna's death all along.

When Maggie heard Gavric's lies, she exploded in rage and told everyone who would listen how Gavric had helped her steal her husband's money and "tidy up" after Shauna's death.

The final blow for Gavric was the evidence that Jamworthy and Cassidy obtained from contacts at the FRAT program, proving Gavric had been denied admission to the special training program. A document expert later established that Gavric's acceptance letter and graduation certificate were fakes.

When I fell overboard that day and believed I would die in Donner Lake, I was filled with sadness that I'd never learn how the stories ended. Stories never really end, but I can tell you the answers to some questions I asked under the icy water.

As soon as the winter snow melted in the spring sunshine, Baggie carted her wooden tulips out of her garage. Every one of them had been brightened with a fresh coat of paint. In hindsight, I never should have asked that question because the replanting of Baggie's wooden tulips is as much an annual occurrence as the spring equinox.

Pierre and his popcorn lady got married about the same time as the tulips reappeared in Baggie's yard. It was a small wedding. Dom and I stood up for them, and Ben and Claire McAdams walked the bride down the aisle.

The McAdams family and Charlie moved from the Riverbend Motel to my suite.

When Shauna's estate was settled, Noel sold the ranch to me. We didn't use a realtor. I paid him five million and agreed he could use the ranch once every other year to film a movie. I demanded and got veto rights over the type of movie he filmed on the property.

We've been in construction for a few months and the place should be ready for everyone in three or four weeks. The *Victoria and Grace Ranch* will welcome guests who want a casual, rustic experience in the High Sierras.

In addition to expanded stables and a barn, crews are building two bungalows for live-in staff and six cottages for guests. I have a fabulous landscaper and chef duo in Duncan and Samantha McAdams, who will live in the four-bedroom bungalow.

When I asked Mel Jamworthy if he'd help manage the *Victoria and Grace*, he said, "Mebbe. Mebbe not. What's it pay?"

I told him.

He spread his arms out and turned in a tight circle in the Airstream. "Hmm, I dunno if that's enough for me to give up all this. Lemme think. Do I wanna be in a tin can and stare at rusting metal all day, or be out in the temperamental weather wrangling horses, kids and dogs? And you say my wife and I gotta live there on that ranch?"

I nodded.

He grinned. "Bring on the weather."

It won't be long before Dom regains his spot on the homicide squad. The Police Advisory Committee is actively searching for a new Chief but while they look, Dom has assumed the role of Acting Chief. "I'm happy to be off that frikkin' boat," he said, "but administrative work is dull beyond words. And it's all day, every day. I don't even have time to look into the allegations in Shauna's files. Frankie Cassidy's doing that. She gets to have all the fun."

The question that may never be answered is whether Dom will become a father. The barrel I'd stashed at Pierre's had kept the vintage bassinet safe and out of sight for a time. During the terrifying moment when I saw Dom dive off the Sea-Doo into Donner Lake without a life vest, I knew I wanted him to live and for us to try to repair the shambles we might have made of our marriage. When I returned home after the Open Water Swim, it seemed right to retrieve the bassinet from its hiding place and bring it back into the house. It will be there when Dom moves back into the house once construction at the ranch is finished and I have moved to the ranch.

I wonder which is the worst sin: my years-long lie about starting a family or his betrayal with Shauna. All I know is each of us has caused the other grief and created distrust.

We've been working on rebuilding trust and reconstructing our story for eleven months now. There doesn't seem to be an end in sight. Dom firmly believes that's a good thing. And I agree.

The End

Acknowledgments

All the characters, businesses, and organizations in this novel, and the town of Prospect itself, are imaginary. Occasionally, for the purposes of story, a character in authority may act dishonourably, but this is not intended as a reflection on the real-life people in those positions.

I took many liberties with the geography of the area around Donner Lake, and plunked businesses and cabins around the lake that in reality do not exist.

I was the person who sat at the keyboard, putting words onto the screen, and editing the first draft (and the second, third and more) for this novel. But alongside were many, many colleagues, friends, and experts who generously shared their knowledge and commented on the plot, the characters, the setting, the whole enchilada. Writing may be a solitary thing, but the actual *making* of a novel is a collective effort.

Robert Leftwich, former Chief of Police in Truckee, California, generously and enthusiastically shared his knowledge about the area and the atmosphere surrounding Donner Lake, as well as investigative and forensic matters. Of course, any mistakes in investigative approaches are mine.

A huge shout out to Robert Dugoni and Steven James, and their Novel Writing Intensive, which is a writer's dream retreat. I workshopped part of this novel at the Novel Writing Intensive and the insightful feedback I received from those two stellar authors helped immensely with plot and structure. Don Brobst, an author (and a colleague from that retreat), asked me the vital question, "How does one person load a heavy, concrete-filled barrel into a boat?" and then brainstormed the solution for me. Without Don's help, I don't think that barrel would have made it from the shore to the middle of the lake.

The talented Karen Abrahamson not only coached me about horses but also designed the cover.

First readers are so important. Kobbie Alamo, with her superb eye for structure, pinpointed where the opening of the story needed to be. Marcelle Dubé not only shared her knowledge about newspapers and reporters, but flagged sections of the manuscript that needed serious attention. Whenever Marcelle says, "you're laying it on a little thick," I tend to pay attention.

I'm so grateful to all my family, friends and writing colleagues for being part of my life. And thanks to organizations such as Crime Writers of Canada and Sisters in Crime for all they do to support writers of crime fiction.

About the Author

Charlotte Morganti is a Canadian writer of crime fiction. She has been a burger flipper, a beer slinger, and a corporate finance/mining lawyer.

Charlotte writes novels and short stories, ranging from gritty investigations to lighter capers. She usually sets her stories in small towns that miraculously harbour both villains (often cunning, occasionally inept) and the sleuths who pursue them.

Charlotte's works have been shortlisted for various awards, including the Crime Writers of Canada's Awards of Excellence. She is a member of Sisters in Crime and Crime Writers of Canada, and is a past president of Sisters in Crime-Canada West.

Charlotte and her husband live in a small town on the Sunshine Coast of British Columbia, where it's mostly sunny, except when it's raining.

You can find Charlotte's books at most retailers. Check her website for links to retailers. https://charlottemorganti.com

Also by Charlotte Morganti

The End Game

Persimmon Worthing Short Mysteries, Vol. 1